COMING HOME

PATRICIA DIXON

BLOODHOUND
— BOOKS —

ALSO BY PATRICIA DIXON

For Harry,

May all of your Christmases be truly magical.
Hold on to the spirit of Santa.
Believe that everything is possible.
Make your dreams come true.

I love you so much.

Grandma
x

PROLOGUE

Tilbury, London. Christmas Eve 1969

The glass bauble on the tree catches my attention first. It always begins like this. I know exactly where I am, the year, the day. I'm alone in the parlour. I recognise it instantly as the house where we all lived, where we had our last Christmas. The rain is lashing against the window, so loud I can hear it through the drawn curtains. The fire is roaring in the grate and the heat from the flames warms my legs. I'm wearing brown bell-bottoms and a stripy skinny polo from C&A. Mum bought them for me as a treat.

To my right, greetings cards line the mantel and the clock in the centre shows 5pm. To the left, underneath the window and in front of our black-and-white telly, Dad's newspaper is on one arm of his chair, an ashtray on the other, waiting for him to get home from work. *Blue Peter* has just finished and behind me I can hear Mum humming along to a tune on the radio.

I go over to take a closer look at the bauble and get so near that I can smell the pine oil that leaks from the needles. This is the ridiculous part because we never had a real tree. Ours was artificial, from Woolworths, about two feet high and stood on the sideboard inside an old biscuit tin wrapped in last year's Christmas paper. My senses are always heightened, sucking in the atmosphere, soaking in the memories, grasping on to every single thing I see, hear and feel. I am intoxicated by the pungent scent of a pine forest and mesmerised by the most beautiful bauble which is hung on a red velvet ribbon. A perfectly formed bow frames the glass that is so clear and polished that I can see right inside and watch the scene as it plays out.

A child is seated at the kitchen table, that's me. My mother, Sylvia, with her blonde beehive and candy-pink lipstick is opposite. She's beautiful, like the lady on the Fairy Liquid advert who doesn't have to wear gloves when she washes the dishes. Mum is happy, I can tell. She's peeling vegetables, a cigarette burns in the ashtray and every now and then she takes a drag and nods to another woman, older, who is sitting at the end of the table and chatters in between sips of sherry. That's Aunty Beryl from next door. Not my real aunty but I call her that.

I know exactly what happens next. When my nose touches the glass it breaks the barrier, like when you pop a bubble. I leave *Blue Peter* behind as I'm sucked inside the bauble, through a shimmering, undulating, wibbly-wobbly time warp. Now, instead of looking in I am part of the scene, seated at the table, in front of humming Mum, my legs dangling from the chair.

From this moment on I have to focus, concentrate, hold on tight to the memories like my life depends on it because in a way, it does.

I am six. I know this because pinned to the larder door is one of my birthday cards from November. It's in the shape of a six.

Me and Mum love it because it has all the colours of the rainbow and she says it brings the sunshine into the room. And inside, written along the curves is my dad's writing. I know exactly what it says. I read the words over and over on my birthday. I still know them now. They remind me of the sea, and the sea reminds me of my dad.

To Daddy's little darling, Daddy's little girl, Daddy's little sweetheart, Daddy's little pearl.

The clock on the kitchen wall says 6.45. Time has moved on. There is a lovely aroma in the room, mince pies, pastry and a hint of orange. I look down and there they are. The tangerine segments lined along the table and the curls of peel on top of the newspaper that's already covered in carrot scrapings and sprout leaves. I always put the segments in a row and eat them one by one so I can savour the tangy sweetness of the fruit. They are a special treat and Mum says we have to make them last like the dates and nuts in the fancy basket we bought from the market.

A sound distracts me from what Aunty Beryl is saying. One of her big, long stories about the vicar's wife and her daft hat. Music is playing in the parlour and I hear a cough.

Dad. He's home and this simple realisation, that my wonderful most perfect dad is in the house fills me with such immense joy. It's like it spreads through me, so powerful is my love for him that I could cry. He's playing one of his records, Bizet. Mum isn't keen and prefers the radio but Dad adores it. That's why I'm called Carmen.

My tummy tickles with excitement reminding me that it's almost here. The big day. The one me and Mum have been talking about for weeks. Our big magnificent feast. We have a chicken. It's under a tea towel on the draining board and the veg on the table is from Dad's allotment. There are so many treats, too. Like a tin of ham and a box of shortbread. Mum has saved her Co-op stamps all year and we even have a tin of Quality Street. I can't even think about Father Christmas and what he might bring but I hope it's a Tiny Tears.

All I have to do is close my eyes and go to sleep and it will be Christmas morning, the Christmas it should have been before the knock on the door that ruins everything. No, don't think that, but it's too late.

I glance again at the kitchen clock and know what I've done. I have broken the spell.

It's almost time for bed. 6.56pm. But tonight there won't be any sleep and Christmas mornings will never be the same again. The second I acknowledge this the edges of the scene start to close in, darkening, casting shadows into the corner of the room, across my mum's face. Beryl's voice slowly begins to fade like someone is turning the radio dial, drowning her out.

And here it comes.

BANG BANG BANG. So loud on the front door that it makes my ears hurt and my brain rattle inside my head and my heart. I'm sure it stops for a second or two while I hold my breath, my chest tight, spine rigid, eyes wide.

Don't open the door. Don't open the door and it'll be okay. I shout the words but nobody hears me even though my neck strains with the exertion of trying to be heard and in my clenched hand, a segment of tangerine squashes against my skin. The scent from the juice makes my nostrils tickle and my eyes start to sting. Tears prick as I watch my dad dart from the parlour and rush to open the door and when he does, a storm enters the house and blows hate right up the hallway, chilling my ankles, swooshing upwards to my wildly beating heart.

From my chair I can't see the woman, just my dad's jet-black hair, neatly cut, curls greased back in a wave, the cap collar of his white shirt, sleeves rolled up, black braces crossing his back.

4

He is preventing whoever is at the door from coming any further.

'Where's your wife, Geordie? Where's Sylvia? Out of my way.'

My dad jolts, takes a step backwards but holds firm.

'I want to speak to her right now. Or shall I stay out here and tell the whole street what your wife needs to know? You want that, do you?'

'Martha, please, stop this. My daughter is here. It's Christmas Eve, for God's sake.'

'I don't care what day it is, and don't you try to wriggle your way out of this, Geordie Wilson. You think you can go around ruining my life while you play happy families?'

I look across the table at my mum and want to ask who Martha is but somehow I know not to. Mum's eyes are wide, round green circles outlined in black kohl with wings at the corner, set against a very pale face. She doesn't speak but stands quickly and pushes back her chair before almost running down the hall, her body blocking my view of Dad and whoever is making such a racket.

Aunty Beryl moves next and all I can see is her big bum wedged between the door frame before she closes the kitchen door, creating a barrier between me and my parents. This is when I panic because I want to be with them so badly, even amidst the shouting. I need to hold on to the last few hours, to them. To the three of us.

Then the shouting begins again and the room darkens further, like someone dimmed the lights and I remind myself to listen carefully because there might be a clue, one I've missed before.

'What's going on...?'

I run to the door and kneel, peeping through the keyhole as Aunty Beryl grabs my arm and tries to guide me away. I stiffen

5

and resist, for a moment anyway.

Yellow. That's the colour I see first. Then brightly coloured birds, and flowers, reds and greens, a block of dress fabric. No body, no face, just a screeching banshee with the angry voice of a woman who is cross with my dad and wants to tell my mum something really important.

The next voice is my mum's. She sounds angry, or is she scared? More likely embarrassed that the neighbours will hear. She slams the front door before trying to calm things down. 'Martha. I'm sorry but I have no idea why you're here, but let's go into the parlour and talk there. You'll be upsetting our daughter, so please, if you will.'

The bird lady moves, and then my mum and the last thing I see before Aunty Beryl heaves me upwards and takes me out the back door to her house, is my dad's arm, hanging by his side. The anchor tattoo that I love to trace with my finger as he tells me stories of his voyages across the sea, disappears from sight.

Blackness swallows me. I'm not scared. This is how it goes. Every dream the same.

I open my eyes and I am upstairs in my bedroom, covered by a blanket but still wearing my clothes from earlier, not my nightie. I have no recollection of how I got there, or when I came back from Aunty Beryl's. It's cold so I sit and pull the thick eiderdown and wrap it round my shoulders. There's a light on in the hall: I can see it under my door. And then I hear voices coming from next door, Mum and Dad's room. And crying, soft and low.

Then Mum speaks. 'I knew, I knew. I just wouldn't admit it. I kept telling myself I was wrong and you wouldn't do this to us. I thought Christmas, us all being together would make it right. I tried so hard to make it perfect. I wanted to stick us back together.'

My dad mutters something and whatever it is makes my

mum erupt. 'Then go. Go now. Go on. Get out. I don't want you here for a second longer if that's how you feel. You make me sick, do you know that? You disgust me–' She stops, interrupted by three loud thumps on the wall. Not from Aunty Beryl's side. It will be nasty Mrs Smith who nobody likes.

Mum says terraced houses have ears so when she falls silent I understand why. Whatever Dad has done is bad and she doesn't want anyone else to know, especially Mrs Smith.

I hear footsteps, Mum's. She goes to the bathroom, the light clicks on and then she closes the door. Movement in their bedroom, drawers being opened and shut and I can't bear it any longer. I have to see him. I have to see my dad one more time so I push back the covers and slide off the bed. The wooden floor is cold beneath my socks but I don't have time to put on my slippers. If I don't hurry I will miss him. I might be able to change his mind. This time.

Four steps along the landing and I am at the bedroom door and I watch him in silence as he pushes clothes into a duffel bag that lies sideways on the bed and my little heart breaks.

'Dad. Where are you going?'

He turns and runs one hand through his hair, pushing the quiff back over his forehead. His face is a mix of worry and shock but he carries on with his task, takes a sideways step and grabs socks from the top drawer, answering as he stuffs them inside the bag then pulls the cord, sealing in his belongings. 'I just need to go away for a bit. Nothing to worry about, pet. You go back to bed. Go on, there's a good girl.'

'But it's Christmas Eve so you can't go away now. You'll miss all the fun.'

He pulls the bag off the bed, steps towards me then kneels. Both his hands gently rub each of my arms while he speaks. 'I'm sorry, pet, but I have to go now. You and Mum will have a nice day, don't worry. Father Christmas will be here soon so you have to get back in bed and go to sleep.'

'Are you going back to the sea? Is that why you have your sailor's bag? Mum doesn't like it when you go away. Stay here, Dad. Go after Christmas. Please, don't spoil it. Me and Mum have made it all nice. It's going to be special.'

And then it happens. The most terrible thing because Dads aren't supposed to cry. But my dad does. I see tears that make his eyes look like glass, then they leak and roll down his cheeks, like someone is pouring a jug of water on his face. No more words. Just the force of him pulling me to his chest, holding me so tight I can't breathe and I think my back will snap. And into my neck, a sob, his warm breath on my skin.

Then he lets go, stands and picks up the duffel bag and before I can speak he rushes, almost runs, from the room. Fast now. Everything happens at once.

Mum opens the bathroom door, a bright light shows the lines of black kohl that run down her face and she holds out her hand for me to go to her. Instead, I follow my dad who takes the stairs at a run. He's in the hall, wrapping his scarf round his neck, pulling on his donkey jacket, picking up the bag and I get to the bottom step just as he opens the front door.

One last try.

'Dad, Daddy, please don't go. Please Daddy, please stay here for Christmas.' But as I look at him one last time, at the face I'll try so hard to remember, it's as though his tears are washing away his features. A watercolour fading to white. So I hold on to his voice, his words, some hope.

'Be good for your mum, pet. Be a brave girl. I'll be back soon, okay.'

'Daddy, no. Please.' The door opens. I know I have failed so I ask the same question I have asked so many times before. 'When, when are you coming home?'

He pauses, looks up the stairs and I follow his gaze to my mum who is standing there, halfway, mute, frozen. Then back to my dad but it's too late, his face has disappeared, a white misty hollow is all that remains. He doesn't answer my question. I start to sob so hard my throat hurts, reaching out as he steps into the night, slamming the front door.

And then he is gone.

1

CARMEN

Appleton Farm, Cheshire
2021

Carmen's eyes snapped open. It was over. The dream. Relief allowed her heart to beat a steadier pace as she swiped at her eyes, brushing away the tears of a six-year-old and the lingering touch of old ghosts.

It took a moment or two to adjust to the light in the room that without the grey-white glow from the moon would have otherwise been cast in complete darkness. Carmen never closed her upstairs curtains: there seemed little point because in such a rural setting there was nobody around to peer in and anyway, they'd have to have a ladder to be able to see into the first-floor windows.

The square, symmetrically fronted Georgian house once belonged to a gentleman farmer who, the records and legend said, built on the highest ground available so he could survey everything he owned from each side of his home. Carmen thought he'd done a fine job because from all of the upstairs windows she had a fabulous view of the Cheshire Plain and the fields and farmland that now belonged to her.

Most days, when she reached the landing she stopped and took a moment to gaze at the lowlands that extended from the Mersey Valley in the north to the Shropshire Hills in the south. And on a clear day she could just about see the Welsh peaks to the west and the foothills of the Pennines to the north-east. The view always gave her immense pleasure. It also provided an overwhelming sense of achievement while she humbly acknowledged one undisputable fact: that she'd been thoroughly blessed when she inherited the house and land and remained duly thankful for all the things it had brought her since.

Turning, she saw that it was 5.35am – at least two more hours until dawn – but there would be no more sleep for her, not after the dream. She knew the score, had got used to the routine and owing to the time of year accepted there would probably be more. December was always a tricky month. Nevertheless, if she stayed in bed she would go over and over the past and no good ever came of that. It was best to shake it off, get up and go downstairs. A cup of tea and two slices of toast would see her right and the dogs, Arthur, Mitzi and Petra would be glad to see her, regardless of the hour.

Flinging back the quilted eiderdown she swung her legs out of bed and pushed her feet inside her slippers, pulling the dressing gown from the bottom bedpost as she made her way over to the window. It wasn't cold in the room, the double glazing repelled the season's icy breath and the heating system was set to tick over and created a steady, gentle heat.

Being warm was one of Carmen's luxuries. Regardless of the bill she was determined to be comfortable in the sprawling six-bedroomed house. The days when she and her girls shivered in the mornings were never to be repeated. She remembered only too well living with a barely functioning boiler, huddling around the old range for warmth. She'd hated the winter months even before they arrived and always longed for the spring.

Nowadays the rooms never felt chilly or damp and Appleton Farm was a welcoming place, a home. It had been in her deceased husband's family for two generations before he'd inherited it and even though he was no longer there, his name lived on. And while that fact sometimes grated, she'd lived there for almost forty years, happily, fulfilled. Recently, though, she'd felt a shift. An unsettling sense of time running out and decisions to be made.

Take your time, you've waited this long. Carmen must have repeated the same words a hundred times over the past few months yet they didn't calm the impatience that constantly nudged her subconscious.

Shrugging on her dressing gown, heeding the words in her head, Carmen lingered, peering at the world outside her window as she fastened the tie around her waist. As she suspected, the softly illuminated driveway and garden below were covered with a slick layer of frost and had the lamps on either side of the door allowed her to see further, the surrounding fields would be the same.

The view in the daytime was spectacular and even the sunset was worth taking time out for. All year round Carmen was treated to her very own painting, like a landscape in oils, a rich carpet of earth, a lush forest that, with a magical stroke of his brush, the artist tinted in ever-changing hues, the colour wheel of Mother Nature's glory. She lived her life by it.

Carmen would go to sleep or wake with the seasons, watching them turn from her bedroom window courtesy of the oaks which lined the garden. The twiggy barren branches that reminded her of forks of lightning currently signalled it was winter, as did the dusting of frost on the corners of the square panes of glass.

Looking up, Carmen could see the brave and hardy moon, a crescent hidden behind ghostly wisps of cloud, and imagined it shivering in the cold night air, not giving up, determined to stay on duty till dawn, another special time of day. When life kicked in, the birds awoke and night creatures – foxes, voles, badgers – sloped off to their burrows. And simultaneously, over on the other side of the gentle hill, at the rear of the house and just out of sight but never out of mind, Appleton Garden Centre sprang into action.

Yawning loudly she turned away from the window and as she headed for the stairs, stopped to straighten one of the frames that adorned the top of her chest of drawers. It contained a black-and-white photo of her dad and she'd been looking at it the night before, reflecting on the face of someone she hadn't seen for more than fifty-one years and no doubt the cause of her dream.

She only had two photos but her favourite was of him on the deck of the *Atlantic Conveyor*, a merchant navy cargo ship, the vessel that sailed her dad to the land of the rising sun and home again to his week-old baby daughter. It was one of the tales he'd told her as she sat on his knee, gazing at the atlas as he traced her finger across the map of the globe, passing far-off lands, crossing oceans she'd never heard of but memorised ever since. The South China Sea, Strait of Malacca, Indian Ocean, Red Sea.

Sometimes they'd listen to the shipping forecast and, while she had no clue what it meant, the sombre voice of the man who read out the names, Finisterre, Dogger, Shannon, Fastnet, conjured images of fisherman being pounded by waves on ships battling through a storm. She would snuggle into the strong, tattooed arms of her dad, held safe by calloused seaman's hands.

He was her hero then and he'd remained so ever since. No matter what he'd done.

Her eyes then fell on the other rogues in the gallery: her grandchildren, Darcy, Max, Tilly, Ella and Lola and more central, next to her dad, were her precious daughters, Rosina, Violetta and Leonora.

Naming them was something Sebastian, her late husband had no interest in. They had his surname and that was enough. This left her to carry on a tradition that her dad had started so Rosina was a tribute to Rossini's *Barber of Seville*, Violetta from Verdi's *La Traviata* and lastly Leonora, from *Il Trovatore*.

Touching the frame, Carmen traced the face of Rosina, dark-haired like herself with eyes to match. Her whippet-thin eldest was a linchpin, reliable, hard-working and maternal, she always had been. Mother's proverbial little helper. Next to her was Leonora, the kindest soul, with identical colouring yet where Rosina was willowy, the youngest was petite, fragile really, a legacy of premature birth most likely brought on by unhappy circumstances. And in the centre as always was Violetta, their auburn-haired firebrand who kept them all on their toes. She favoured her father in many ways. And just like Carmen, Violetta's memory of a man she'd adored might be faded but it was something she had clung to with indomitable determination. For a while anyway.

Carmen understood how that felt more than Violetta knew, which was why she'd never sullied Sebastian's memory as her sister had, and allowed her dead husband to live on in a way that gave their daughter comfort.

Her own mum had done the same, albeit through gritted teeth which was why the photo of Sylvia was positioned at the edge of the collection. Even though it was just a photo, Carmen imagined her mother's pursed lips, her squinted eyes glancing sideways along the row with a look of disgust aimed at her unfaithful husband. Instead of bringing her down, the notion made Carmen smile because that's exactly how her mum was, who she was and she still loved her for it.

Right, enough of that. Tea, toast and Radio 4 is what you need right now, not starting the day in the past.

Yawning as she opened the door and stepped onto the landing, Carmen was glad she had the choice to get up with the lark or lie in till the barking of dogs forced her out of bed. Her days of early starts at the crack of dawn were over, being half asleep, pulling on work-clothes and boots to start a shift that stretched into twelve hours, sometimes longer, working non-stop to establish her business while bringing up three children.

It had all paid off though, and twenty years later her market garden was thriving and the garden centre booming, as were all the other offshoots that had sprung up over time. The café was always popular, the farm and gift shop even more so, the children's petting zoo was a huge draw and a personal favourite of her five grandchildren. Even the campsite was fully booked for the year ahead while the nature and cycling trails looked after themselves.

Thanks to a brilliant team who ran the whole shebang, Carmen's input was surplus to requirements but always heeded, even after she had handed the reins to Rosina. Everyone knew the business was Carmen's brainchild, her labour of love. She still liked to wander down there to say hello to the staff, most of whom she regarded as friends. She'd get her hands dirty in the greenhouses, was always on hand in an emergency or if they were short-staffed but on the whole her days were spent at the house, sedate and leisurely. And that was how she liked them.

All that was about to change, though, and as she began her descent of the wide stairwell, flicking on lights as she went, there was a tickle of excitement in her stomach that brought a smile to her lips.

Christmas was only eleven days away and soon the house would be filled with family. Celebrations and get-togethers had been planned, making up for lost time and then in the new year there would be a huge white wedding – but before that, Carmen would face another hurdle. There it was again, a tickle in the tummy.

It had been a long time since she'd felt like this about Christmas. The previous year's festivities had been a washout. Lockdown rules that had everyone's hopes hanging in the balance, gloom and fear, no real light, just a tunnel that separated people from their loved ones or worse, took them away for good.

No wonder Carmen had a morbid fear of Christmas. She couldn't lay the full blame on an evil virus, though, it went further back than that. Ever since her sixth Christmas, memories of a day that should have been filled with joy and happiness were doused in gloom and unshakeable, gut-swirling misery.

It had never left her, what happened on that Christmas Eve. Her father didn't come back. Not once. Afterwards her whole life changed, her mother changed, Carmen changed. Even if, for 364 days of the year she somehow managed to live without her dad there was no escaping Christmas, one special day that tormented her for weeks before and days after.

In adulthood Carmen had forced herself to smother the demons that taunted and threatened to derail Christmas for her own children but they still lingered in the corners of her mind. Right up to the last minute she would wait for something to go wrong, ruin it all. The saving up, the wrapping up, the waking up on Christmas morning, knowing it had all gone wrong.

And then in a weird and ironic twist, totally unexpected and unplanned, a pandemic broke the spell. In a 'eureka' kind of moment, or maybe it was an epiphany, when she was at her lowest, Carmen decided that enough was enough.

Her own family had been touched by the curse that was covid. From the worst tragedy of losing a loved one, not being there to say goodbye to her mother or hold her hand in the final moments. Then a postponed wedding, cancelled holidays, the lack of human contact, hugs, conversation with a real-life human. Right down to irrelevances, trivial stuff they missed that suddenly meant so much.

But they had emerged. Still the same family yet Carmen felt altered in, for want of a better word, a spiritual way. More resilient, quietly determined, most definitely eager to embrace a new way of life.

Which was why this year was going to be different. This year Carmen fully intended to laugh in the face of adversity. She dared fate to spoil her plans, knock itself out because she had made lists, checked them more than twice, second-guessed, prepared contingencies and given the Grinch a two-fingered salute.

She had been mentally ticking boxes since October, taking stock and counting blessings. Her three daughters were all happy, settled, waged and, apart from one, in love. Her five grandchildren weren't a moment of trouble but then again find her a grandma who didn't think that. She was fortunate and in a position to spoil all of them rottener than ever before – hence a Christmas weekend extravaganza that they would never forget.

Last Christmas, they couldn't all be together. Rosina had tested positive two days before so all of her family had to isolate. Violetta and her daughter were able to come, as well as Leonora, minus her fiancé who was showing symptoms.

The Appletons had been forced apart at a time when Carmen needed them close. They'd made do with Zoom. Not this year. Nothing and nobody was going to ruin the day for her or her family, least of all her own fears and foibles. Her overactive imagination had been stuffed in a box, padlocked and the key smelted down.

Finally and not before time, Carmen was breaking the cycle that had dogged her for so long and marred fifty-odd Christmases. She had ordered half the farm shop – including two turkeys, just in case one was off like in 2017. There was nothing in the festive food chain that wasn't stocked in her larder – she'd checked.

And if Boris made a new and unexpected rule, she would pretend she hadn't heard and smuggle them in across the fields under the cover of darkness. Whatever could go wrong, she'd thought of it and was hell-bent on having a good time. So God help anyone who stood in her way, and quite frankly the mood she was in even the Lord Almighty should watch his step. And if, by some long-awaited miracle, the grown-up Baby Jesus rode in to town on a knackered old donkey, a tsunami washed over the Cheshire Plain or a meteorite landed on Appleton Farm, somehow the show would go on.

Christmas was going to be perfect because at Carmen's request she would have everyone under her roof. This year, for one special weekend, all her family were coming home.

2

LEONORA

Manchester city centre
Present day

Leonora headed towards Joel's in rush-hour traffic, cursing other drivers but knowing he would wait patiently, all night if necessary. Still, it didn't rid her of the panicky sensation that made her neck go tight or the flood of irritation that swam through her veins like poison. Due to some total knobhead blocking the junction while he had a row with another knobhead who had cut him up, she was twenty minutes late. Twenty precious minutes with Joel had been lost and it would piss her off all night.

Turning onto Joel's road she scanned it for a space and was further disheartened to see that the whole row on either side was rammed. The terraces were a stone's throw away from the Trafford Centre where she was supposed to be shopping. But the car park there was chock-a-block, so shoppers used the residential areas. Sucking in her irritation Leonora drove around the block and willed there to be a space. Three streets later she found a spot and reversed in.

Turning off the engine she sighed and took out her phone and sent a text to Jolene, her imaginary friend from work and Joel's alias, just in case Caspar, her fiancé from hell scrolled through her phone.

Be there in five. Just parked up.

Then taking a deep breath she made a perfunctory, or more accurately, obligatory call before she left her car. Riddled with anxiety, terrified he'd change his plans and decide to come and meet her, Leonora kept the conversation light and swift.

'I've just arrived at the Trafford Centre. Are you busy? I won't keep you if you are.'

Caspar's sigh was loud enough to demonstrate how under pressure he was. 'You wouldn't believe how much I need to get done. Seriously, I think I'm the only one who does any work around here. Are you shopping alone or meeting someone?'

The change in pace was swift and she'd expected an interrogation. 'Like I said in my text earlier, Jolene is going to try and meet up at some point but if not I'll be fine. I want to try lots of things on and maybe pick up some extra pressies for the kids. I'm starving too, so I'll grab a bite to eat.'

Leonora had to stick to what she'd already said. And she was glad to have Jolene as an imaginary backup, her social-media phobic friend. Innocent remarks from her friends in conversation, or a casual post on Facebook or a tweet had made him suspicious of all sorts of stupid things and then the questions would start, delving, trying to trip her up. He was sly like that.

'Sounds boring as hell but at least you'll get something

decent to eat. I'll have to make do with something on the way home. Are you staying at mine tonight?'

'No.' The word escaped rather more quickly than Leonora had intended and she immediately tried to soften the blow. 'I'm on an early again. I'll go home so I don't disturb you. It's not fair especially as you'll be tired by the time you leave.'

The sound of another phone ringing in his office brought the conversation to a swift end when Caspar became distracted. 'Look, I have to go, I'll text you tomorrow. Happy dress-hunting, oh, and don't buy anything too revealing like that one you wore for my works party. The last thing I want is everyone gawping at you while we eat Christmas dinner. It was bad enough my boss leching over you. Be good.'

The disconnected tone brought Leonora immense relief. She was still raging inside though. Locking her car she set off, her stride purposeful. At least for the next few hours she was free, supposedly trawling every single dress shop in search of a new outfit for Christmas Day. What really irked was that Caspar still might actually turn up out of the blue.

She could imagine him ringing and his fake-as-fuck voice saying, *'Hey, I'm here. Let's get something to eat.'* So at least her car would be close by and she could say, *'Oh bugger, I'm outside, just leaving.'* The ridiculousness of her meticulous planning really pissed her off and so did her freakshow fiancé.

Bullets of hail nipped at her legs and drenched the hood of her parka so she ignored her paranoia, bowed her head and hurried onwards, determined to make up for lost time. She wove between parked cars and then along the path towards Joel's, niftily sidestepping dawdlers.

Christ, why is everyone so slow?

The urge to shove the woman in front to one side and chuck her wheelie trolley under the shuttle bus was overwhelming – and out of character because Leonora wasn't prone to aggression. But at that moment, her only desire was to be with Joel.

The hail turned to sleeting rain and her jeans were soggy, the denim rubbing her skin as water seeped into her boots. It was as though someone up there was deliberately thwarting Leonora's plans, intent on preventing an illicit liaison.

The idea of being watched from above turned Leonora's thoughts to her grandmother and if anyone was prone to meddling, it would be her. Not content with spreading rumours and ruining everyone's day up in heaven, her gran probably felt the need to niggle the evildoers who still dwelt on earth too.

That was how Leonora imagined her dear departed grandmother, and even though she was a cantankerous, opinionated pain in the arse at the best of times, Leonora and her sisters really loved their Granny Sylvia. She was tough as a pear drop on the outside, but once you knew how to wince through the acid layer there was a surprisingly squishy core of mush in the middle. And as much as she tested everyone's patience, her behaviour was borne purely from love, the result of a bruised and broken heart, and the desire to protect her family from hurt of any kind. Which was why they always forgave her.

Oddly enough, even though she wasn't a believer, it gave Leonora great comfort to think of Granny Sylvia zooming straight up to heaven in the arms of her beleaguered angel who couldn't wait to dump her charge and finally, after seventy-five long and trying years, be done with *the* most pious and bigoted woman in Cheshire. Despite all that, Leonora really missed her. They all did.

Saint Sylvia. That was what Leonora and her two older sisters secretly called their gran. She had come to live with them after their dad was killed in a horrific accident. Their mum was heavily pregnant with Leonora and had two children and a rattling leaky house to care for. And as much as she was a stickler for routine, manners, early bedtimes, cod liver oil – basically everything most things children absolutely hate, nobody could deny that she had arrived at Appleton just at the right time. Granny Sylvia had swept in like a blonde, cockney Mary Poppins to take care of her grieving daughter and shell-shocked granddaughters and set about putting the world to rights. Once she was ensconced at Appleton Farm she became an integral part of the family, someone they couldn't do without which made losing her so much harder to bear.

Leonora swallowed down the blob of sadness that had welled in her throat. She cheered herself with thoughts of Joel, who was just minutes away, only to be plunged back into misery when she thought of Caspar and his whiny voice. It was as though his self-pity had stuck to her eardrums. Lately, it seemed like everything he did or said irritated her and his negativity soaked into her pores, dragging her down like soggy trainers.

He was like a limpet who spied on her and on more than one occasion had turned up unannounced at a wine bar when she was with her friends. Or by pure coincidence in a packed Arndale Shopping Centre he would 'bump into her' – fancy that! Leonora sensed he was following her and was increasingly obsessed with her whereabouts and routine, making it easier for him to pin her down.

Then there were the questions about her colleagues and who she talked to during the day, gave a lift home to, where they lived. The guy was seriously giving her the creeps, turning up at her mum's unannounced like he was trying to catch her out and poking his nose into family affairs, never mind their business.

The rain was easing slightly. She couldn't wait to be inside the warm home that Joel was house-sitting for his brother who was in Italy skiing. They were making the most of having a place where they could escape from everyone, real life, and Caspar.

The traffic in and around the huge shopping centre was ridiculous but would suit Leonora's purposes because everyone knew that at Christmastime the place was packed with shoppers, diners and cinemagoers; therefore if she was delayed getting home, her tragic story of roads being blocked would be totally believable.

'Honestly, Caspar. It was bumper to bumper in and out, and you should have seen the crowds inside. My feet were killing me so I stopped in the food hall and had something to eat, I was knackered. I know, I can't believe it either, that in all of those lovely shops I still couldn't find a dress I liked. You know I prefer to try things on so I might nip over to Cheshire Oaks at the weekend, otherwise I'll have to take a chance online.'

There was no way Leonora could stay the whole night with Joel: it was too risky. And as much as she was looking forward to Christmas, it would also mean being apart from Joel and putting up with Caspar tagging along. The whole family would be there and Christmas Day fell on a Saturday, which had thrilled her mum no end.

Usually the garden centre would remain open until 4pm on Christmas Eve but this year it would close on the Thursday and all of the staff and their families were invited to a 'thank you' party in the café. It had been a tough year and her mum wanted to show everyone who'd worked so hard to keep the garden centre ticking how grateful she was.

It was going to be 'open house' and Leonora and her sisters, nieces and nephews could invite anyone they wanted, the more the merrier. The only thing was, the person Leonora didn't want to be there was Caspar, and the one she did want to be there couldn't even show his face because all hell would break loose. And that was the last thing anyone wanted. A pre-Christmas Eve punch-up!

The Big Weekend (as they'd all taken to calling it) meant a

lot to her mum, who'd been planning it since the end of summer – that's what it felt like anyway. Ever since Leonora could remember her mum had made Christmas Day special. According to Rosina, even when everyone was grieving the loss of their dad, a dad Leonora had never met, she pulled out all the stops to make sure it was a happy day. Being a single mum would have been tough – especially once she started building the garden centre – but she was their absolute rock who never let them down and was an inspiration to all of the Appleton women. So no way was Leonora's illicit affair with the man who broke her heart when he ran off to the Far East, going to ruin it.

That little drama was scheduled for after Christmas, as soon as she plucked up the courage to tell Caspar *and* her mum that the big white wedding which had been halted the year before wasn't going to happen this year either. And then, while she was on a roll, she'd hit her family with the double whammy. She and Joel were back together, madly in love and this time it was for keeps.

To be fair Leonora hadn't expected Caspar's proposal but as she imagined thousands, maybe millions of blindsided people had done in the past, she'd said yes to save embarrassment. For Caspar and all the people in the Parisian restaurant. It wasn't wrong to have accepted when she wanted to scream, NO! It was merely an act of panic-stricken kindness.

Two months later, the terrible virus that was ravaging the world helped her avoid the massive mistake of marrying someone totally unsuitable. She wasn't remotely upset when they'd had to shelve their wedding plans and her mother's new notebook was stuffed in the kitchen drawer, permanently as far as Leonora was concerned. They had watched the big lockdown announcement in the kitchen of Appleton Farm and while her mother commiserated and Caspar cursed Boris, Leonora wanted to hug the tatty-haired bearer of bad tidings, even if it wasn't allowed.

Her future didn't lie with Caspar even though he one hundred per cent believed that his lay with her. Or, as she'd come to realise, he believed his future lay with the Appleton Farm family and the thriving business that his wife-to-be would one day inherit.

On paper, Leonora knew that the garden centre, its land and tenanted properties put her mother in the millionaire bracket. And, unfortunately, so did Caspar, because he worked for the firm of accountants that looked after their financial matters.

Leonora also knew that she and Caspar were completely mismatched and had she not been recovering from a broken heart, wouldn't have given the handsome and suave accountant the time of day. At the beginning, if she were honest, she'd hoped that word of her new relationship would filter across the airwaves and oceans via mutual friends. She wanted to piss Joel off and make him rue the day he chose Thailand and an internship at a wildlife reserve over her.

The nice half of Leonora, because she did have one, had begrudgingly accepted that Joel's trip was an opportunity he couldn't miss and she tried hard to be pleased that he was going to live his dream. But she'd loved him too much to let him go.

Every bone of his beautiful body, his unruly fair hair that he had to tie in a bobble while he worked in the pine forest at Appleton, and those soulful brown eyes that couldn't look at hers when he told her he was thinking of leaving. The same eyes that danced with excitement when he explained about the elephant sanctuary and how the local villagers would teach him about bio-diversity and sustaining the environment.

So to begin with, nice Leonora waved him off and promised she could live without him for six months, convincing herself that it would go in a flash. Then when he came home he could put his skills to good use at Appleton where her mum had already promised him a job managing the forest. And his own brand-new Land Rover. Who could resist?

Joel, that's who.

When she received the phone call, telling her he'd been offered a full-time position by a global conservation trust, nice Leonora disappeared in a puff of angry black smoke and nasty Leonora emerged from the flames. This version was riddled with disappointment while humiliation whispered that she was a gullible fool, whipping up fury that vented itself in angry, intolerant words.

No, she didn't believe that a job wasn't already on the cards the day he boarded the flight to Bangkok. No, she wouldn't consider joining him over there. No, she wasn't prepared to give him another six months to see if it worked out. And no, they couldn't be friends. Leonora didn't regret calling him a dirty perv who was probably enjoying the backstreet pleasures of Thailand. Or insinuating stuff about ladyboys. And hoping he'd catch something that would make his dick drop off, just before jabbing the red phone icon and ending the call.

Yes, messages were sent back and forth for a week or two but in the end they both accepted it was over. It still didn't make loving someone, every day, any easier to bear.

Leonora was still annoyed with herself for going to pieces and hibernating in her room like a smelly hermit that only came out to drag itself to work, or to nibble at food slumped at the kitchen table in her pyjamas. She was tutted at by Saint Sylvia and mollycoddled (as the holy one put it) by her worried and angry mother. Three months of wallowing later, two stone lighter and looking like a bag of bony rags in her whites, the sallow witch with grown-out roots was called upon to do a favour.

Her eldest sister, Rosina, who managed the garden centre, had come down with a bug. The young man who was doing the audit would be arriving early and someone needed to let him into the office so he could crack on. Cue Leonora.

Not only was she taken aback by the good-looking guy who didn't mind a bit that she was ten minutes late when she shuffled to the office door, Leonora was surprised that she noticed him. She was also rather chuffed he was flirting and felt ridiculously glad she'd worn her bobble hat. The next morning she applied a bit of make-up – nothing that the hawk-eyed Saint Sylvia would notice – and was ready and waiting for Caspar, as she now knew him to be, when he arrived to get on with the audit.

One appointment at the hairdressers later Leonora was ready and willing to be wooed and maybe, just maybe, Joel would panic and come home.

Leonora miscalculated, badly. And had she not been such a desperate, game-playing saddo who was on the rebound and determined to punish Joel for his stupidity, she wouldn't have given Caspar the time of day and ended up trapped in a relationship with an utter control freak. Or a complete bore. Her total opposite in every way. A vain, self-obsessed social climber. A man intent on doing the least possible for the greatest gain.

She could see Joel's car outside his brother's house and for the umpteenth time asked, *What have I done?* Why couldn't nice Leonora have given Joel a bit longer and, in the meantime, focused on her career and followed her own route. Catering college, then some real-life experience in a restaurant before opening her own bistro in the grounds of the garden centre. It was all set aside for her. Funds to renovate and refit the old mill where she could make her mark on the Cheshire dining scene.

But no. Instead she'd had a paddy and lost the most lovely guy with a heart of gold who might have eventually come back to work at the family firm, once he'd had a chance to live his dream, which he deserved. And everything would have been perfect.

And to add insult to injury, Saint Sodding Sylvia had been right all along because she never liked Caspar from the off and wasn't shy about saying so. 'He's a shifty get, and smarmy with it. And his suits are shiny, like a lounge lizard. Never trust a man in a shiny suit. Or who drives one of them cars that the roof comes down. Poncy poser. You want to watch him, my girl.' Sylvia pursed her lips as she eyed Leonora across the kitchen table.

Her mum had her back to them, stirring a pan at the Aga, saying nothing but tutting loudly. Leonora imagined she was rolling her eyes as she added more salt to the vegetables.

Leonora picked up the bread and the carving knife with the other, pointing it as she spoke. 'Gran, you've only met him once so how can you tell? And what are you going on about, shiny suits? And I have no idea what a bloody lounge lizard is and loads of men drive convertibles. Seriously, you can take generalisation to the next level.'

'And he talks funny, in a know-all voice, like he's cleverer than us.' Sylvia turned the page of her newspaper, keeping her eyes on the print.

'No he doesn't!'

A Sylvia shrug meant her gran thought she was right, as usual. 'Suppose there's no accounting for tastes.'

Determined to make her point Leonora continued to bat for Caspar's team. 'And anyway, he was only here for half an hour and you can't make an assessment based on clothes and cars, and voices for Chri– crying out loud.' Leonora knew better than to take the Lord's name in vain. 'I thought he was very polite even when you started interrogating him. You shouldn't ask people who they vote for or where their parents are from. It's sod-all to do with you.' Leonora began chopping the bread into cubes to make croutons and was glad that Caspar had declined the invitation to stay and eat with them.

Her toes were actually curling throughout the visit especially when the holy one had asked if he was financially stable and had he been christened. Seriously embarrassing.

'Well, I'm only looking out for you, Leo.' Her gran shortened all her granddaughters' names because she didn't like them, or opera, or the female characters they and their mother were named after.

'The last thing we want is you getting dumped by another feller. Once is enough. I know that better than anyone.' Granny Sylvia flipped another page of the *Sunday Express* and raised an eyebrow.

Leonora wouldn't back down, determined to make a point. 'And thanks so much for telling him all about Joel and how devastated I was when he left to follow his dreams because *that's* what really happened. He did NOT dump me, remember! And was there any need for the bit about me sounding like a wailing banshee and not having a wash for twelve weeks? Jesus, Gran. Could you have made me sound any more sad and gross?'

Her hand coming down hard on the newspaper told Leonora that her gran was cross. 'Leo! Do not say "Jesus" in that tone of voice.'

Leonora winced. 'Sorry Gran.'

Mollified, her gran continued. 'And I'll have you know that I am very well informed about how that man has been sniffing round and asking our Rosie all about you. You shouldn't forget that he has access to facts and figures so he knows he's onto a good thing with a young girl like you. Like a rat up a drainpipe he is.'

'Gran! That's gross'

'And he's too old for you, like your dad was when he met your mum and did she listen to me? Course she didn't and look what happened there! Men, they are the road to ruination, mark my words.'

It was at this point Leonora saw her mum swing around, waving the wooden spoon as she spoke. 'Leonora, just ignore your gran; and Mother, give it a rest, will you. If you've got nothing better to do than criticise, come and stir the soup. You and this spoon are made for each other.'

It was impossible not to notice the glare aimed at her gran, who finally shut up and got on with reading her paper while Leonora received a conspiratorial wink from her mum. It was common family knowledge that their self-appointed head of the clan hated all men in general. In fact, unless you were white, straight and a Christian, Sylvia operated a zero-tolerance policy with regards to the entire human race.

The funny thing was, despite her sometimes cutting ways, she was often on the money. Definitely where Caspar was concerned and even though Joel had broken Leonora's heart, and according to her gran, dumped her, she never really had a bad word to say about him. Before or after. And at Appleton Farm, that was as close to a miracle as you'd get. Ever!

Manchester. Present day.

Leonora was grasping at celestial straws because even if her gran had given Joel a second chance, she certainly wouldn't condone cheating on her fiancé no matter how shifty he was. Maybe if she'd confided in her gran that she was right about Caspar, she'd have forgiven her. That he was insanely jealous of Joel, and a nasty drunk who had once or twice made her feel unsafe. Plus the twisted belittling comments that came naturally to someone who was a controlling bully. Leonora imagined her gran giving him a taste of his own medicine. In fact, she was sure she'd have stood by her and Caspar would have come off worse.

Seeing Joel at the door she wiped the rain from her face and thoughts of Caspar from her mind because for the next few hours she would pretend he didn't exist. They both would. As she almost leapt into his arms and made his jumper as soggy as her, she reminded herself, *Not long now. All you have to do is get past Christmas, not ruin anything for Mum and then you'll be free.*

3

_____

GEORDIE

Geordie picked up the post from the hall mat and sorted through the various envelopes, separating the takeaway flyers from Christmas cards and a squishy parcel in a brown bubble pack, until he came to the one he'd been expecting. He recognised the writing on the front immediately but instead of opening it, he placed the rest on the stairs and made his way upwards, legs creaking as he took each step.

A voice from the bathroom called out, 'Was that the post? Did my parcel come?'

'Yes, it's on the stairs.' The swish of the shower curtain and then the clunk of the boiler as hot water gushed into the bath told Geordie he had a few minutes of peace and quiet, time for himself and his thoughts.

Opening his side of the wardrobe he crouched and from the bottom shelf pulled out a battered box. By its side was a Quality Street tin. It was scuffed by time and full of photographs that he'd once salvaged, scraping all of them together like a scavenger who needed to feed on images of what once was. Stiff, formal snaps of his parents and grandparents, sepia tones and sparse in number, but at least he could see their faces, hold onto a fragment of his history. Others were of him as a young man, again few and far between as were the ones of him and Sylvia and Carmen, his long-ago family.

The other box once contained a new pair of Dr Martens work boots. On the lid was a faded black-and-yellow emblem, an iconic brand name that was once worn by factory workers, postmen and labourers. Geordie smiled when he read the price label on the end, £2/6s/4d and gripped by nostalgia he said it out loud, 'Two pounds, six shillings and four pence. Those were the days.'

Taking the box to the bed he sat, then lifted the lid, pulling away the crinkled brown wrapping paper to reveal a post office savings book and the piles of letters inside. Each one held a message of love that he'd written to his little girl, every Christmas since he'd left.

The fifty envelopes differed in size, always containing a Christmas card, a letter, a twenty-pound note, a photograph taken in a booth or a Polaroid and later, developed at Boots. The handwriting on the front was either black or blue biro and the addresses were like a road map, a trail that tracked his life's journey for just over half a century.

Placing the envelope that had just been delivered on top, Geordie rested his hand on the pile knowing that underneath were lines and lines of words telling of his travels, a shipyard, another rented room or flat.

He'd bared his soul, shared hopes for the future and dreams that they would meet again. Been honest about his regrets for the mistakes he'd made and explored solutions, worked out how he could have done things differently.

And even though she couldn't reply there were many questions. A one-sided conversation that parents, not ones like him, were lucky to have with their children, in the same room, not somewhere out of reach. He asked about school and her friends and interests, what pop groups she liked or he tried to guess. He wondered what she was good at, was she artistic, academic, sporty? Was she built like him, tall and stocky or willowy and petite like her mum? Her hair had been blonde when she was little but had it darkened a shade? One thing Geordie knew was that her eyes would still be brown, nothing could change that. So many questions. No answers. Just the face of a tearful six-year-old who for him never grew up.

Realising she would be in the same predicament, he'd include a yearly photo of himself so she'd know what he looked like, even though the booth ones made him look a bit rough, like a mugshot of a criminal. And there were others, of the places he lived, stately homes and gardens he'd visited, scenes from the top of a hill during a walk, his allotment, all the stuff he would have said in person or on the phone.

He shared with her his love of opera, films and books and would list the titles he thought she might like. He hoped she knew why they'd named her Carmen, his choice of a beautiful name for a beautiful baby. Did she remember the rhyme about the pearl? He would always write it on the back of the last sheet of paper, just in case.

Then later, when she would be in her teens he'd tentatively broached the subject of how much she knew about why he left, worries over what she'd been told and the unfolding of his side of the story. It was ridiculous in a way because if her mind was set, if Sylvia had broken her promise then the words were all for nothing. But then there was always a chance that knowing he'd taken the time to lay it all out, to converse with his living, breathing yet part-imagined daughter, she would understand and forgive him.

When he'd felt brave enough there was an introduction to the love of his life, along with an apology for not loving her mother as much, and an assurance that he had tried so hard to make things work if only for her, his little pearl.

Geordie swore that he would have gladly stayed, sacrificed his own happiness for hers and lived a lie for the rest of his life if it had meant not losing her. He swore this as his oath.

The hardest part was explaining why he had never searched for her after she disappeared with her mother. It was harder in those days with only house phones and letters to keep in touch. But Sylvia had been so bitter, rightly hurt when Martha had barged into their home and tore their life apart.

Bitterness. It was like a plague that infected all of them because he'd felt it too, towards Martha who had been riddled with it, as well as being jealous and insecure but with age Geordie came to realise that she was also a victim. He never saw her again after that night in Tilbury because he'd fled, ashamed and unable to bear the look on the face of his wife and child and by the time he'd found the courage to return and talk things through, they were gone. No forwarding address, no telephone number. The cord was cut.

Geordie felt suddenly weary so closing his eyes, rested back onto the pillows. Against the blackness of his eyelids the past played like a reel of cine film, taking him straight back to 1969.

Tilbury, London 1969

The shock of finding them gone was actually worse than when he'd opened the door to find Martha on the doorstep. It was the day after Boxing Day. The house was a land version of the Marie Celeste. He'd sneaked back under the cover of darkness, still sheepish and unsure what the neighbours had heard. As Geordie moved from room to room he tried to work out what Sylvia had taken. Going by the looks of it, anything she could carry in the three suitcases that were no longer stored under the bed.

It wasn't as though they had a lot. They were just getting started really. Money was tight so there wasn't much in the way of valuables or knick-knacks but knowing she'd left her precious crockery and some of Carmen's toys made Geordie hopeful that Sylvia was coming back. And she hadn't smashed his records or ripped the pages out of his books. The two things that confused him, that pulled him both ways were the missing titles and the photos. Why had she taken two of him yet left the one of their wedding day? And Sylvia didn't read the same books as him so why take the copies he knew were gone?

Carmen! Had she taken them? Because if she had, it meant only one thing: she didn't think she was coming home. The thought of his little girl taking things that linked her to him broke Geordie in two, sobs wracking his body as he sat in the darkness, praying for them to walk through the door.

Once he'd composed himself he lit a fire and settled into his armchair, resolute, clinging to hope. He was going to wait for his wife to calm down and eventually she would bring their daughter home. Then they could talk, make sensible arrangements and part on good terms.

Three days later she still hadn't turned up and Geordie began to panic. He'd suspected they'd gone to stay with Sylvia's elderly aunt in Brighton so after remembering their address from a day trip he rang directory enquiries and got their number. Geordie rang there constantly, begging to speak to Sylvia, or Carmen, or for an address where his wife and daughter might be but Mavis vehemently denied they were there or any knowledge of their whereabouts.

Unconvinced, he took the train to Brighton and marched straight up to her front door in a row of identical terraced houses, convinced they were there and determined to see

Carmen and make Sylvia promise to keep in touch. Instead of an agreement, he got a punch in the face from Roy, Mavis's husband.

Geordie didn't give up, though, and waited all night at the end of the street, watching the house from an alleyway. The doors opened straight onto the pavement so he would see clearly if they came outside. The only other way out was via the back alley and from where he lurked, he had a view of one entrance.

By midnight he was perished and starving but being skint, had to sleep in the bus station. After a cup of tea offered to him by a kindly caretaker, Geordie returned to Mavis's the following morning and kept vigil all day, hoping Sylvia and Carmen would reveal themselves. Nothing. After one more night shivering in the bus station he trudged back to the street and watched the milkman on his rounds, then Roy leaving for work and later mums walking their kids to school. There was no sign of Carmen and Sylvia. Geordie accepted it was hopeless.

He was about give up, frozen, tired and starving when he spotted Mavis opening the front door, and beckoning him over.

Looking from side to side, worried that Roy was going to ambush him, Geordie took a chance and raced across the road to be met by the beady eyes and pursed lips of Mavis. She had a line of rollers down the middle of her hair and the one on her fringe bobbed as she wobbled her angry head, her voice harsh. 'You'd make a rubbish spy, Geordie Wilson. I've been watching you for the past two days, you daft apeth. You'd best come inside, I've got Sylvia on the blower.' Mavis turned and marched up the hall, pointing at the green phone on the stand.

Wordlessly, Geordie made his way along the gloomy hallway, his eyes trying to accustom themselves to the light and the hideous orange-and-brown swirly paper that made the walls feel like they were closing in, or was that hunger and nerves? He glanced at Mavis who stood firm at the bottom of the stairs, arms folded across her chest, obviously going nowhere. Picking up the receiver he spotted a birdcage in the corner of the parlour opposite, a yellow budgerigar flicked his bell. Ding ding. Let battle commence.

'Hello, Sylvia.'

The voice on the other end seemed to have hardened, her tone sharp, her words precise. 'I want you to leave us alone, Geordie. Stay away from my family, do you hear me?'

Geordie had only one aim and that was to find out where she was because no way was he abandoning his daughter. 'Sylvia, we need to talk. Please tell me where you are and I can meet you, discuss things like adults and make arrangements for Carmen. That's all I ask.'

'No. I don't want to see you ever again so I'm telling you one more time, leave us alone.'

Despite her warning he had to persevere. After almost freezing to death he wasn't giving up his daughter without a fight. 'But what about money? I need to look after Carmen and the house. I can send it there.'

'Geordie NO! We won't be going back there ever, not after the shame you brought to our door. Don't you see it's only a matter of time before people start gossiping about us? Walls have ears and rumours spread and I won't be laughed at, Geordie, and neither will Carmen. Kids are cruel and I won't have the others saying stuff. It's over. We've gone and it's all your fault. I will never, ever forgive you for what you've done, not as long as I live.'

Geordie began to panic. He could hear the venom in Sylvia's voice yet at the same time he heard a sob, felt her heartbreak and hated himself for what he'd done, for giving in to lust, for being weak. 'But it's your home, Carmen's home. You can't take her away.'

'Well I have. It's done.'

The walls felt like they were closing in, the hallucinogenic swirls of orange and brown making him nauseous while the ceiling threatened to flatten him, like his lungs that were having trouble catching a breath. Steadying himself, he forced out a plea while his heart drummed in his ears. 'Sylvia, please, I'm begging you. Give me a chance to explain... what will you tell Carmen? Please don't turn her against me, please Sylvia, I beg you, don't do that.'

There was a long silence down the line. All Geordie could do was wait and pray, not throw up or cry, and ignore Mavis's steely glare that was boring holes into the side of his head.

Then Sylvia spoke. 'If you leave us alone, don't try to find us, I promise I won't turn her against you. But if you ever bother me again, I swear to God I will do everything in my power to make her hate you. Do you understand me, Geordie? Let us go, let me go. No child deserves a disgusting dad like you. You made your bed, so lie in it.'

For a second his lips wouldn't move and the moment would always be frozen in time.

Foot-tapping Mavis, orange and brown, sick swirling inside his stomach, trembling hands grasping the receiver of the pea-green GPO phone, the tinkle of a bell, the chirp of a caged bird in the corner of a room, the end of life as he knew it closing in.

Geordie, barely able to speak, whispered his answer. 'Tell Carmen I love her and I'll never forget her. She'll always be my pearl.'

'Goodbye, Geordie.' There was a click on the line. And then she was gone.

Geordie made his solitary way back to Tilbury but couldn't settle. His restless soul was constantly hounded by a guilty conscience so he'd set off for pastures new, hoping to make a fresh start, away from gossips and pointing fingers, whispers and insinuations.

Every year at Christmas, no matter where he was, Geordie would write his daughter a letter and send it to himself. That way the postmark would show the place and date and if she did track him down, he would give her the box of letters to prove he had never forgotten her.

He marked the years in envelopes and when there were twelve in the pile he prayed that her eighteenth birthday might be a turning point and she'd seek him out. Three envelopes later he clung on to the possibility that turning twenty-one might mean she was a bit more independent, confident enough to try and find him. But as the envelopes piled up, the corner of his heart that was reserved for hope began to shrink. Logic took up residence in the space where daydreams once dwelt and Geordie realised that it might be hard for Carmen to find him, especially when he was at sea. Regardless, he kept up his tradition and waited patiently. The thing was, time was running out or was it catching up with him? But either way he'd made a decision. The past twelve months of living through a pandemic had taught him many things, least of all that you can't afford to linger, have regrets. So he would get this Christmas and New Year over with and then, he would try to find his daughter even if it meant using up the last of his savings.

He'd kept his bargain with Sylvia, the promise she'd extracted at the lowest point in his life but everyone had the right to change their mind, and he'd changed his.

The slurping of water going down the plughole and the bathroom cabinet door slamming shut told Geordie he would soon have company. So with a sigh, he folded the brown paper over the letters and replaced the lid. Was it worth a prayer to ask that this would be the last time he'd add an envelope to the box? Prayers had never worked before so why try now?

Geordie stood and placed the box back inside the wardrobe and wondered if all his good deeds could be recouped and cashed in. And what about the snap of many wishbones; and the four-leaf clover that was tucked in the back of his wallet next to a photo of Carmen; or every shooting star he'd seen as he'd sailed the oceans; the seventy-six candles he'd blown out last May? Surely at least one of those wishes would come true. Surely he'd waited long enough.

4

VIOLETTA

Macclesfield, Cheshire
Present day

Violetta had just closed the front door when Darcy, her daughter, realised she'd not opened the window on her advent calendar and was refusing to budge until they went back inside.

'But I'll be the only one who hasn't opened the window and it's bad luck.' Darcy's feet seemed to be welded to the step, her folded arms glued to her chest.

Violetta rolled her eyes as she picked up Darcy's schoolbag and pointed the fob at her car, jabbing the button. 'No, it's not bad luck at all. And just think, it will be an extra treat when you come home tonight. Now come on, we'll be late.'

Darcy stood firm. 'It is bad luck. Kyra told me that if you don't open your windows every day the Christmas ghost comes and steals all your presents and anyway, I'm going to Grandma's after school and I'll have lots of treats there.'

Bloody know-all Kyra strikes again. The precocious child ruled the class and her word was like law that Darcy followed to the letter. Closing her eyes in defeat, Violetta span around and strutted back to the door. Arguing with a five-year-old about a chocolate reindeer seemed futile so glaring at her triumphant child, she took out her door key.

Minutes later, the spoils of war were dribbling from the corners of Darcy's lips, the set of which betrayed utter contentment and victory.

Eyeing Little Miss Chocolate Face through the rear mirror, though the stand-off had made them late, Violetta smiled and a familiar glow of pride washed over her.

Darcy was her whole world: the reason for getting up in the morning; the person she thought about last thing at night and did her best to please and provide for; always her number one priority. Violetta was determined to follow in her mum's footsteps because she'd set her three girls a fine example. The bar was raised high and Violetta had striven to do her best, better if that was possible.

And so far Violetta thought she had done okay with Darcy who was a good girl despite her stubborn nature. But what could anyone expect being brought up surrounded by women and strong ones at that.

Violetta often felt a bit sorry for the menfolk in the family who were in a minority. When her gran was alive it was seven against three. Rosina's husband was a lovely bloke but outnumbered at home by three daughters and his wife. Their son was his only ally. Then there was Bern, her mum's bit on the side as the sisters affectionately referred to him. He was a great guy who'd been part of their lives forever but resolutely refused to move out of his cottage on the edge of the forest.

To be fair Violetta didn't blame him one bit, especially during their teenage years. What single man in his right mind would want to move into a house full of screaming girls who fought like cat and dog, made up, then fought like cat and dog again. And then there was Granny Sylvia. No wonder he preferred the luxury of going back to his cosy home for a bit of peace and quiet.

Poor Bern. Everyone knew he was their mum's rock and had been by her side from the early days of the garden centre. Nobody had a bad word to say about him, not even Granny Sylvia but really, she didn't have to. It only took one of her looks and you'd know.

She was like their gatekeeper, the indomitable matriarch whose mission in life was to protect her girls from the scourge of the earth (men) and the last thing she'd wanted was one moving in. On the other hand, had her mum wanted him there, Violetta was sure that's where he'd be because if anyone could deal with Granny Sylvia, her mum could.

Just thinking about her gran made Violetta feel maudlin so she was glad when a squeaky voice in the back piped up. 'Mummy, guess what we're doing tonight, at Grandma's?'

Violetta knew exactly what it was but Darcy liked to go over things. It was her way of making damn sure nobody was going to change their minds.

'We're going to the farm shop to get everything we need for Christmas baking and Grandma says I can go in the grotto and sit on Father Christmas's knee again because I need to make sure he's remembered everything on my list.'

'Darcy, I've told you Santa can't remember what every single child wants. That's what the postbox at school is for, so you can send him a letter and you've already put three in! So I think he's got the message now. The elves will make sure.' A quick glance told her that Darcy was mulling it over.

'But I've thought of an extra thing and I have to tell him.' Her legs kicked as she spoke, her grey socks pulled high up to her knees.

'And what is this extra thing? Don't you think your list is long enough, you cheeky monkey?' Violetta was having visions of a mad dash to the shops or panic trawling online for a last minute, must-have present. She was a soft touch and Darcy knew it.

'It's not for me. It's for you, Mummy.'

This revelation took Violetta completely by surprise. 'Me... what on earth are you going to ask for?'

'I'm not telling you. It'll be a surprise.' Darcy smiled mischievously, which set alarm bells ringing.

'Give me a clue... go on, just a teeny one.' Violetta knew only too well that Darcy was rubbish at secrets and clues.

A dramatic sigh and a wobble of the head accompanied by two raised hands, reminded Violetta of Granny Sylvia. 'Okay. Here's your clue. You will have to kiss a boy.'

'WHAT! Why on earth would I do that?'

Darcy giggled. 'Because that's what you do when you get married.'

'I'm not getting married. I don't even have a boyfriend.' Violetta shook her head and pulled into a side street by the school to look for a parking space.

'That's what I'm asking Father Christmas for. I want my real daddy to come and find us then you will have a boyfriend then you can get married and I will have a daddy. Like Kyra.'

In one fell swoop Violetta's morning crashed and burned. Lost for words, her heart dropped like Wile E. Coyote off a cliff. Silence descended on the car but Darcy didn't seem to notice or care because as always she was too busy searching the cars for Kyra who right now was at the top of Violetta's shit list.

Ten minutes later, back in traffic, Violetta switched on the radio and headed towards work and thanks to her daughter, had yet another problem pecking at her brain.

She was hurt, too. Darcy hadn't meant to cause upset and in her sweet and innocent way would've thought that she was bestowing the perfect gift on her mum, and at the same time herself. But her desire for a daddy had wounded.

Violetta always held her head up at parents' evenings and even though she wasn't the only parent attending alone, she was acutely aware that some of them would have partners waiting at home. Same at school events. She was always manless and even if Leonora or their mum accompanied her, she couldn't help notice the couples, the family units, especially Mr and Mrs Perfect Parents to Kyra, the best-friend-forever-from-hell. They always made a point of coming over and saying hello and they were probably only being polite when they asked if Violetta and Darcy were going anywhere nice for the holidays, before making damn sure they banged on about their hidey-hole cottage in Cornwall.

Stopping at the traffic lights, Violetta sagged against her seat, asking herself the same old questions. *Will I ever be good enough? Why can't she be happy with what she's got? I try so bloody hard to be perfect and give her everything.*

It was true. Ever since she found out she was pregnant Violetta had striven to be the best mum, even when she knew it was going to be a solo venture, even when she knew that her baby would never know who its father was. Simply because Violetta had no clue either.

Pulling away from the lights, she felt like Darcy had really put the mockers on the day, more or less forcing her into an arranged marriage organised by Santa. Sighing, Violetta perused her options. She should try and get Kyra expelled from school, or spread malicious rumours about her obnoxious parents so they'd leave the area and Darcy would never see the uppity little monster ever again. That might help solve the daddy equation and having to put up with Mr and Mrs Smug. Violetta liked this idea, two birds, one stone.

Added to her failings in the marriage department, it also irked her immensely that no matter how hard she tried she always felt like the underdog, the family's loose cannon, the one who messed up. Sometimes she wanted to scream, 'Hey, I'm actually doing okay.'

Darcy was, hands down, her greatest achievement but apart from that and without the help of a man, or her mum for that matter, she'd bought a two-bedroom town house on a new estate in a nice area on the outskirts of Macclesfield. And she was able to send Darcy to a private day nursery before she started school, and take her on holiday every year and afford treats like weekends away and days out.

Violetta wasn't flash, though, because if she knew one thing about her mother, she wasn't stupid and if she started living the high life questions would be asked. That had to be avoided at all costs. This was another reason Leonora's fiancé, Creepy Caspar, was given short shrift when he started dropping hints about taking over the bookkeeping for her own business. He would do it for mates' rates, a nice little earner for him and it'd save her money. Not a chance. It was bad enough that her future brother-in-law knew the ins and outs of her mum's business, let alone hers.

Her investment in the artisan bakery had paid off and she was able to work her hours around Darcy so for both of them, life was sweet. Well it had been, but all that was about to change since her best friend and business partner had quite frankly lost her mind; and maybe her daughter had too. Suddenly, to ice the cake, one wanted to go on an adventure and the other one wanted a sodding dad.

Turning on the radio to numb the boredom of crawling along in what looked like a never-ending line of traffic, half listening to the local news, Violetta weighed up her options. There was no way she could buy Candy out. For a start her friend was the backbone of the business, the master baker while she flitted in and out. So if the bakery closed it'd mean finding a new job; and where the hell was she going to store the equipment for her other one? Certainly not at home that was for sure.

Home. That word made Violetta's stomach flip. What if she couldn't pay the mortgage? She would have to let her house and move back to her mum's. Would that be such a bad thing? Certainly not. For a start Darcy would love living at her grandma's, seeing as she constantly begged to stay for sleepovers in the big house.

Truth be known, Violetta hadn't wanted to move out in the first place and would have happily remained under her mum's roof with her toddler. Who wouldn't want to live in a gorgeous house in the countryside with dogs and ponies and your family all around, yes, even Granny Sylvia. It had been her desire to prove herself that eventually led to her moving out, showing the world that despite her circumstances and change of career she could stand on her own feet.

Oddly enough, she still saw her mum's as home and loved staying over just like Darcy so if push came to shove, she could go back. That was at least a short-term option and eased her tension down a notch. She really needed to have a sit-down chat with her mum as soon as possible but knew that the second she explained her predicament, it would taint The Big Christmas Weekend. Her mum would start worrying and that was the last thing she wanted hanging over her head. This family get-together meant a lot to their mum so Violetta's problems would just have to wait a while longer.

The traffic was moving faster now and seeing the turning for the bakery, Violetta indicated and pulled into the car park at the rear of the building. She wasn't stopping long. Her shift in the shop didn't start until midday and she was only popping in to get changed and collect her case of equipment.

She needed to head back out of town and towards an exclusive boutique hotel where she had a client booked. Leaving her car, Violetta hurried towards the steps that led to the flat above the shop, waving as she did to Candy who'd spotted her from the bakery window.

'I'll see you later on. Is everything okay?' Receiving the thumbs-up sign from Candy she carried on and when she reached the top opened the door to the flat.

Inside, she went straight to the bedroom and took out the uniform hanging in the wardrobe and began to change quickly. Her work was specialised and catered for a range of customer requirements which is why she needed somewhere to store her equipment, which varied from one session to another.

That day, her client was new and she wanted to make sure she was there in good time so hurried, checking her watch as she flicked off her boots. Violetta had taken her time getting to know him online before agreeing to take him on. It was a two-way thing. Making the client feel comfortable but more so she could get a measure of them. They usually lied about their age though: vanity and the fear of getting old wasn't confined to the female race.

Buttoning up her white overall and pinning on the name badge, Violetta checked her image in the mirror that told her she looked fine, pristine and professional and after slipping on a pair of flat black shoes, put her coat on and pulled the Gladstone bag from the shelf. Being organised was essential and made her life easier, meaning she was ready to go within minutes.

She intended to use the drive to prepare and go over everything the client had told her via email. He'd been seeing someone else for a while but they were away on holiday and he required a session to get him over the festive break. Even though the procedure was straightforward and she'd performed it many times before, she expected the client to be nervous and therefore explained each step. All practitioners varied slightly so it was best to be thorough.

Once she was back in the car and driving towards the main road she switched on the sound system and selected a playlist to get her in the zone. The money for the session was already in her account and the thought of her big fat fee made her smile as she tapped her hand along to the throbbing beat of Guns N' Roses.

The hotel was indeed exclusive and smelled divine, of expensive reed diffusers and fresh flowers that stood on plinths lining the corridor. Glancing again at the room card, Violetta checked the door numbers and looked for 308. Two doors along she paused before placing the card in the lock and once the light turned green she let herself in as arranged.

Inside the silent room she looked around and got her bearings. The king-size bed was made up with what she assumed was high quality bedlinen but that was of little concern because they wouldn't be needing it. The windows were covered with organza, good. That gave them privacy but still she walked over and drew the curtains across.

After switching on the bedside lamps she placed her case on the mattress and eyed the bathroom door which was closed. Next she undid the silver clasp and began taking out her equipment which she laid out on the bronze bedspread. Slipping off her coat she laid it by her bag and took out the old-fashioned nurse's cap which she placed on her head and fastened with clips before picking up the restraint and the long silver chain that was attached.

Walking to the middle of the room she positioned herself

outside the door to the bathroom where the client was waiting, just as she'd told him to. Taking a fortifying breath, because it was always a bit of a moment when she met them for the first time face to face, lowering her voice a couple of octaves, sounding commanding, she summoned him from the room.

'You may come out now.'

The door opened slowly and a hooded figure appeared, the bathrobe open at the front and underneath the man was completely naked, head and shoulders bowed as he shuffled forward three paces, his hands covering his genitals as instructed.

Violetta swung the chain by her side, the neck restraint in her other hand as she gave another command. 'Stop. Take off the hood. You may look up. Do not speak.'

The man obeyed and then slowly lifted his head. All she could see was the crown of his hair, brown. Nondescript. She didn't pay much attention to the rest of him. It was of no consequence or interest. She was there to do a job, nothing more.

When it happened, coming face to face was almost in slow motion and instantly Violetta wished she could press rewind. The gasp that filled the room came from him while she remained mute, catatonically rigid. The only responsive parts of her body were her brain which prayed for it to be a dream while knowing in her wildly beating, panicked heart that it wasn't.

It could have been anger, that she had been caught out and her carefully constructed world was about to come crashing down, or maybe it was a simple mouth-jerk reaction that made her ask possibly *the* most stupid question ever.

'What the hell are you doing here?'

The answer was accompanied by a sly smile, one that immediately told Violetta that the man before her was the worst kind.

Even though they were both in a very unfortunate predicament, only one of them found it amusing and that did not bode well.

'I suppose I could ask you the same?' Turning, standing straight and... proud, he walked over to the mini bar and as he looked over his shoulder gave her a wink. 'I think we both need a drink and little chat, don't you?'

Swallowing down bile, Violetta nodded because even though her instinct was to run, she knew she had to stay and sort this out. She also knew something else. No matter what the cheating, lying scumbag said, he wasn't getting his fucking money back! That was for sure.

5

ROSINA

Appleton Farm, Cheshire
Present day

Closing the door to her office Rosina rested against it, shutting her eyes for a second, glad that she had her own little space where she could escape the madness that Christmas brought to the garden centre.

They were busy all year round but December was off the scale when it felt like the whole of Cheshire descended on them. In recent years, pandemic aside, they'd had to employ parking marshals so that the queue of traffic didn't block the road or the entrance otherwise they'd have complaints from the residents of Gawsworth village. Still, it was a great way for Max, her son, and a couple of his mates from college to earn a few extra quid and he loved doing his bit for the firm. His favourite place to be, though, was in the greenhouses, literally getting his hands dirty, up to his wrists in compost.

He watched all the gardening programmes on the telly and was hoping to study horticulture but in the meantime had sourced new varieties for the online side of the business, assuring his grandma that they would sell, and they did. All the family had him pegged as the next Monty Don and even though it might be a pipe dream, Rosina secretly hoped the eldest grandchild would one day play a bigger part in the business, maybe taking the helm. As long as he was happy she didn't care, as long as he never felt like she did.

Returning to her desk Rosina pulled open the top drawer and looked at the Tupperware containing the lunch that she should have eaten hours ago, then pushed it shut. She had no appetite and even if she did manage one of the sandwiches there was a chance it'd make her nauseous. Combined with the panic attacks that were coming more frequently Rosina was on the verge of a meltdown.

She actually understood what people meant when they said that the walls were closing in because that's how she felt, surrounded. From all corners of a dark room inside her mind came the whispers, reminders, warnings. And as if to reinforce the threat, her brain taunted her with images and each time she looked up the threat had taken another step closer.

Echoes of the past floated in her ears, the game her children loved to play when they were little: 'What's the time, Mr Wolf?' and they would scream and run when Rosina would turn and roar 'Dinner time.'

Looking at her watch she saw it would soon be time to go home and make dinner, and how ironic it was that a real-life wolf might actually come knocking at her door.

Resting her pounding head in her hands, Rosina tried to banish the demons, smother their incessant chatter, wipe them from her mind. No matter how many times she averted her eyes, clamped her hands to her ears, they lingered. The worst one, the biggest mistake she'd ever made, sneered from the shadows. There wasn't an hour of the day she didn't think about him, because he was always on the periphery, humiliating her, holding her to ransom.

And instead of lifting her up, the image of her husband Lou would make her weep, privately, of course. He would be so disappointed if he found out. She couldn't bear the thought of how he would look at her, the things he would think, the trust lost. And to make matters worse, just out of sight, hovering behind their dad were her children. The respect they had for her, all the lessons she had taught them, the boundaries and rules she'd laid in place would become a mockery.

And there stood her mum and if that wasn't enough, the essence of her beloved Granny Sylvia.

Shame consumed her as the final and biggest nail was hammered home when Rosina admitted how stupid she'd been. If only she had gone to her mum straight away and asked for help; if only her gran was still alive. She'd have confided in her, without a doubt, no matter how awkward the conversation would have been. They'd always had a special bond, been able to communicate with a look and share confidences. And while everyone in the family agreed that their mum was their rock, to Rosina, her Granny Sylvia had been a mountain. Touching the silver bracelet she wore on her left wrist, Rosina ran her thumb over the charm, a letter R. Her gran had given each of her granddaughters one.

I miss you, Gran. I wish you were here to tell me what to do.

Cutting through the moment, the vibration of her phone caused Rosina's body to stiffen and if it wasn't for the fact she had four children she would have ignored it. However, despite her other failings she was still a good mum. Yanking at her handbag that lay under the desk, Rosina placed it on her knee, and praying it was school to say that one of the girls was ill, because that truly was the lesser of all evils, she unzipped the top and took out her phone.

Seeing the name on the screen Rosina exhaled and answered. 'Hi Mum, what's up?'

'Nothing, love. I just wanted to double-check a few things.'

Rosina smiled, indulging her mum. 'Okay, fire away.'

'What time are you all going to the churchyard on Sunday? I've already been?'

Grateful for the distraction and taking comfort from her mum's voice, Rosina confirmed their plans. 'Me and Vi will pick Leo up on the way and then come back for lunch, about one-ish. Is that okay? Darcy and the girls are going to watch Christmas movies at ours and Max will be working here.'

'Perfect. I'm so looking forward to the four of us having some special time together before the run-up to Christmas week.'

'Me too.' The notion of being back at home in her mum's kitchen brought Rosina some much needed comfort.

Intuitive as always, her mum asked a question that could only be answered with a fib. 'Are you okay, love? You sound really tired. I bet it's manic over there. Don't forget to delegate.'

Rosina put on her best cheery voice. 'Yes, I am tired but we all are really, and I do delegate, I promise. I swear if we stayed open twenty-four hours this place would still be heaving. But don't worry, once we get the last weekend before Crimbo over, we should start to wind down. And it's a Monday. I hate Mondays.'

'As long as you're sure everything's okay. I do worry about you and I know Lou is a love but it's not easy having a full-time job and four kids. So if you need some help, even if it's a bit of housework, I can nip over to yours. Just give me a shout.'

Rosina felt the sting of tears and the wobble of her bottom

lip but mustered a quick reply. 'I will, Mum, I promise. And thank you.'

Her mum always had one more question. 'We can have a quick chat when I pop down there on Wednesday, same time as usual?'

They met once a week in the café for a coffee and a catch-up. 'Yes, it's a date.'

Another question. 'Oh, and while I'm on, have you spoken to Leonora?'

Rosina loved that her mum never knew when to go and always used their full names, not the shortened versions favoured by the rest of the family. 'No, just texts, why?'

'She's been a bit off these past couple of weeks, quiet and not her bubbly self. Perhaps she's working too hard, too, because she's hardly here and whenever I ask about Caspar she's vague. Do you think they've had a falling out? Has she said anything to you?'

Knowing that their mum was the only person in the family who liked Caspar, Rosina didn't voice her hopes that he and Leonora had fallen out and then none of them would have to put up with him on Christmas Day. She could have strangled her sister for hooking up with their accountant. It was just weird, having the guy who sifted through their finances suddenly sitting in their kitchen acting like he was one of the family. Caspar had unsettled Rosina from the start because he had an enquiring way about him, like he was looking into your soul when he asked a question and then didn't believe a word when you answered. Maybe everyone felt like that around accountants: guilty conscience syndrome.

'Nope, not a thing but if it will settle your mind I'll do some subtle digging on Sunday. It's probably just work: the restaurant will be hammered this time of year.' Talking of being busy gave Rosina the nudge to get on with some work, that was if she could shake off her mum and focus. 'Right Mum, if that's all, I'll get off.'

'Yes, that's all. I have loads to do here. I'm getting your rooms ready one by one and today it's Max's turn. He told me he doesn't mind having Gran's old room as long as he doesn't have to share with four girls, bless him. And you're all still staying from the Thursday aren't you, after the party?'

The thought of her gran's bedroom nearly finished Rosina, clenching her fist to her lips, scrunching her eyes in an effort not to cry. 'Yes, nothing's changed. We will all be able to stagger back to the house after the party and wake up with you on Christmas Eve, I promise.'

'Marvellous, I'm so excited about you all coming home, I really am. Right, I shall let you go. Love you, and get some rest later. That's an order.'

Hold it in, hold it in, don't let her know something's wrong.

'Will do, Mum, love you too, bye.' Dropping her phone onto the desk the second it disconnected, Rosina leant her elbows on top of a pile of invoices and covered her face with her hands, sucking air through the gaps of her fingers while she tried to get it together.

Why was it that when you're down and on the edge, the second someone is kind and understanding it has the worst effect, acting as a catalyst that unleashes all those carefully guarded emotions. But it was the reference to her gran's room that had been repainted and her personal belongings removed that was hard to bear.

She understood why her mum had done it. None of the kids would have wanted to sleep in a room that was an homage to their dead great-grandma. The flowery wallpaper behind her bed was faded and nicotine-stained, as were most of the fixtures and curtains. Granny Sylvia's Ciggie Den: that was what she and her sisters had called it when smoking around children suddenly became reprehensible. Old-timers, set in their ways, were shuffled to the back door to have a cigarette and the birth of smoking shelters doomed workers to shivering through their lunch breaks.

The thing was, even though they all went to school ponging of Granny Sylvia's Benson and Hedges that she'd smoked while they ate their cornflakes, Rosina never minded. Even though it had been just over a year since they lost her, whenever she caught the whiff of cigarettes in the air Rosina's brain transmitted a cipher, the code word for Gran.

Once again, the vibration of her phone interrupted a moment of reflection, a flicker of solace. Looking through her parted fingers at the screen, as soon as she saw the words NC, Rosina began to tremble. Unable to drag her eyes away she watched as her phone jiggled on the polished surface, holding her breath as she willed it to stop which was stupid because she knew exactly what would happen next. Immediately the vibration ceased, a message appeared on the screen.

Time's up. I want my money. Answer your phone. I know where you live. I know where you work. Last chance.

Closing her fingers over her eyes, blocking out the phone and the world, Rosina began to sob while her whole body shook. She couldn't take it anymore. She didn't know what to do. She could get up right now and walk out of work and up to her mother's and confess everything, or go home and wait for Lou to finish work and tell him what she'd done. But then it would be out there, her shame laid bare and she couldn't do it. Not now, not before Christmas.

As she cried, she spoke not to herself but to someone who would have helped her out of the mess, kept her secret and made it all right again. 'Please help me, Gran, I don't know what to do. I can't go on like this and I'm running out of time. Show me what to do. Please Gran, I need you to make it stop.'

When nobody answered, as she expected, Rosina wiped her eyes and after finding a tissue, blew her nose then picked up the phone, took a deep breath and made the call.

6

LEONORA

Manchester
Present day

The rain pelted the windows of the break room, smudging the glow from the Christmas lights that straddled the city centre roads and pedestrianised areas below. Whatever the season, Leonora loved working in Manchester. There was a vibrancy that she thrived on – the buzz of the hotel and the bustle of life beyond its walls was a complete contrast to the countryside where she had grown up. It had been quite a teenage revelation that, although she lived on a farm and thought herself stranded in the middle of nowhere, only thirty minutes away by car was a whole new world. Leonora and her friends had embraced their inner city like it was their salvation. They'd lived for Saturdays when they would get the train in, all dressed up in their best gear so they could trawl the shopping malls and check out boys.

The vibrancy of Manchester inspired Leonora, who was the career girl of the family. She had always known what she wanted to be when she left school: a chef. And she always knew where she wanted to work: in a big city. She'd since achieved both her goals but now she had others, her focus was elsewhere. And while she could hold her own as a sous-chef at the hotel, Leonora was sensible enough to realise that going it alone in Manchester was a step too far. So now, having earned her stripes, it was time to make two life-altering decisions.

Turning away from the window she sipped her coffee, savouring the peace and quiet of an empty room as she relaxed into the sofa, slipped off her clogs and rested her achy feet. The evening shift was just as manic as the day but for the purposes of avoiding Caspar, she had swapped with two of her colleagues who were grateful to spend time at home with their families. All she had to do was avoid him as much as possible until they'd got Christmas done with, then she was telling him it was over, goodbye and here's the door. And she couldn't wait.

Her best friend Daniella knew the whole story and wasn't in the least bit surprised that Leonora and Joel had rekindled their relationship, although if it had been up to her, she'd have given Caspar his marching orders straight away. Smiling, she recalled their latest conversation and wished that everything was as easy as Daniella made it sound.

'Dan, I can't dump my fiancé before Christmas! It's not like when we were fifteen and we wanted a boyfriend just so we'd get a present. You were a monster and dumped poor Dale Cole on Boxing Day; at least I waited to dump Martin whatshisname till we went back to school. I have a heart.'

The loudest tut ever echoed down the line. 'But you're going to have to put up with Caspar at your mum's on Christmas Day while poor Joel will be sat at home with his ready meal for one, sobbing into his runny gravy and pulling a cracker all by himself – which is really hard because I've tried. Just tell Caspar to get lost and have it done with.'

Leonora stifled a giggle. 'Seriously, could you be any more unsubtle?'

'No! Because he's annoying. Last week he drove past me in the village in his stupid sports car and I know he saw me but instead of waving back, he revved it up like a boy racer then sped off. He looked a right pillock because he only went a few yards and got stopped at the pedestrian crossing by the lollipop lady. About a hundred kids took their time dawdling across while he had to wait. He's a complete arsehole.'

'I'm cringing.' Leonora really was.

'And I'm just saying it like it is. Anyway, I don't think your mum will give a stuff if you ditch him. Carmen is so cool and as long as you're okay that's all she cares about. No way will she take the huff about a wedding and anyway, you and Joel are soulmates and one day you'll get hitched. I know it.'

'Okay, Gypsy Rose Lee, but let me get rid of Caspar before you start planning my second hen party. And I know you're right about Mum but it's *him* I'm worried about. Don't forget how awkward it's going to be professionally. The firm he works for have been our accountants forever and it could cause problems there.'

'What, like he's going to fiddle the books and report you to the taxman and have your mum thrown in jail?' Daniella chuckled, clearly finding this scenario most amusing.

'I don't know. He might want revenge, or be so broken-hearted he loses his mind and the last thing I want is him causing a scene at the farm, or the garden centre, or turning up in the middle of Christmas dinner or ringing me every two minutes. He's a control freak and I reckon he might turn nasty.'

Daniella immediately had the solution. 'Okay, okay, I get the message. But the way I look at it, he won't take it lying down whenever you tell him and that's why I think you should do it now. And if he gets nasty I'll send my Chris round to sort him out. And I'll come too. He's already scared shitless of me.'

Leonora laughed, picturing her beautiful best friend, a petite brunette whose sensitive and caring nature was a complete bluff because she had the heart of a lion and the roar to go with it. 'Never mind Caspar. I'm scared shitless of you. All of Gawsworth is scared of you, Dan.'

'Well, just you remember that if knobhead causes trouble. I'll bring my gun.'

Taking a sip of her coffee Leonora couldn't help but smile as she remembered the conversation and once again indulged herself with the mental image of Daniella chasing Caspar off the farm on Christmas morning, pointing her dad's old hunting rifle, blasting the tyres of his shiny sports car and taking out the back window as he sped off.

The door of the break room opened and pulled her from her dreams and for a second she was disappointed that her solitude was about to end, until she saw who it was.

Sam was their kitchen porter, an extremely genial man who got on well with everyone but away from the hubbub he came across as shy and very private. They'd become friendly ever since she spotted him reading one of her favourite books, *Robinson Crusoe* and she'd asked if he was enjoying it. He said he was but had read it many times. She said, 'Snap!'

Leonora was reading a book by Keri Beevis – one of her favourite authors – and she promised to give him her copy once she finished. They had bonded over literature, forming a tentative friendship – mainly one where she chattered on and he for the most part nodded and listened. And then boom. Lockdown.

Their fledgling friendship was curtailed and she had worried about Sam, hoping he'd stayed well so when they all finally came back to work Sam was one of the people she'd been looking forward to seeing the most. Normal service was resumed, catching a few minutes between shifts, one usually heading off as the other came in and their conversations remained light, a way of passing a few minutes while they relaxed.

Once again Leonora found herself drawn to her introverted friend. Her gran would say it was a father complex, the same one her mum had. Apparently Granny Sylvia had never approved of her daughter's choice of husband, saying he was far too old and predicting it would end in tears – which it did, but not in the way she meant. But none of the sisters ever talked about that. Not in front of their mum and gran, anyway.

Never having had a granddad either, Leonora didn't rule out that the reason she enjoyed Sam's company was because he was around the same age as Granny Sylvia. She'd surmised that Sam was in his seventies. Handsome in a rugged way, perhaps you could say he'd had a hard life, outdoors. His brown soulful eyes seemed wise, knowing and kind. Leonora imagined his grey curls were once dark, maybe black, and he wouldn't have been short of female admirers in his youth. He had a gentle voice, sort of mesmerising, that betrayed a faint accent when he spoke. He took time to enunciate, almost eradicating traces of his roots. That was his business though.

This subtle misdirection reminded her of Granny Sylvia who rarely talked about the past, or her life before she left London. She'd been adept at swerving the subject entirely, refocusing the conversation elsewhere. It was like she wanted to wipe it all out and start afresh which was fine, her business and nobody else's and they'd all accepted it. Her mum was the same.

Their new life had begun when they both moved from

London to Manchester and their painful past was simply left behind. It never seemed to bother her mum, so there was no reason to ask especially if it might upset her. All they knew was that their granddad had run off with another woman and was never seen again. Which was why as she got older, Leonora made sure to respect everyone's right to privacy. She abhorred insensitive nosey parkers who didn't take the time to think before they spoke. One stupid question could open wounds or ruin a day, cause embarrassment. If someone wanted to tell you about their private life then fine, if they didn't, that was okay too.

Leonora applied this rule to Sam and sensed that whatever information he had shared was enough for him and he wouldn't appreciate her prying. In fact, he didn't delve into her private life either which was a good thing because at the moment it was a hornets' nest. For the most part they talked about the news, the weather, work and books.

She had gleaned from snippets that Sam had been a dockworker at the shipyard in Tilbury. He then moved north to Manchester where he remained until the Salford Docks finally closed in the eighties. Ever since, he'd worked at the hotel where owing to his loyalty they'd kept him on part-time. Sam hadn't wanted to retire and remained convinced that having a routine and a focus kept his mind active and his body from seizing up.

Just like Sam, Leonora stuck to facts if she referred to her family, avoiding deep and meaningful insights about her dead dad and disappearing granddad. He knew that she had two older sisters and her mum owned a garden centre. Leonora never bragged and played down how huge a concern it was, talking more about the fresh produce that she wished they could use there in the restaurant. And she'd even confided in him that soon she'd be taking the plunge and opening her own bistro and then her wish would come true because Appleton Farm, and other local producers would supply most of her ingredients.

Sam had seemed genuinely interested and in an unguarded moment told her that he and his better half had an allotment near their home. Gardening was their passion and they spent most of their free time there. It was then that Leonora noticed Sam didn't wear a wedding ring. He saw her glance at his hand, but didn't embroider. The moment, the opportunity to take another step evaporated for both of them and he never mentioned his better half again, or whether they had any children, so she didn't either.

Smiling as he approached, knowing he would take a seat opposite her, she watched as he sat and placed his mug of tea on the table by the side. He took it with lots of milk and two sugars. Sighing the sigh of an exhausted man who was glad to be taking a break he yawned as he spoke.

'My, it's busy tonight. I'll be glad when this shift is over with.'

Leonora nodded. 'Me too, we've not stopped since two. Do you want a lift later? The weather is atrocious.'

'That would be very kind. I don't relish the thought of walking from the bus stop if this rain keeps up.'

She had assured him a while back that it wasn't any trouble diverting to Altrincham on her way home and anyway, she enjoyed the company. Sam had also assured her that for the most part he didn't mind the twenty-minute bus ride to wind down after a shift but graciously accepted her offer, saying he, too, enjoyed their chats. Leonora loved their polite exchanges, like playing a gentle game of conversational ping-pong. Nice and safe, refreshing really.

'Have you got your ticket?' She nodded to the far side of the room where sat the huge hamper rammed with food and wine and next to it an array of the other prizes up for grabs in the staff charity raffle.

'Oh yes, have you?' Sam began unwrapping the tin foil parcel on his lap.

'No, I didn't get one but I still made a contribution. I'd rather someone else be in with a chance of winning. Oooh, what have you got there?'

'Jerk chicken, here, have a piece.' Sam held out the package.

There was nothing that Leonora would have liked more but her break was over and she didn't want Chef giving her the evil eye if she was late. 'I'm fine thanks, you enjoy. I'll see you out the back at ten, okay.' Picking up her mug she waved at Sam who gave her the thumbs up and as she left him to eat, she was already looking forward to their drive home.

Leonora was so glad she'd been able to give Sam a lift because the rain was coming down in sheets, dousing the windscreen and causing the wipers to swish like crazy. They were heading out of the city and even though it was gone ten, they were stuck in a steady stream of traffic caused by late-night shoppers and diners.

'Are you working over the Christmas break? I'm not. But I'll be in for New Year and all the mayhem that entails.' Sam was looking up at the coloured decorations that adorned Deansgate and the route out of the city.

'Same. Aren't we the lucky ones!'

The lights had changed to red and while they waited in the queue there was a period of comfortable silence. For no good reason other than it just came out, Leonora decided to break their usual code of conduct. 'I'm actually dreading Christmas this year. It's always been a bit of a weird one because my dad was killed in a car accident two weeks before. Well, actually it wasn't really a car accident; it also involved a train. Anyway, I'm sure it's on my mum's mind each year, not that she ever shows it or lets what happened spoil the day – but it must be hard.'

For a second or two Sam remained quiet, like he was thinking of the right words to say. 'Well, I'm very sorry to hear that, Leo. It must have been terrible for your mum and family. How old were you when it happened?'

The lights changed to green and Leonora drove on towards the ring road. 'It's okay, I wasn't affected by the accident but I could have been. My mum was eight months pregnant with me and my dad was taking her to the antenatal appointment when he had a heart attack at the wheel of his car.'

'Oh my, that's dreadful.' Sam was giving Leonora his full attention, his body turned slightly to the side.

Concentrating on the flow of traffic, Leonora shared a piece of often unspoken family history. 'There's an unmanned level crossing near our house and he crashed the car into the fence at the side of the barrier. The warning lights started to flash, you know, saying a train was coming and then the barriers on each side of the road came down. Mum got out of the car and tried to drag my dad out but he was too heavy. He was a big man, and stocky with it. She's only tiny and being pregnant, had no chance, so she ran to the emergency phone box and tried to get help, but it was too late.'

'Oh Leo, that's awful.' Sam sounded genuinely shocked.

'They couldn't stop the freight train and there was a terrible crash. The driver survived and I'm sure you can imagine what happened to my dad. Mum was lucky, too, because she only just got to safety. She saw everything though.'

'Oh my dear, please don't say more if it disturbs you.'

Leonora shook her head. 'No, it's fine. I think because I wasn't born yet and I've heard the story via my sisters, in a way it doesn't affect me as much. I never even knew my dad. It's like I'm emotionally removed from it – although I do understand how awful it must have been, especially for my two sisters. Vi, the middle one absolutely idolised him. My elder sister Rosie was fifteen at the time and closer to my mum and my gran, who we lost last year. But I do feel like I know him, if only from my family and photos.'

Sam sighed. 'Nevertheless it's still very sad that you never got to meet your father or spend time with him. I am glad that your mum wasn't injured, though, and you were delivered safely.'

'Yes, I'm here to tell the tale. And I promise, I'm fine. I can't miss someone I've never had and my mum and gran made up for everything and everyone.'

Again Sam lapsed into thought as the car sped along, free from traffic.

The only sound was of the wipers scraping the screen and amidst the silence Leonora once again found her voice and as she spoke, wondered if saying things out loud might actually be a way to ease her burden. 'And, to make Christmas even more weird, I'm working up to ending things with my fiancé. Once I've done that I'll probably upset my mum even more when I tell her that I've fallen in love with my ex-boyfriend who broke my heart. There, that's an unexpected late-night confession. I bet you wished you'd caught the bus now.' Turning sideways Leonora smiled but when she caught the shocked expression on Sam's face her heart lurched. 'I'm sorry. Have I really offended you? I don't know why I blurted that out, I really don't. I bet you think I'm a really bad person now.'

After checking the road ahead she stole another glance and saw that his expression had changed to one of slight amusement, allowing her to relax a little.

'No, you haven't offended me at all, Leo. Please don't think that. These eyes have seen plenty over the years and I've heard stories that would make my hair straight.' His smile was genuine and as they turned into his street, a flash of lightning lit the row of terraces on their left as Leonora pulled into a space outside his house.

Placing the car in neutral and before Sam got out, she tried to reassure him in return, not wanting to end the night on an awkward note. 'Phew, I'm so glad. It's on my mind all the time and even though I've already decided to wait until after Christmas, I think I needed to say it out loud rather than bottle it up. I haven't told anyone apart from my best friend – but don't worry, next time I see you I promise I'll keep things light and not totally depress you.'

Then, in a move that both surprised and comforted her Sam placed his hand over hers where it rested on the gearstick. 'And I promise you that I don't mind and if you need an ear over the next few days, I am happy to listen. This time of year is tricky for lots of reasons. So many mixed emotions are stirred up, memories of good times and bad, missing the people you love, regrets, mistakes... the list goes on. I know this only too well and have my own ghosts who without fail come to visit at Christmas, year in, year out. That's why I understand. More than you know.'

Touched by the moment of rare frankness, Leonora had to compose herself before she replied. 'And the same goes for you, Sam. Perhaps this is the time of year we all need to be there for each other, more than usual, just in case someone is struggling.'

A moment of understanding passed between them before he patted her hand and undid his seat belt. 'I'll see you at work tomorrow. Take care going home, Leo, and thank you for the lift. Goodnight, dear.'

Above, the sky continued to flash and rumble but Leonora paid little attention because she was transfixed by the shadowy figure who, as Sam opened his front door, was cast in a halo of yellow-gold light that glowed from inside the hallway.

When the door closed on that brief portal to his life she pulled back onto the street and drove away. She hoped Sam's lady friend was a good soul like him. He deserved a woman who loved him, looked after him, would be his best friend. She hoped that was the case but more than anything, on the most sodden of winter nights, she was just glad he had someone there, to welcome him home.

7

CARMEN

Appleton Farm, Cheshire
Present day

C armen had reached the end of the private footpath so called the dogs to heel and slipped on their leads. The track led from Appleton House, along the side of the field that backed onto the garden and then downhill towards the garden centre in the shallow valley. She always stopped to take it in: the little empire she had created from an expanse of neglected farmland.

The main building that housed the pet and gift shop, café and country clothing store was at the centre and from there the extensive plant shop and greenhouses spread out from the east side. The car park was at the front and three-quarters full, not bad for a Wednesday. In the distance was the petting zoo and farm, then the forest and beyond that the woodland trail and lake. It was her legacy, her pride and she would leave it to her children and hopefully it would remain in the family for generations to come.

Setting off again, she opened the gate that led to four large potting sheds at the rear of the centre. After weaving through the middle two, she let herself in through the side door of the admin centre and once she'd settled the dogs in Rosina's office, closed the door and headed towards the gift shop.

It had been transformed in early November into what she could only describe as Winter Wonderland that was dedicated to all things Christmas: artificial trees, lights, decorations, you name it, they sold it. There was even a miniature steam train that wound around the garden centre, a massive attraction all year round but more so in December when children clambered aboard The Santa Express. And then there was the grotto, Winter Wonderland itself, her favourite place. Big Dave the head gardener was roped in every year to be Father Christmas and even though he huffed a lot and made out it was a chore, he thoroughly got into the part. And, as his wife attested, he put a lot of effort into his pre-Christmas training, bulking up on mince pies so his red-and-white suit fit like a glove, size XXXL.

Carmen had always made Appleton Farm a special place for her girls at Christmas but had wanted to create something for other children to enjoy, somewhere that was steeped in the magic of Christmas. She knew only too well how it felt to be a child. The thrill and expectation, believing, then not quite believing but wanting to hold on to the hope that Santa was real, that he really did fly through the sky and squeeze down your chimney. She still felt those things, and she was fifty-seven!

From the moment you walked into the Winter Wonderland, and it didn't matter if you were young or old, your senses were heightened by sights, sounds and smells of Christmas. The dry-ice machine puffed wisps of white clouds along the path to the North Pole that was covered in snow, and twinkling lights lit your way towards Santa's workshop and then the man himself, Big Dave and his well-practised, if not rather melodramatic, ho-ho-ho.

Resisting the urge to nip inside, Carmen headed into the café and stopped to ogle the cakes in the chiller, pondering what to have when Rosina turned up. It was something they did once a week to get them over the Wednesday hump. Carmen insisted on it because when the grandkids were about neither of them could get a word in edgeways and there, they had an hour of total bliss, a nice cake and a catch-up.

Seeing that Rosina wasn't waiting at the reserved table by the window she decided to nip behind the counter and spend a minute with her longest-serving employees and now, after almost twenty years, special friends. Waving as she passed Christine who was serving a customer, she found Jan and Toni hard at work preparing lunch.

'Hello ladies, are we all ready for Christmas? And let's not forget our party next week?' Carmen hovered by the door, observing kitchen hygiene rules.

Toni waved from the counter where she was slicing sandwiches. 'You bloody bet we are! It's been crazy here all week and we're fully booked for Christmas lunches right through to Thursday.'

Jan was loading a tray up with plates as she spoke. 'And my lot can't wait. If our Maya asks me one more time if Darcy is coming I'll go daft!'

'You're already daft, mate. That ship's sailed.' Toni winked at Carmen who stepped further back against the wall as Jan bustled past.

'Right, I'll leave you in peace. I can see you're busy and remember, the four of us have a bottle of fizzy stuff with our names on, so until next week, be good.'

To calls of 'we'll try', Carmen hurried to her table, smiling at

77

diners as she passed them by. She was early so rather than ring Rosina to hurry her up, she took some time to observe the customers milling about the store. It never wore off, the pride she felt at her achievement and she never got tired of telling her five grandchildren stories of how it all began.

Out of a terrible tragedy, the Appleton women had pulled together, with the help of a Wilson, of course, and once Bern joined the team there was no stopping them. That's where their history began.

Appleton Farm, Cheshire. December 1999

It was late, the mourners had finally gone home. The remnants of the cold buffet had been cleared from the dining room and Rosina and Violetta were settled in bed. Carmen and her mum were taking a moment for themselves in the kitchen. Sylvia was perched on a kitchen chair in front of the battered old range; Carmen was on the sofa they'd dragged from the lounge when they moved in. Those were the days. When she and Sebastian had laughed and at least tried to make their marriage and the house work, even though he'd hated being confined to the kitchen during the winter months so they could keep warm.

She hadn't cried all day, in fact she hadn't cried since the day of the accident when she'd seen her husband killed in the most shocking and gruesome way. All she could remember were flashes, like teasers from a movie trailer, scenes in her head before, during and after. One of them was the kind policewoman holding her hand, saying, 'At least he was unconscious and he didn't suffer. Try to focus on that.' And she had.

From the second she arrived home in a police car, a switch had been thrown and her only concern was for Rosina and

Violetta and the baby who waited silently inside her, curled into a ball, hands over its ears. That was how she imagined it because throughout her baby's gestation, through the layers that protected it from the outside world, most of what it had heard would have been the angry words of a father and the tears of a mother who was hanging on by a thread. Now, the baby would only be meeting one of them. For this, amidst the carnage, Carmen was glad.

The kindly policewoman, who insisted on being called Rebecca, had wanted Carmen to go to the hospital to get checked over and have her bruises looked at, worried that she'd have concussion after hitting her head on the dashboard. She had refused, wanting only to go home, to Appleton.

Sitting at the table, half listening to Rebecca, she lifted her hand to her sore lips and cheek. It was painful but bearable, like most things had been for a long time.

Rebecca had bustled about the kitchen, making tea, promising to wait until the girls were brought home from school so she could help Carmen tell them about their father. She had been grateful for the sensitive intervention of the policewoman who had told two children the worst news in the kindest possible way.

Afterwards, it was easy really, pretending to hold it together for Violetta who had been distraught while Rosina looked shocked, yet accepting, like she was simply relieved to have him gone. Carmen knew exactly how that felt.

In the days that followed the accident she'd asked her eldest many times if she wanted to talk about it and she'd declined, and when Granny Sylvia had broached the subject she'd been met by the same response. Who could blame her though?

Rosina had been picked on and shunned by Sebastian, physically abused on more than one occasion so as with herself, his passing was a blessing. Since that day they had got on with life and focused their attention on Violetta who needed their love and support and never shut up about her dad. Even though her words of adoration and moments of despair were hard to bear in different measures, Carmen did her best. She kept up a front, like she had done since the day he died. It was for the best.

To those who'd attended the service and wake earlier that day, Carmen would have appeared brave and stoical. To others she was simply a mother guiding her children through a very difficult time and not wanting to overly distress herself or her unborn baby. It was also evident from the way her mother had been scrutinising her for most of the day that she was worried about her daughter's well-being, or, was she merely biding her time?

When Sylvia spoke, Carmen realised it was a bit of both. 'Rosie seemed pleased that I'm going to stay on for a while. Her little face lit up when I told her. She's a pure diamond, that girl.'

Carmen forced a jovial tone. 'Sometimes I think she prefers you to me. I don't mind though. As long as she's happy and I can't blame her for being glad. I've put too much on her shoulders of late and now she can just get on with being a teenager. So thanks, Mum, for offering to stay.' Her words were genuine as was the rush of emotion that took her by surprise after feeling nothing all day, nothing at all.

'Well, as if I'd leave you in the lurch right now especially with Christmas coming up. We need to give those girls a good time regardless of what's happened and you look exhausted. I'll ring in sick tomorrow and then get stuck into helping here while you have a rest. I think you need one, body and mind, don't you?'

When the tears came, like lava from a volcano they wouldn't stop, prompting Sylvia to dart from her chair and sit by Carmen's side, holding her tight while she cried it out. 'That's good, you need to get it all out in one big go and then you'll feel better.'

'Do you think they'll be okay? The girls and this one, too.' Carmen placed a hand on her belly.

'Yes, of course they will, they have us and once the dust is settled you and I will sit down and work out what to do going forward. We need to decide if you can manage here or you'll have to call it a day and sell up – but for now, let's just take one step at a time.'

The thought of leaving Appleton immediately filled Carmen's heart with dread and now Sebastian, the wage earner was gone, everything hung in the balance. Panic came next to the party, pricking at her conscience, reminding her of mistakes, marrying the wrong man, trapping him in a house he hated, filling it with children he had no time for.

'I hope I did the right thing... that it wasn't all for nothing... the girls are my everything, and you.' Carmen's words were barely a whisper, pushing through a layer of fatigue and conjured by an exhausted brain.

'What do you mean, love, the right thing?' Sylvia pulled away and regarded her daughter, confusion flickering across her face.

Carmen didn't answer immediately, rubbing her tired eyes, blowing her nose, sighing before she replied. 'Trying... trying to make it work, hanging on to a man who didn't love me anymore and then this–' Once again she indicated the baby within. '– bringing another child into a loveless marriage and a broken home because I thought it would stick us back together.'

It was true, that's what Carmen had done but admitting it didn't ease the guilt. 'I did it for all of us but most of all for the girls. I wanted them to have a dad and be a proper family. I thought it was the right thing to do.'

'My darling girl, of course it was the right thing to do. You tried, for the sake of the girls you did what you thought was best and nobody could ever accuse you otherwise. You made a choice and put them first, and were prepared to sacrifice your happiness for them. So no more worrying, okay. And we *can* be a proper family and between us you and I will make up for anything they think they are missing, like I did with you.'

Carmen wiped away tears as she realised how her words might have sounded. 'Mum, I'm sorry. I didn't mean to bring up the past or make you feel bad and you're right, you've been a mum and a dad to me, you filled all the gaps. So together, we'll do the same. You were hurt too, all those years ago and did what you thought best at the time, just like me. I understand that more than ever now.'

A moment passed between them, mother and daughter, woman to woman, decades of history and memories of things they wished to forget or alter, binding them even closer together.

'Well there you go then, we make a right pair, don't we. Now, how about I make us some toast and another cuppa and then we'll get off to bed and when those girls get up in the morning, we'll be waiting with a smile on our faces and a bit of a spring in our step. Is that a deal?' Sylvia stood, still watching Carmen closely.

'It's a deal and yes, tea, toast then bed. Thanks Mum.'

Sylvia patted her hand then bustled over to the bread bin. Relaxing her tense body into the sofa, in the glow from the kitchen lamp, the room warm from the logs that burned in the range, Carmen drew comfort from her mum's words and being in the heart of the house that she couldn't give up on. It was their home and she would find a way to stay.

A few days later, when the solicitor arrived to go over the details of Sebastian's will, in one fell swoop all, or most of Carmen's worries melted away. Perhaps the huge payout shouldn't have come as such a shock because her husband had sold insurance for a living and therefore made a shrewd move. It was more the fact that – for once – he'd actually done the decent thing and ensured his family were provided for that came as a shock. Perhaps he did care after all. It was Sylvia who popped that bubble the second she'd seen the solicitor out and returned to the kitchen to sit with her shell-shocked daughter.

'Well at last, he came good. Doesn't surprise me though. I can imagine him now, making sure he screwed the insurance company for as much as he could and at the same time thinking he was invincible and the policy wouldn't be cashed in. That's how arrogant he was.'

'Mmm, I know what you mean but let's not dwell on that now. We've been handed a lifeline and that money means we can stay here. I need to make it work for us, though, not just leave it in the bank to pay the bills. The farm rents are a bonus and would have tided us over for a while but this is a pure godsend and a golden opportunity to change our lives. So get your thinking cap on, Mother.'

Sylvia nodded. 'That's all very sensible but let's get Christmas over with first, and I for one fancy a trip into town. Come on, let's go get the girls some nice bits and bobs. For once in our lives we won't have to pinch the pennies and that in itself is a cause for celebration. We can have some lunch in BHS too. You're paying. Chop-chop, get your bag and coat, you've pulled.'

They'd laughed for the first time in ages that day, and it wasn't until the New Year that Carmen caught her breath, quite literally puffed out from hauling herself and her humongous baby bump up the stairs. She'd stopped on the landing to look out across the fields that now belonged to her when an idea popped into her head as she imagined them full of home-grown produce. A giant vegetable patch rather than a square in the corner of the garden.

It had been something she'd longed to do but looking after the girls and renovating the house had come first. Now, though, she could easily afford to have someone else restore Appleton, from the leaky roof down. And her mum could help with the girls and the baby (whenever it decided to make an appearance) while she started a business.

If she utilised the land that surrounded the property Carmen could open a farm shop which would sell what they grew, along with the meat and poultry produced by the neighbouring farmers. She had the capital to do it properly, start off small and grow a business that would provide jobs for the locals and give her an income. Never had Carmen been so energised and focused, driven and desperate to get back down the stairs and start making a list. Which would have happened had her waters not broken, right there and then on the landing.

One year and another daughter later, Carmen stood watching the diggers as they began scraping out earth for the footings that would be the foundations of her farm shop. Baby Leonora was fast asleep in the pram, rocked to and fro by Granny Sylvia who had given up her job and flat in Manchester and moved to Appleton permanently. The house was almost complete after being fully restored, rewired, re-plumbed and revalued by the bank who, going forward, would be happy to consider lending against Carmen's considerable assets.

There had been another development with regards to her business venture and that was the hiring of a project manager who would oversee the planting and farming of the outlying fields. She had intended advertising for the role but word had spread of her plans and one autumn evening, she'd been surprised by a knock on the back door and found Bern waiting outside, looking bashful.

'Sorry to impose, Carmen, but I wondered if I could have a quick word?'

'Of course, and you're not imposing. It's great to see you. Come in and take a seat.' Carmen quickly removed the knife and bag of potatoes from the table to make room for their guest.

Pulling out a chair Bern said hi to Rosina who was finishing her homework while Violetta played with Leonora on the floor by the new Aga.

'So, how can I help? Do you fancy a coffee, or I have some wine.'

'No, it's fine, I won't be stopping. I can see you're busy. Thing is, and I know it's a bit of a cheek but I wanted to throw my hat in for the job as project manager. I heard you were looking for someone and seeing as we know one another, hoped I could wangle an interview first.'

Carmen was taken aback. 'Oh, I see. I've not actually advertised for it yet. Are you unhappy at the dairy farm? You've been there for such a long while.'

'Yes, but I've been thinking now might be a good time to try something new, take on a challenge and as you know, I've worked on farms all my life so I reckon I could help with your project. And I'm local so know these fields like the back of my hand.'

Two hours later they were still at the kitchen table after she'd brought out her maps and plans and lists and explained them all to Bern. So engrossed were they in ideas for the farm shop and land that Rosina ordered everyone pizzas when it became clear that dinner wasn't going to happen any time soon. Rosina had also dropped a huge hint about saving money on adverts so once the girls were in bed, Carmen offered the job to Bern.

It was the start of their working relationship and later, both admitted that if they were honest the spark was there while they drank a celebratory bottle of Blue Nun, hunched over the map of Appleton Farm.

It had been hard work and thanks to having Granny Sylvia living with them, Carmen was able to get her hands dirty and grow not only her crops, but later, bedding plants, adding potting sheds and greenhouses to her quickly expanding garden centre. Bern suggested they plant a forest. By adding saplings each year they'd eventually have a sustainable rejuvenating crop of Christmas trees.

Word spread throughout the county and soon it became a thriving business that over the next twenty years, grew year on year, a bit like her and Bern's love for one another. Everyone insisted it was a foregone conclusion, Carmen falling for the man who was perfect for her in every way. The garden centre became a part of village life and offered jobs to the community just as she'd hoped and going forward, life seemed rosy.

From the ashes of a failed marriage that, unlike what she had with Bern, was wrong in every way, she had built something good and wholesome, of value and worth that gave back and would do so for many years to come.

Tutting as she checked the time, Carmen wondered where on earth Rosina had got to. Ignoring her annoyance and rumbling stomach she scanned the contented diners and then the busy gift shop beyond in search of her daughter's face.

She couldn't help compare it to the start, those chilly nights at Appleton when their toes still froze in two pairs of socks, and pans lined the hall and landing to collect leaks as faded wallpaper peeled and mould appeared on ceilings for fun.

Thoughts straying back to her mum who she missed like a limb and who had played a huge part in Appleton's history, Carmen recalled once more the night the two of them sat around the old range. She'd asked her mum a question and all these years later, knew that Granny Sylvia was right. Enduring the bruises and the tears and the heartache hadn't been for nothing. She'd given her girls a secure future and a happy family life and for this reason alone, Carmen knew without a doubt that everything she'd done had been worth it.

8

ROSINA

Gawsworth Village, Cheshire
Present day

Rosina checked her watch, knowing she had to hurry. Her mum would be on her way for their coffee and cake date and she hated it when people weren't punctual – but the sudden urge to come and speak with her gran had overwhelmed her. Without thinking it through she'd grabbed her car keys and coat and nipped out the back door, not caring if she was missed.

It was ridiculous that in her desperation she'd resorted to asking advice from the dear departed who refused to answer. For as long as she could remember, her gran, Saint Sylvia, had always been there to make things right and it was hard to get her head around the fact she wasn't at the end of the phone, or the kitchen table.

She'd even tried praying. It had worked once before, while she'd lain on the kitchen sofa, a fifteen-year-old keeping guard over her mum who was heavily pregnant, battered and bruised.

Rosina's prayer had been simple. That it could be just them. Her mum, Vi and the baby when it came. She prayed that her dad would go away and leave them in peace. A few weeks later he was dead.

At the time, her teenage self felt not an ounce of guilt and actually believed her wishes had been granted through divine intervention. Unfortunately, her most recent request had fallen on deaf ears. Taking a seat on the bench opposite her gran's headstone, Rosina allowed herself a few more minutes before she went back to the garden centre. She needed to prepare, rearrange the mask she'd been wearing for months and find some way to calm the maelstrom of worry that swirled inside. Deciding to give reaching out to her gran another shot, Rosina dredged her memories in the vain hope that Granny Sylvia's voice and some words of wisdom would somehow filter through.

Appleton Farm, November 1999

Rosina sucked air in, deep breaths of November mist that lingered on the fields around their house, the pale grey clouds overhead blocking out the morning sun, making the day seem bleaker than it already was. She didn't even attempt to quell the sobs and hiccups that had made her chest ache as she'd raced from the house, clutching the side of her face as she stumbled towards the village. She needed to let it out, all the anger and hurt and disappointment.

Entering the village, running along the main street, she kept her head down, not wanting anyone to notice her distress or the red hand mark imprinted on her stinging cheek.

Seeing the phone box was empty, relieved not to have to queue up, she flung open the door and dug out a ten-pence coin from her jeans pocket. Inserting it into the slot she dialled the number she knew by heart. It answered on the third ring and as soon as she heard her gran's voice at the other end Rosina sobbed and stuttered into the receiver, desperate to get it all out and make her gran understand how bad things were getting.

'Gran, you have to come and help Mum. He's hit her again and I don't know what to do. I found her on the kitchen floor last night and she has a big bruise under her eye. I stayed with her all night to protect her and we slept on the settee. Then this morning he went mental and called Mum a lazy bitch for not making his breakfast and when she did, he tipped it all over the floor because she'd burned his fried eggs... I hate him, Gran, I hate him so much.' All Rosina could see as she cried into the receiver was her poor mum with her big belly, kneeling on the floor, crying silent tears as she wiped up grease and bacon.

Sylvia's voice was the opposite to Rosina's, calm and in control. 'She's not said she feels poorly? The baby is okay?'

'I think so, but she's just being brave for our Vi. She walked her down to the road to wait for the school bus, to get out of his way. Vi thinks Mum banged her face. Mum told me I had to go along with it, again.'

'It's for the best... no point in upsetting Vi if she's not realised. It's bad enough that you've seen.'

'Well, I'm not going in today. I need to stay with Mum. He came into the kitchen when they'd gone and asked me why I wasn't at school and lost his shit again when I said it was because he was a nasty bully and someone had to take care of Mum.'

'And what did he say to that?'

Rosina hesitated... then decided that there were enough lies knocking about and she was sick of hiding what her dad was really like. 'He smacked me across the face, Gran. It made my head rattle it was so hard. So I ran out the back door and down here to phone you.'

If rage could be transmitted down a phone line, Rosina

swore she felt it echoing in her Gran's voice. 'Where is your father now? Has he gone to work?'

'He's packing, he's going on a trip today.'

'Good. I'll be there by this afternoon. I'll ring work and tell them I won't be in then I'll set off. How long is he going for?'

'A week but I wish it was forever. I hope he leaves and never comes back.'

'I know, love, I know. Right, you go home and keep out of his way and look after your mum till I get there. Tell her I'll see her soon. You did the right thing, Rosie, ringing me.'

Hearing the pips on the line, Rosina said her goodbyes. 'I've run out of money, Gran. I'll see you in a bit, love you so much.'

'And I love you, too.'

The line went dead and after replacing the receiver, Rosina stepped out of the phone box just in time to see her father's car shoot by and to get a glimpse of his face. She despised him so much and couldn't bear to look at his jowly cheeks, swollen and red from drinking too much whisky and eating like a pig. He didn't even care that her mum was pregnant. Smoking in every room, leaving a trail of cigarette fumes everywhere, making their clothes stink. He was a selfish pig and a nasty, lazy slob. He did nothing to help around the house and acted like her mum was his slave, Rosina too.

It was like the older she got, the more he treated her with disdain. Perhaps it was because he knew she could see through him and wouldn't pander to him like Vi did. God, it irritated Rosina so much that her younger sister hero-worshipped their fickle father and in return he focused all his attention on her, like he was playing a game, conning a ten-year-old into believing he was a nice person and rubbing their mum's face in it at the same time.

It was Violetta's birthday in a week's time and he would no doubt turn up bearing gifts he'd bought in London, acting like he was the best dad in the world. One week. That's all they had to relax. Not dread him coming home, be able to breathe easy without that tight feeling in your chest when you heard his car on the drive and not walk around on eggshells from the minute he came through the door.

It would be so good, to have Gran there. She always cheered everyone up in her own bossy, no messing kind of way and Rosina knew that within a day of her arrival the washing and ironing would be up to date and her mum would be able to put her feet up and get her strength back.

Rosina did her best to help out. The house was huge and her dad expected it to be clean and tidy always, inspecting things for dust and going apeshit if he found a tidemark in the bath or pots in the sink. It was like he was punishing her mum and used his favourite taunt as often as possible. *'You were the one who wanted to live in the big house so you can look after it.'* That was why in between studying for her exams, she tried to ease her mum's burden but she was tired too, of being scared most of all.

Running, eager to get back to her mum, Rosina hoped she wouldn't be cross that she'd told what was going on and be glad that Granny Sylvia was on her way. It wasn't the first time, though, that Rosina had rung her gran in tears. It was their little pact. To keep an eye on things and report back ever since the first time her mum had 'walked into a door'. The truth was a completely different story.

Witnessing the scene from where she hid on the stairs, Rosina had peeped through the spindles as her dad threw a glass full of whisky over her mum, then, after he'd slammed the lounge door, she'd heard the sound of more glass breaking and her mum crying.

The very next morning, while the house was empty, she'd picked up the hall phone and rang her gran, telling her what she'd seen. In her fifteen-year-old eyes, the solution was simple.

'Mum should throw Dad out, or we could leave and come and live with you in Manchester. I know your flat is tiny but we could squash in and we'd be really good, I promise.'

After assuring Rosina that they were all welcome any time, Sylvia had then gone on to explain a few home truths. 'You see, love, when you're married and especially when you have children, life isn't always that simple and you can't just up sticks and run away. And let's face it, your dad's a big bloke and from what you say, nasty with it. So I think we'd have a struggle chucking him out.'

'But you left London with Mum, when her dad ran off with that woman.' The moment she said it Rosina winced, it was a taboo subject with Gran that even her mum rarely discussed. The silence down the line was excruciating, like her gran was either annoyed or thinking what to say.

'That was an entirely different situation, Rosina, and I know that's one of the reasons your mum won't leave, why she will keep trying with your dad. She doesn't want you to feel like she did. She may not say it out loud, especially to me but she always missed her dad and probably still does. But that's my cross to bear, and his.'

Rosina remained silent, knowing not to push her luck. She could already see her dream of squishing into a flat and being near her gran every day clouding over as she listened to more words of wisdom coming down the line.

'And even if your mum did leave, she would worry about money and paying the bills. I know I did when me and your mum arrived in Manchester and I only had one little girl; she'll soon have three children. So for now, that big old house you live in gives you girls some stability and a roof over your head. Do you see what I mean, love?'

When Rosina countered with another idea, saying they should ring the police, her gran once again spelt it out. 'Making the call in a moment of desperation or fear is a solution, however, it only solves the problem short term, gives you a few nights of peace. The thing is Rosie, lots of women worry about what comes after, making statements, going to court and folks finding out, gossipy people, like neighbours and at school and work.'

This imagery brought Rosina up short. She got it, and knew her mum would hate being talked about and so would she and Vi because some of the girls at school were total bitches. 'Okay, Gran, I get it. But we can't just do nothing, can we?'

When she answered, Rosina imagined her gran doing that smile, the one she did when she was pleased with you, chuffed with a present you'd made or taken her a mug of tea with two big sugars. 'Good girl. I'm glad you understand and I'm so sorry that you've got all this to deal with but you have me to share it now. So, I'm going to pack a bag and I'll be there tomorrow, a surprise visit from the mother-in-law from hell should clip his wings for a day or two. And I'll try and talk some sense into your mum while I'm at it. And from now on, you and I can keep our eye on things. Is that a plan?'

Rosina's body sagged with such immense relief and she wasn't sure whether to laugh or cry, her voice croaky when she replied. 'Yes, Gran, it's a plan.'

True to her promise, Sylvia had turned up out of the blue that Friday afternoon looking exhausted from her six-two shift and a three-bus ride to Appleton. After depositing her various carrier bags of treats and supplies in the kitchen she gave her daughter a hug, watched closely by her eldest grandchild. Rosina saw her mum's body fold into her gran's arms and inside she rejoiced. For a couple of days, they could relax, they were safe. Saint Sylvia had arrived.

That night as she lay in bed, enjoying the reprieve from

forcing her eyes to stay open while her ears strained for the sounds of trouble, she went over the events of the past few days.

The hardest thing to get her head around, out of all her gran's erudite advice was that her mum's ultimate goal was making her children happy and this meant patching things up and somehow getting her dad to change. Rosina didn't hold out much hope for either and was still convinced they would all be better off without him.

And then another thought. If her mum did make things work, in the long run it meant sacrificing her chances of being happy by settling for second best, doing anything for a quiet life just so that your kids would have a dad and the family not be torn apart.

Of all the things that her gran explained Rosina thought that was the most sad and she realised that being married, or deciding not to be, wasn't as easy as she'd thought. As her eyes drooped, she made a vow to herself never to settle for second best. She'd look out for someone who was the complete opposite of her father, a good man who she would love for all the right reasons, and someone who truly loved her back.

Seven months later, not long after her sixteenth birthday, she met Lou. He was playing football for the visiting village team. As she cheered from the sidelines her eyes never left the tall, sandy-haired centre forward who, after he'd scored the first goal gave her a wink as he ran back up the pitch. And that was that, the start of her and Lou, someone she loved for all the right reasons and who truly loved her back.

Gawsworth Village, Cheshire. Present day

A speck of rain and the sound of a digger in the background spurred Rosina into action, groaning when she checked her watch again and realised she only had minutes to make it back.

Wiping her eyes with her scarf she stood then gave her gran a wave before heading towards the car, already dreading lunch and picking her way through food she would have trouble keeping down.

Opening her car door she whispered under her breath, *'Come on, Saint Sylvia, you've never let me down before and I don't think I can keep this up much longer, please, Gran, I need you.'* Turning the key in the ignition she waited a second and sighed. The rumble of her engine drowned out the unmistakable sound of silence.

9

VIOLETTA

Macclesfield, Cheshire
Present day

Turning her phone over so she couldn't see the screen, Violetta took a huge gulp of wine, draining the glass which she topped up again, right to the brim. An immense ball of anger rested firmly in her chest. At the forefront of her brain was the memory of a smarmy smug face, pouring himself a drink. The only thing preventing her from crumbling or, giving in to the temptation to scream so loudly that she'd wake the neighbours was Darcy who was fast asleep upstairs.

Instead she focused on her hate for men, all of them because she couldn't be arsed sorting out which was which anymore so it was easier to generalise. It was wrong, she knew, as was getting drunk on a Wednesday when Darcy was in the house. Her conscience told her to stop after that glass. Conscience got told to piss off.

Her daughter was all Christmassed out and snoring like a

reindeer after her trip to the garden centre to get the ingredients for 'The Great Appleton Christmas Bake Off', so Violetta knew she would sleep straight through. Resting her head in her hands she wished Christmas would also piss off. And Santa and all his elves who were probably a load of bastards, too. She wouldn't put it past them – because let's face it all the men in her life had let her down one way or another and those who hadn't, like Lou and Bern and Max, were probably just biding their time.

Take Darcy's dad. He was a bastard because he'd not worn a condom and he hadn't even bothered looking for her the next day and he definitely knew where she was staying because he'd picked her up from the sodding reception. Was she being harsh? Most likely because even though it was six years ago, Violetta did have some glimmers of recollection from a balmy summer night of passion.

They'd met by the pool. He was a soldier. He'd joined up when he was seventeen, not much of a home life, had been fostered and had one sister. He loved the army, it was his home and family where he felt secure with his mates. He took her for a meal, they went to a bar and she woke up the next morning on the beach, inside a dinghy, covered by a smelly piece of tarpaulin. She'd lost her knickers and the silver bracelet her gran had given her. Then spent the next few days chucking up. And that was that.

Hence, the arrival of a beautiful baby girl nine and a half months later. Poor Darcy. Her bright-as-a-button daughter had only ever asked about her dad once before. Violetta had prepared herself for the moment when it came, but she hated every second of the lie she'd told her four-year-old, green-eyed girl.

'Where does my daddy live? Can I go and see him one day, Mummy? And what's his name, and what does he look like?

Have you got a photo?' In between the bombardment of questions, Darcy ate her tea, sucking macaroni through her lips.

Violetta could still hear the slurping noise, see her daughter's curious face and smell the cheesy sauce. Instead of answering straight away she took her empty plate to the sink, cursing the school and the nosey bastard teacher who'd asked the kids to draw a photo of their house and their family. That's where it had stemmed from when Darcy had noticed that someone on her drawing was missing. She wouldn't be the only one with a missing parent, but that wasn't the point. The point was that on Darcy's stick figure painting that was stuck on the cupboard door, there were only two people and she wanted it to be three.

Knowing that this was probably going to be the hardest thing she'd ever said and there was a chance, knowing her daughter, that it would lead to more questions, Violetta told Darcy her first fib. 'I'm sorry, Darcy, but I don't know.'

'Why? Kyra knows where her daddy lives.'

Fuck off, Kyra.

'Yes, because they live in the same house but I only met your daddy once when I was on holiday and I don't have his address.' That was all totally true and Darcy was mulling it over while she chewed her garlic bread.

'Do you know his name?'

'Yes. It's Gabe.'

'I like that name. What did he look like? Is he nice?'

Violetta could feel her cheeks burning under close scrutiny. 'Yes, he was a soldier and very handsome.'

'Like Prince Eric off *Little Mermaid*?'

Please let this stop. 'No, he had blond hair.'

'So, my hair is red the same as yours and my daddy's is blond?' Darcy seemed happy with this news.

'Yes, that's right. Your hair is strawberry blonde, a mix of both.' *Please do not start calling him Daddy Gabe, that's all I need.*

'Does he have tattoos like you?'

'Yes, he did.' It was a dagger, his regiment badge, but no way was she telling Darcy that because she'd only want the same. She had a thing about tattoos and loved nothing more than covering her arms with transfers.

'I'm going to have *Frozen* tattoos. Anna on this arm and Elsa on the other.'

'That's lovely, I'm sure they'll look ace.' And that was precisely why Violetta hadn't mentioned a dagger!

And then came the words more stomach-churning than the first question itself. 'I think one day my daddy will come and find me, and you too. I bet he's busy being a soldier and when he's finished he'll come and see us. I'm gonna watch for him on the telly if there's soldier men on the news.'

Oh, you poor, sweet child, if it was only that easy. 'I don't know about that, Darcy. He doesn't know where I live so don't get your hopes up, okay. Now eat your dinner then you can have some jelly. I made strawberry.' How could she add that he probably didn't even remember her name, never mind admit that he'd buggered off and left her in a boat, pissed and semi-comatose. Not a good look!

'Can I have ice cream on top, too?'

You can have whatever you want but please don't ask me any more questions. 'Yes, and rainbow sprinkles. Right, be quick while I nip upstairs and get some laundry. Then it's jelly time.'

It was the coward's way out, rushing from the room to avoid further interrogation but it had worked because when she came back down Darcy had finished her tea and was already engrossed in her colouring. Violetta prayed it wasn't a new family portrait but to her relief, there were no more questions apart from a cheeky request for some squirty cream that, under the stressful circumstances, was duly granted.

Every now and then Darcy would mention her long-lost dad but only a passing comment, like: *My daddy is a soldier, isn't he, Mum.* Or, *Is my daddy's hair the same colour as Granny Sylvia's?* So when Darcy mentioned asking Santa for a dad, Violetta's first reaction was to feel affronted, that a mum wasn't enough. Then, after she'd calmed down, it dawned on her that Darcy, in her hankering after a daddy, had resorted to Santa – or as everyone else knew him, Big Dave. This had made Violetta so sad, and that anger surged.

She had never wanted this for her child because she knew exactly how it felt, pining after her own dad when he'd been away on a business trip and worse, when he'd died and she knew he wasn't coming back at all. Darcy was suspended somewhere in between and none of it was her fault.

What silently killed Violetta was the awful realisation that in Gabe, she might have found a gem but let him slip away like the sand she'd washed from her hair and clothes when she finally staggered back to the hotel that morning in Croatia. She had considered trying to track him down, but how? With no idea what regiment he was in, or where he was based. The only place that might have been any help was Facebook although she didn't fancy posting a status saying: *Hey, can you help? I'm trying to trace the father of my child. He's a blond-haired soldier called Gabe and we had a one-night stand in Croatia six years ago!* Her mother would have a fit. And imagine the conversation if she did find him. He'd probably think she was after maintenance payments and run a mile.

It was as though history kept on repeating. Dads didn't last long in their family. First, her granddad had an affair with a woman called Martha and buggered off, never to be seen again.

At least her own dad had stuck around. It wasn't his fault he was killed.

That's what she had believed at first. She had clung on to her memories, idolising him in life and death – until Rosina had ruined everything.

Appleton Farm, Cheshire. 1999

Being the middle sister, Violetta had always been protected by the eldest, Rosina, the mother hen of the family whose role expanded when Leonora, the surprise baby, came along just after their dad was killed. Even though it happened when she was eleven, those terrible days were scorched into Violetta's memory and had tormented her for the next twenty-one years.

Christmas had been two weeks away and, as always, her mum had made the kitchen look lovely, decorating the warmest room of the house. They'd ordered the turkey from the butchers and in that jokey way that mums use when they actually mean it, she'd asked Violetta and Rosina to pray that their knackered old range didn't conk out before she'd made their Christmas dinner.

Times must have been tough and her parents were scraping by. Her dad worked away much of the time while her mum stayed at home and tried to renovate an old, leaky house. It wasn't as though they went without, they just didn't have a lot. Nevertheless, each year belts were tightened and a happy day was had by all and with a new baby due any time, Violetta and Rosina were even more excited. Then everything went wrong.

Her dad was killed, her mum wandered around like a zombie and the house seemed to be plunged into darkness. Gloom lingered in every room and ghostly shadows waited in corners and for the first time ever, Violetta was glad to go to school.

In the days leading up to the funeral, half of Violetta was grieving her dad while the other half was cross with him for being killed and spoiling Christmas. She thought it wise to keep these bad thoughts to herself so during the funeral service, when the vicar asked everyone to pray for her father, Violetta had bowed her head, clasped her hands and prayed hard for a miracle. The thing was, instead of asking for her dad back she had begged God and his angels to grant her a happy Christmas Day. And that her mother would stop crying and Rosina wouldn't be in a bad mood because she was tired from looking after everyone. And lo and behold. It worked.

Instead of going back home to her council flat in the city, after the wake Granny Sylvia said she would stay a while to help out, until the baby came at least. And the very next morning when Violetta and Rosina came down for breakfast they found their mum in the kitchen, humming to the radio, cooking them egg on toast and smiling. From that day, her mum rallied, wiped away their tears and held in her own. And it was all down to Violetta's prayers and God actually listening for once. That was the Christmas their lives changed and their mum took control of the family and their futures and became a legend.

Not that Violetta didn't revere her dad, too. She adored him and always would, once she'd forgiven him for dying and almost ruining Christmas. Soon, she learned to get along without him, making do with memories and a box of his treasures, knick-knacks that her mum had allowed her to keep. His lighter, a hip flask, some fancy sunglasses, his wallet, all kept inside his briefcase along with a photo album. And in order to assuage the guilt she felt at being so angry with him, Violetta made sure she thought about him every day.

She also took it upon herself to ensure that her baby sister loved him too, passing on everything she remembered, showing Leonora videos so she could hear his voice and his laugh, see him smile. It annoyed Violetta that when she talked about her dad at the kitchen table her mum didn't really join in, maybe a bit, a nod and a smile but it felt like she changed the subject too quickly.

Maybe Granny Sylvia was right when she'd taken Violetta aside and explained that talking about her dad might make her mum sad, and everyone dealt with grief in their own ways so not to be cross with her. It made sense and knowing her gran was always fair, Violetta took it on board.

About a year later, Rosina was in one of her bad moods (Granny Sylvia had said it was hormones) and she'd made Violetta cry by saying that their dad wasn't a saint and she should stop talking rubbish to Leonora. She'd hated Rosina that day and they'd actually fought. Hair-pulling, face-scratching, rolling around on the carpet while their little sister wailed until Granny Sylvia had pulled them apart and made Rosina apologise. When they'd both calmed down she'd asked Rosina what she meant only to be told it was nothing. However, deep down Violetta knew something was wrong.

Preferring to stick to her version of her dad, and heeding her gran's words she'd let it go and found other ways to vent her frustration, easing the little balloon of anger that every now and then filled with hot air, swelling, fit to burst inside her heart.

Violetta wasn't what you'd class as a troubled teenager, more headstrong, prone to flare-ups, a borderline drama queen who chose the best opportunities to make a statement. Granny Sylvia simply called her a pain in the arse and she was right.

It began with the black clothes, studded boots and kohl-pencilled eyes. Then came the piercings, as soon as the law allowed without parental consent. At fourteen it was her lobes and then at sixteen her nose and as many studs as she could fit in her ears. Her tongue and whatever other bits remained unpierced had to wait till she was eighteen.

Rosina had been furious when her chief bridesmaid refused to take them out for the wedding, and was horrified by the red Dr Marten boots that peeped from beneath the peach bridesmaid dress. They'd had a stand-up row about it. Violetta sulked all day and took further umbrage when her mum walked her sister down the aisle. It should have been her dad, the dad nobody talked about and nobody missed. At least it wasn't Bern. That would've sent her daft because it was bad enough him hanging about the house without him muscling in and acting like he was their stand-in father.

During the reception, she managed to stash two bottles of wine and after sneaking away as soon as the speeches were done, rang Candy, told her to bring vodka and meet at their favourite haunt, the graveyard. Here, basking in the summer sun, the chief bridesmaid and her partner in many crimes proceeded to get totally smashed. And it didn't end there.

Deciding to honour her dad, seeing triple, Violetta and Candy staggered through the graveyard and into the village church. It was empty, too early for evensong, so they proceeded along the pews, unhooking the floral wedding decorations from the end and liberating the two large arrangements that stood on the altar and lectern.

'Well, I think that looks bloody frantas– flabul– great, don't you, mate?' Violetta slurred and swayed, leaning on Candy.

'Yesh... it's very flowery now. I like it a lot.' Collapsing into a heap, Candy lay down next to the grave that was covered in ribbons and carnations.

Flopping by her side, Violetta lay prostrate in her bridesmaid dress, red Dr Marten boots poking out the bottom, her eyes closing against the early evening sun. When the vicar discovered them later, he drove Candy home and then took Violetta to the golf club where the evening reception was in full swing. Her mother was already out of her mind with worry and really didn't need the disapproving looks from the vicar or to hear that he'd be sending her the valeting bill after Candy had vomited over the back seat of his car and Violetta, too, going by the state her dress.

The following afternoon Rosina turned up at Appleton. She and Lou wanted to say goodbye before they set off on their honeymoon to Tenby but first, after bursting into the kitchen she tore a strip off her sleepy, hungover sister.

'What the hell do you think you were playing at, stealing my flowers from the church and putting them on *his* grave, of all places?' Rosina was leaning on the table opposite Violetta who was sipping water.

'It was just a prank, a bit of a laugh and you didn't need them after the wedding so what's the problem?'

'Oh, a prank. Well, that's okay then! The problem, Vi, is that I'd promised the flowers to the vicar's wife who was going to give them to the old folks' home. You are so bloody selfish and you can sodding well pay for that wine you pinched because I'm not.' Rosina stood straight and folded her arms, glaring at her sister just as her mum and gran came rushing into the room.

Violetta gave a shrug of her shoulders. 'Oh, stop going on. You're just pissed off cos I put them on dad's grave so stop making out it's all about the old biddies. I put them there to include him in the day because nobody else mentioned him, as usual. Don't you think he would've liked to be part of his eldest and most *perfect* daughter's day?'

Rosina slammed her hands onto the tabletop, her face puce. 'Oh, for God's sake do not turn this into another "poor dad" speech! It's pathetic. And actually no, I don't think he'd have been too bothered about missing it, unless you count the booze because, just like you, he'd have loved knocking it back and ruining my day.'

At this point Carmen stepped forward and intervened.

'Rosina, that's enough, love. I know you're annoyed but let's not spoil what's been a lovely weekend – and you need to get going. Lou's waiting in the car.'

'Well, he'll have to wait a bit longer, Mum, because I've had just about enough of pandering to Vi and her hero worshipping. It's about time she knew the truth. If she's big enough to get pissed and steal things she's big enough to face some facts.'

Violetta's head snapped up in time to see her gran place a hand on her mum's arm, as if preventing her from silencing Rosina.

'What do you mean, "face some facts"?' Violetta felt as though she'd been slapped. They'd been lying about something. All this time, her family had been keeping secrets.

Temper flaring, she stood and just like Rosina banged her fists on the table, addressing her sister, rage flowing through her veins as she shouted across the table. 'Go on then, Mrs Wonderful, tell me all about my big bad dad, go on, go on!'

Not missing a beat, Rosina did exactly that. 'He was a drunk, a slob and a bully who was too handy with his fists, okay. He beat Mum black and blue for years, even when she was pregnant and before he died started taking his temper out on me, too. He was a nasty, spiteful man who had no time for any of us, apart from you because you were the only one who still liked him. He didn't even want our Leo to be born. I'm sorry, Vi, but it's true.'

The only sound in the kitchen was the clock ticking as Violetta looked from one to another and when her mum and gran failed to dispute Rosina's words, she knew without a doubt that her sister was telling the truth. Her heart plummeted, her legs gave way and she sat.

And as quickly as her temper had flared, it dissipated. All the resentment that she'd kept trapped inside began to seep away, replaced by a glimmer of understanding. What they'd done was kind, keeping secrets because they loved her. Now she knew why they never joined in. It made sense. She wasn't cross with them, not anymore, and it felt quite nice, to let it go.

Her mum put it all into perspective as she came and sat by Violetta's side, taking her hand. 'No matter what we knew, you were entitled to your memories and I'm glad you have them, I truly am, despite how he behaved towards us. You must understand that.'

Next, Granny Sylvia. 'And you were so good with little Leo, passing on your stories and giving her a sense of belonging, a little bit of knowledge about a dad she never met. It was hard for us to do that, knowing what we did, so we were grateful that you were there to fill in the gaps.'

Rosina spoke next, but softly this time. 'But you're so angry, Vi, all the time and it has to stop because it's spoiling the lovely person you are inside. I don't know if you're mad at us for not being in Team Dad, or mad at him for dying but whatever it is please don't let it wreck your future. Talk to us and let us help. We all love you so much even though you are a complete pain in the bum.' Rosina had come around the table and had placed her arm around her sister who accepted the gesture willingly.

Wrapping her arms around Rosina's waist she rested her head against her stomach and before the tears escaped, made amends. 'I'm sorry, Rosie, for being a pillock at your wedding and being angry all the time. I'll buy some new flowers for the old folks' home and take them up, but I might have to pay for the wine next month cos I'm skint. Is that okay?'

When Rosina laughed and said it was fine, she'd pay for the wine, Violetta burst into tears and was shushed by her mum while Granny Sylvia put the kettle on and Lou wandered in, saw what was going on and backed straight out again.

Later, once Rosina had gone off on her honeymoon and Granny Sylvia had gone to bed, Violetta and her mum had a conversation that was long overdue. All the questions were answered and a jumbled past laid to rest. And if one good thing came out of being the flower-stealing-chief-bridesmaid-from-hell, Violetta decided that she'd had enough of being a pain in the arse and the rebel of the family. When college started a few weeks later she finally knuckled down, determined to make her mum and all of them, proud.

Present day

The buzz of Violetta's upside-down phone brought her slap back to the present and as she tentatively turned it over, read the message on the screen which only confirmed what she'd known all along. Men were bastards and they could all just fuck off.

Appleton history proved her theory. Not just that, Violetta lived in the real world where nobody was perfect. Her real job had taught her that. She was becoming jaded and didn't believe she would ever find an honourable family man. Someone without demons, who worked hard, would never stray or let her down. A man who would carry Darcy on strong shoulders and care for her as if he were his own. That's what she aimed for – yet all around her, every day, she saw shining examples of why it was far better to remain single. She and Darcy were fine as they were.

10

CARMEN

Appleton Farm, Cheshire
Present day

The storm that had battered all four walls of Appleton Farm was slowly moving away, southwards towards the Shropshire Hills, lighting up the sky in the distance as it bade farewell to the Cheshire Plain with a two-flash encore.

Carmen was untroubled by storms, knowing she was protected by her home that had withstood many an onslaught by the weather. She was warm and cosy, lying in bed next to Bern, a fire roaring in the grate and the scent of cinnamon and bergamot mingling with the unmistakable aroma of coal and woodsmoke. Whatever the season, her whole house smelt divine – another perk of owning a beautiful gift shop stocked to the rafters with the most heavenly of scented bits and bobs. And then there were the decorations.

Her grandchildren were creatures of habit and set great store on their grandma's house looking EXACTLY the same every single year. Carmen knew it gave them comfort, the ritual of bringing the boxes down from the attic. Her twin granddaughters Ella and Lola would unpack their favourites, the nativity scene and the angel, while her eldest granddaughter Tilly took charge of the baubles with Darcy, the youngest as her assistant.

Bern, Lou and Max brought in the trees after the whole family went down to the forest to choose them, a task that always took a while. They had a huge pine in the lounge, two smaller versions in the kitchen and hall and then there was the special tree for her room. A little artificial one that stood in an old biscuit tin that was wrapped in Christmas paper.

It wasn't the same tree she saw in her dreams: that had been left behind like everything else but as soon as she got married and had her own place, Carmen replicated the one from her childhood and she'd kept it ever since.

Turning to her side slowly, she smiled when she saw Bern. Pulling the eiderdown further up to cover his shoulders she spent a moment taking him in. She really did love him so much, her strong and able lover who she'd known since Rosina was a toddler. He had been by her side for the past twenty years, not always in a physical sense but there, watching, guiding, lending support. He had never let Carmen down.

She had the urge to stoke his hair, the soft waves on top that were still chestnut brown, fading to ash and grey at the sides. *Bloody men,* thought Carmen as she traced the wrinkles of his face with her eyes. *How come they grow old gracefully and look better as the years go by?*

Bern put his rugged good looks down to working outside and according to him, hard work and fresh air were the keys to longevity. He was never ill, had the constitution of an ox, ate like a horse, was powered by batteries that seemed never to run out, but most of all he had a heart of gold. That was the real source of his power, Carmen was convinced of it.

The girls loved him. Her whole family did and that included her mother. Not that she ever said it out loud but the mere fact she hadn't said the opposite, spoke volumes. And even though Carmen and Bern had taken their time, a rather long time really, everyone said they were always meant to be.

Looking to the chest of drawers in her room, her gaze washed over the photo frames, a gallery of memories that she looked over every day, her own private ritual, saying thanks for her blessings.

Luckily, her mother rarely entered Carmen's bedroom but when she did, would steadfastly avoid the photographs because at the centre, surrounded by the granddaughters he'd never met, was her dad. She only had two photos that, in a rare moment of defiance, she'd snatched before her mother dragged her sobbing to a taxi.

The face of her father was etched into Carmen's memory thanks to the black-and-white images that she'd since had copied and remastered when her fear of then being destroyed or lost became an obsession.

The time of year always made her reflect more than usual, but going through sequences of events either wide awake or in her dreams was another ritual she had to embrace, get out of her system then move on. She and Bern had spent many Christmases apart, however, from now on they would be together every year, no obstacles, no excuses.

Closing her eyes she rested her head against his shoulder. It was definitely time to move on and once she'd told the girls on Sunday, she would focus on the future. And as she listened to Bern snore – and yes, that was definitely a little whistle – she stifled a giggle as she took her annual walk down memory lane.

. . .

Appleton Farm, Cheshire. 1983

Carmen had fallen in love with the farm the moment she set eyes on it, the day she and Seb, her husband of just over a year, trundled up the drive to their new home. As the only living heir, Sebastian Appleton had inherited the house and extensive swathe of farmland from his great uncle Jonathon Appleton and even though the building had fallen into a state of disrepair, the land agent assured them it was salvageable.

Using all her powers of persuasion, Carmen tried to convince Sebastian that Appleton Farm would make the perfect family home. Placing her hands on her rounded belly, she painted a picture of their children growing up in the countryside, being part of a village community well away from the smoky city and all its perils. Yes, it was a huge project and the clunky plumbing and fire-hazard electrics would need attention but if they did the rooms up one by one, using the money they saved from their rented flat in Manchester, along with the added bonus of his recent promotion, they could do it.

Sebastian had no interest in the farm or the house and its antique mantel clock that ticked so loudly that Carmen said was a sign. He loved city life so wanted to sell the hideous pile immediately and buy somewhere modern. And then Sylvia arrived to cast her beady eye and as soon as she pronounced judgement, his opinion changed. But Sylvia knew that. Later, she'd told Carmen that once she realised how much her daughter wanted to keep it, she did her very best to make sure that happened.

On this occasion Carmen was grateful but it hadn't always been so. From the moment she introduced her boyfriend to her mum, she had resigned herself to being chief peace negotiator. Sylvia was of the opinion that her naïve, eighteen-year-old daughter was far too young for a worldly-wise thirty-two-year-old and made her position on the matter most clear. With hindsight, many years later, Carmen realised that the more Sylvia protested, the more Sebastian dug in his heels, determined to prove her wrong because he wasn't a dirty old man and Carmen certainly wasn't looking for a father figure.

Hence, the about-turn when Sylvia came to visit Appleton and condemned it as a smelly hellhole where Sebastian would keep his young wife and family prisoner while he swanned off around the country flogging business insurance, living it up in hotels and doing God knows what on expenses.

Sylvia always made sure she spoke loudly, her barbed comments and harsh judgements bouncing off the walls, her acid tongue capable of stripping the peeling plaster and paint back down to brick. No doubt determined to prove the hag wrong, and realising that maybe Carmen was right, Sebastian decided that living in the countryside away from Manchester – and his battleaxe mother-in-law – was in fact a positive. So they stayed.

Carmen adored village life and embraced being part of the Gawsworth community. It was bliss. A simpler life. Back to nature. And after channelling her father, imagining him on his allotment she slowly resurrected the vegetable patch so they could eat off the land. She watched the seasons turn, shivering through the winters, embracing spring and breathing in the glory of summer in the countryside. She made new friends, other mothers from the village and in particular Stacey, the wife of one of the tenanted farmhands. It was at a birthday party for their daughter, Sarah-Beth, that Carmen first met Stacey's husband Bern.

Sebastian had no interest in meeting new people. He was happy with his colleagues in the office in Manchester and the clients he saw regularly during his nomadic travels, however, he begrudgingly attended the party and feigned interest in the locals. What Carmen failed to accept, closed her eyes to and made excuses for, was his belligerent attitude, that air of superiority he adopted while making out he was the local landowner who lived in the big house. The very same house he'd told her the night before would serve them better if it was burnt to the ground.

There was something else too. For the first time, amidst a crowd of young parents of a similar age, there appeared a yawning gap between him and Carmen's twenty-three years. As they trudged home, her pushing the pram and him marching ahead, three whiskies worse for wear, she blanked out her mother's voice, the sage advice she'd ignored. Instead, she blinked back tears and couldn't wait to be home so she could close her eyes to her big mistake, and sleep in the bed she'd made for herself.

Five years after Rosina arrived, Violetta was born and although the house was taking shape, progress was slow and they were still managing with two bedrooms, an ancient bathroom and the kitchen. The tenanted farmland brought in extra money but that was commandeered by Sebastian so Carmen managed the house alone, doing what she could while despite her best attempts to avert it, her mother's prophecy was coming true.

Sebastian rose through the ranks but was away more often and when he returned seemed unsettled, disinterested in Carmen's plans for the renovation of the house and unimpressed by her efforts. It was the drinking that bothered her the most, followed by maudlin periods that cast the house into shadows, gloom sticking to her newly emulsioned walls. But the thing she hid most was his ever-increasing bouts of anger, rages that ended with him storming downstairs to sleep on the sofa, leaving Carmen with sore ribs and eyes red from crying.

Her mother, who was a regular visitor but only while Seb

was away, had had enough and wasn't backwards in her interrogation, using information passed on by Rosina, who at ten was far more astute than her little sister. Carmen, desperate to prove her mother wrong, dug in her heels, said it was a blip, an eleven-year itch that they could fix. Sylvia disagreed but respected her daughter's decision to stay, promising to keep her counsel but to wait in the wings if she was needed.

They staggered on for five more years. He was ill, overweight and unfit and even though the doctor had told him to stop drinking and smoking because whisky and forty cigarettes a day weren't helping his heart condition, Sebastian knew best. Deep down she knew they were in trouble, but what rammed it home was hearing that Stacey had left Bern for an old boyfriend she'd not seen since school.

The news that she'd simply gone, taking her daughter while Bern was at work rocked the village. For Carmen it was worse, as though the ground beneath her shook when the truth dawned. Bern and Stacey had looked so happy and content on the outside yet her close friend had kept such a huge secret, been carrying on like nothing was amiss.

In contrast, Carmen was trapped in a rickety, rocky marriage that was as unhappy on the inside as it looked on the out, and that meant only one thing – if Stacey could get up to no good right under their noses, who knew what Sebastian got up to while he was away. They were doomed.

To make matters worse, Carmen had heard the Stacey and Bern news as she left the doctor's, two minutes after he'd confirmed what she already suspected. She was thirty-five years old, baby number three was on the way.

Her husband was a drunk, sickly man and neither use nor ornament. The only person who truly adored him was Violetta, blinkered by love for a father she hankered after, a man who was rarely there and showered her with guilty affection when he was. At fifteen, getting too old for cuddles and hastily grabbed consolation gifts, Rosina was beginning to see through him and his smokescreen, just like her Granny Sylvia always had.

Nearing the gates to Appleton, Carmen looked down and stroked her stomach, imagining the new life inside her. She hadn't planned it. Her baby was the result of a loveless fumble in the dark, one she'd tried to avoid but acquiesced to in order to keep the peace. Yet despite the circumstances of conception, or how weary she was and how difficult the future might be, Carmen was invested in her unborn baby, in Rosina and Violetta and in their home. As for her marriage, all she could do was give it one more try. She wouldn't walk away, or run. History would not repeat. She would stay and hope that life would give her a break and somehow it would all work out.

When it came, her chance to start again, Carmen wasn't expecting it, but knowing it was now or never she grabbed it with both hands, and hadn't looked back since.

Appleton Farm, Cheshire. Present day

Her reminiscing was interrupted by Bern stirring beside her. Turning on his side he pulled her close, kissing the top of her head. 'Have you been lying there making more lists?'

Carmen gave him a gentle nudge. 'I'll have you know all my lists are ticked and up to date. I was actually thinking about the past and how we met. With our big announcement on the horizon, it's like I need to get everything straight in my head.'

'Ah. You're having second thoughts and trying to work out how to tell me, is that it?'

Pushing herself away so she could assure him it was nothing of the kind, one look at his face told her he was joking and she relaxed. 'No, you fool. We've been through all this a million times and I'm one million per cent positive that I want you to move in, so stop fishing for compliments.'

'Well, what is it then? The girls?'

Carmen shook her head and brushed hair from her face. 'The girls will be fine. They love you to bits and I'm excited to tell them and anyway, they've been teasing us for years about living separately so they finally get their wish.'

'And I love them too, like daughters. I know Vi put up a bit of a wall at first but we get along fine now so I don't think she will be a problem, do you?'

Carmen was surprised at his concern over Vi. 'No, not at all. Yes, she idolised her dad but you've been part of the family since Leonora was born and she knows how much you helped us all. Seriously, Bern, there's nothing to worry about. As they love to remind us, you're my old-time, part-time, live-in lover who nips across the field for a cheeky leg-over then out the back door at the crack of dawn. It was their teenage joke, laughing at the worst-kept secret. So stop overthinking things. You're worse than me.'

'Nobody is worse than you.'

'This is also true.' Carmen nestled beside Bern and enjoyed the warmth of his body and she felt him relax, drifting off to sleep.

Once again her thoughts wandered. Had they wasted time? Bern was getting over losing Stacey and the shock of being separated from his daughter. Then Sebastian was killed and Carmen had enough on her plate with a new baby on the way, two daughters and a rambling home.

When finally, they both felt able to trust and love again, their friendship was the solid foundation on which they built a relationship, everything that followed was a natural progression, a combination of mutual respect and admiration, a common aim, and for a long time suppressed lust that eventually bubbled over and sealed the deal.

Bern had kept his cottage for when Sarah-Beth came to stay. And it would have been easy for Carmen to blame her mother for him not moving in. The truth was simple. They were happy just as they were. The years tumbled by, their lives fell into an easy pattern, comfortable yet not complacent, the thrill of attraction remained strong.

But when Bern's son-in-law was made redundant and their landlord gave them notice, Carmen stepped in. 'You know what the solution is don't you?' The blank look from Bern spurred her on. 'I think you should let them have your cottage.'

At this he looked taken aback. 'What do you mean? Actually let them have it?'

'Yes. It will go to Sarah-Beth one day so why not let her live there now and you move in with me. That way she won't have to worry about money or scrimping for a deposit and she can use what she's saved to do the cottage up.'

Rather than reject the idea out of hand Bern looked more offended by Carmen's last comment. 'What do you mean do it up? There's nothing wrong with my cottage.'

Carmen rolled her eyes and tried to be tactful. 'I suppose not, if you like living in a nineties time warp with an avocado bathroom suite and wall-to-wall Anaglypta.' Taking his hands in hers, ignoring his offended expression, she tried to make him see sense without coming over as desperate, or bossy, or suggesting Sarah-Beth might need a skip. 'Look, what I'm trying to say is that we've spent years making excuses why we shouldn't move in together so maybe this is a damn good reason why we should. I think it's time, don't you?'

It hadn't taken long for him to agree, and Sarah-Beth had cried tears of relief and joy when he told her the news. All that was left was to tell Carmen's three over Sunday lunch and then

Bern would be moving in permanently. No more nipping across the fields.

Carmen knew in her heart it was the right thing to do. Her grand plan was coming together, another tick in the box. It was the final piece in the puzzle and would be a perfect start to Christmas, having Bern there for good.

The crackle of the fire in the grate lulled her into sleep. Her subconscious mind drifted, thoughts floating into the land of dreams, nudging old ghosts and buried memories, taking her back to the past. Back to Tilbury and the worst Christmas ever.

11

CARMEN

Tilbury, London
1969

I hate this dream. I need to wake up. Stop the music. I want to get off.

I am standing in the hallway of our house. It's freezing and my legs feel pimply, sticking out of my nightie and when I look down my feet are bare. My hands are bruised from where I banged on the door as I screamed and begged my dad to come back and then kicked and cried even more when Mum dragged me away.

It's like I am a time traveller, borrowing my little girl body, popping in to watch my mum as she clomps up the stairs in her green dressing gown, pink slippers flapping with each step.

I can see her blonde hair, a frizzy hive of white candyfloss, messy with a flat patch at the back that shows her dark roots. She's carrying a cup of tea in one hand, a cigarette in the other leaving smoke swirling in her wake, adding to the stale smell that is so alien to me. Our home is always clean and tidy and yet there's this stench that I can't get rid of, like it's sticking inside my nose.

Don't go in the kitchen.

I ignore my own voice. It's always the same and why my feet automatically take me in that direction, the smell getting worse with every step, my curiosity egging me on. The kitchen is the same as it was on Christmas Eve, two days ago. A pile of peelings lies wrapped in newspaper, a pan of vegetables at the side and at first I think that's the source of the smell. Going over I pinch my nose. It's reminding my brain of the compost heap at Dad's allotment. I take the pan and peelings to the bin, lift the lid and throw the lot inside. It's only when I turn to put the pan in the sink that I realise where the true cause of the stench is coming from.

On the draining board under a bloodstained tea towel is the chicken. Again I pinch my nose and with my free hand I pull back the cloth, stupidly allowing a waft of rancid air to escape from the grey, slimy flesh and my stomach rolls as bile slides up my throat. I have to get rid of it and the forfeit is letting go of my nose so that two hands can grab the plate. In one panicked, nauseating motion I throw the whole thing in the bin, plate included, then grab the lid and slam it down hard on top.

A voice from behind, harsher than the clatter of metal on metal makes me jump.

'Carmen!'

I am jolted forward in time, the next morning, in my bedroom. I am wearing my best coat and woolly tights and on top of the mattress is a suitcase, the lid open and the contents of my wardrobe and drawers folded neatly inside.

'You can take whatever will fit on top. Don't dawdle. The taxi will be here soon.' My mum looks nice today. She's wearing her pencil skirt and black turtleneck, and high heels that make a clomping sound on the floorboards as she goes from room to room.

'Here's your toothbrush and toothpaste, save me buying new. Now, are you taking Tiny Tears? Let's squash her in the end, and pass me Mr Bunny.' She makes a flicking motion with her fingers that I know means hurry up.

'But Mum, why do I have to take my toys? We never take them when we go to stay with Aunty Mavis.' She quickly takes Mr Bunny who is resting on my pillow and I pass Tiny Tears to her.

Why won't she look at me? She fusses with the suitcase and answers sharply, the sting makes my eyes water. 'Because we're not going to see Aunty Mavis. We're going on an adventure and I don't know when we will be back. That's why you have to take as much as you can now.'

I can feel my heart pounding, something isn't right. It's as Mum moves towards my bookshelf and starts to remove my Enid Blytons that I notice the two large suitcases in the hallway.

'Is Dad coming too? Have you packed his clothes? Where is he? The taxi is coming so he needs to hurry up. Mum, where's Dad? Where's my Daddy?' My last question comes out as a shout and my mum responds the same way.

'Carmen stop! Just shut up, please. Just be quiet.' Mum has closed her eyes tight and is pinching the bridge of her nose between finger and thumb. She looks like she's in pain.

I wait.

When she opens her eyes she takes a last look around my room, grabbing the Etch A Sketch and my pack of felt pens, throwing the colouring books on top before zipping up the case, squashing Tiny Tears's face and for a second trapping Mr Bunny's ears.

I start to cry, not because I'm worried my doll can't breathe and my rabbit is hurt and that my Beatrix Potter books won't fit in. It's because I don't want to go. So I tell her. 'Mum, where are we going? Please don't make me go without Daddy.'

Dragging the case off the bed she ignores me for a second but when I don't move she stops. 'Daddy isn't coming with us.'

'Why not? Has he gone to live with that nasty lady who was shouting at him? Why would he live with someone horrible like her, Mum, when he can live here with us?' I am so confused. I want answers.

She holds my stare. My mum always says it's wrong to lie. But I can see she's trying to think of what to say and I panic. I can't bear the thought that she might tell me a fib so I give her a get-out. 'Has he gone to sea? When will he be back?'

Again she wavers and again I panic. 'So if he's gone to sea and we go away I won't get his postcards and letters so we have to stay, then I can read them when the postman comes.' I'm pleased with myself for giving Mum such a sensible and easy solution, until she speaks.

'No, your dad hasn't gone to sea, Carmen, and I have no idea where he is right now. So please don't ask me any more questions. And I don't want to talk about that woman or the other night so go downstairs. Here, take your satchel and wait in the parlour. Go on. Now.'

My lips begin to wobble and so do hers and as much as I am angry with her, I don't want her to cry. So instead of putting up a fight I follow the direction of her pointed finger, holding tight to the banister because I can't see the stairs properly through my tears.

The second I enter the parlour it's as though he's there, the scent of him, his presence is everywhere, squashed into the cushion on his armchair where he was sitting when the woman banged on the door. His ashtray is on the arm, half a cigarette perched on the side and his slippers are by the fire. Looking up I notice that there are photographs missing from the mantelpiece, Mum's mum, me and mum. The happy wedding photo is still there. Mum and Dad outside the town hall.

I turn when I hear a noise, cases bouncing down the stairs and I am going to ask about the photographs when she goes straight back up to collect mine, at the same time as the light dawns. She doesn't want photos of my dad, but I do.

My head flicks towards the sideboard. Knowing there's no time to spare I rush over and pick up two photos of my dad. One on the deck of his last ship, the other of the two of us, the week he came home to see his new baby girl. I put one in each pocket. My eyes then fall on the bookshelf and my heart lurches. I can't leave the atlas behind or his storybooks but mum is on her way back down. I watch and wait, listening as my case is dragged to the door and then her heels clip-clop towards the kitchen and then I pounce on my satchel, dragging it across the floor to the bookshelf where I kneel, fumbling with the buckles.

Hurry, faster, she'll be back soon. My chest is tight and my fingers tremble as I grab the atlas, *please let it fit.* It's a squeeze but it slides in and then I remove the photos from my pockets and put them in, too. Then the books. I take *The Swiss Family Robinson* and *Heidi* but there's only room for one more and I know which I have to choose, *The Rime of the Ancient Mariner.* Our poem.

She's coming back.

I manage to flip the satchel closed but not thread the buckles so I stand and clutch it close to my chest, holding it so tightly I can feel my heart beat beneath the brown leather. Mum is putting on her coat in the hall and I take one last look at the books I have to leave behind. *Robinson Crusoe, Anne of Green Gables, Adventures of Huckleberry Finn, The Old Man and the Sea.* But it isn't only them I'm leaving behind, it's my dad, too.

The noise of the taxi honking its horn outside makes me

jump and now I am at the station. Euston. I don't like how everyone is rushing and Mum still isn't speaking. She didn't say a word in the taxi so neither did I. Instead I fiddled with the buckles of my satchel and fastened it properly.

A porter helps Mum with our cases and loads them onto a trolley and I follow them both in silence to the ticket office where I listen as she speaks to the man at the window. 'Two singles to Manchester, please. One adult, one child.'

Manchester. Why are we going there? My mind races and all I can come up with is that Mum likes watching *Coronation Street* but it's not real, it's a telly programme. Elsie Tanner is made up so we can't be going to see her.

We're on the move again, racing along the platform, the porter loads our bags, Mum gives him a tip and then we find a seat, next to the window, facing each other and I can't bear it anymore. 'Mum, why are we going to Manchester? Where will we stay? Does Dad know where Manchester is so he can come and see us?'

'We're going to stay with an old friend, a lady I knew at school. She's nice. You'll like her. She works at the airport and has a spare room in her house and when we get settled, I'll ring your dad, okay?'

I see her suck in a breath and then I spot the tear that's leaking onto her cheek, just before she flicks it away and I can tell she is sad. And that's when I feel sad too, for my mum who was looking forward to Christmas and had made it all so nice before that nasty Martha came and ruined it all. And it was Martha that stole my dad, and made him go and live with her so it wasn't really his fault. He had to choose. But he didn't choose me. Perhaps Martha doesn't like children. That will be it. And that's why I start crying and Mum rushes over and puts me on her knee, holding me tight while she cries too.

The train jerks, then starts to move, slowly at first but within seconds it's picking up speed, going into a tunnel, then back into the light, leaving our life behind, taking us away from London and my dad and before I know it, before I can wake up and make it all stop, we are gone.

12

VIOLETTA

Cheshire
Present day

The fourteen-minute drive from Darcy's school to Appleton had never seemed to take so long, getting stuck at every single traffic light on the route and now she was crawling along behind a tractor. Violetta sighed her irritation. Her brain throbbed as another Christmas tune came on the radio: 'It's the hap-happiest season of all...' *No it's fucking not!* Jabbing the button on the console she switched off the sound and tried to clear her head, put things into perspective.

It was a glorious wintery morning. The sky was cloudless and blue, and even though the sun was low and unable to warm the frost-covered fields, the sight of the yellow orb was guaranteed to lift anyone's spirits. Unless your name was Violetta.

To start with she'd lied to her daughter and she never did that but the situation called for it. Darcy had picked up that something was wrong. So Violetta had pleaded a migraine and put on dark glasses to hide her puffy eyes.

Violetta also felt guilty about asking one of the other mothers to walk Darcy in but she simply couldn't face anyone, faking it wasn't an option, or throwing up in the bin in the yard. Not today. She'd cried again, behind her Ray-Bans but forced a smile as Darcy happily jumped out of the car and after a quick wave, held hands with her friend Mabel and chatted all the way to the gate. Vowing to make amends, Violetta was glad it was a Friday, Darcy's favourite day of the week when they had a chippy-night tea but the mere thought of food turned her stomach.

Pushing the button that lowered the window, she welcomed the gust of icy air that whooshed around the car as she inhaled deeply to calm the swell of nausea. It came in waves, a toxic combination of Pinot Grigio and nerves. On either side of the road that wound towards the village where she grew up were fallow fields that stretched for miles and miles, some of them belonged to her mum, the knowledge of which always filled her with immense pride.

God she loved her mum, her wellie-wearing, tractor-driving indomitable force who, when she was at her lowest ebb, bereaved, pregnant and skint, had forged a new life for herself and her daughters. And as always Violetta was the one who let her down. She'd been brought home twice in a police car: once when she and Candy had passed out in the village after a cider binge; the second time when they had spent all their money in town and got on the train without a ticket. The village bobby had brought them back, told them off and that was that. Then the shoplifting from Boots, green glittery eyeshadow of all things. Her mum had grounded her each time, and Granny Sylvia had her ten-pence worth too. Apparently Vi carried the rogue gene which was code for, *She's like her dad and granddad.*

But in the end she'd been forgiven. They were childhood misdemeanours, though, not a huge, great, grown-up cock-up.

She was a mess, and in a mess. That was for sure and the only person she wanted to be with when she felt like this was her mum, although what the hell she was going to say when she got to Appleton was another thing entirely. She'd been up all night, thinking, crying, typing texts to her mum then deleting them, ringing Candy but getting voicemail, pacing the lounge, drinking too much wine then chucking it back up.

At some point in the early hours of the morning, while she stared blankly at the ticker-tape bulletins on Sky News and tried to keep a cup of weak tea down, she'd come up with half a plan and made a firm decision about her future.

As for her moral dilemma she was no further on. How could she tell her mum one thing without divulging another? To expose a liar and a cheat she would have to expose herself and she couldn't. Her mum was her hero. What she thought of Violetta mattered and in the past, no matter how badly she'd messed up, her mum had supported her, never blinked, just dusted herself down and helped sort things out. But this was different.

To keep a huge secret like hers from her mum and sisters was a form of betrayal but one she had deemed necessary. There was no way of turning the clock back, of being honest from the start. That was what bothered Violetta the most, knowing that they would look at her differently, be hurt by her dishonesty. They might be disgusted, definitely shocked, maybe even turn their backs. And then, wrapped up in all of it was someone else's little secret and as soon as it was out, there'd be trouble.

Pushing the button that closed the window, Violetta shivered. The fresh morning air had pinched her face, her eyes watery from the cold, while the chilly hand of conscience tweaked her heart. *Why couldn't you just be like Leo and Rosie?*

Why do you have to be different, the one that messes up? Greedy Vi, always wanting more, never settling for normal, ruining everything.

Finally the tractor indicated and once it turned off the narrow road, Violetta put her foot down, racing towards Appleton and her mum, her mind keeping up the pace, zipping in and out of the past as she tried to make sense of it all.

Macclesfield, Cheshire. 2012

Candy's sister was jetting off to Australia, taking a whole year out and if her master plan succeeded, she was going to bag herself a hot Aussie husband and never come back. Jenny was sorting through her wardrobe and Violetta and Candy were sitting on the bed of the flat the two sisters shared, staking claim to the best bits and ramming the tat into bin liners.

It was no secret between the three women what Jenny did for a living and they'd had many a giggle over what she got up to at work, and how much she earned as a dominatrix. Her family thought she worked at a recruitment agency in the city and only Candy knew the true source of her income that provided her with a ticket out of there and a very healthy bank balance.

'What are you going to do with all your equipment? If you're not planning on coming back, you should sell it on eBay. I bet you'd get a few quid for it.' Candy was holding a cashmere sweater against her boobs, trying to work out if it would fit.

'Nah, I might take it down to the Sally Army. Can you imagine their faces when they open the bin liner and find all my outfits... and the whip.' At this all three of them fell about laughing until Jenny had another idea. 'Or you two could take over where I left off. I'll gift you my set of collars and leads as a leaving present and anything else you fancy.'

Candy responded first. 'Sod off, and anyway as if I'd fit into any of your gear. This body is a temple to my pastries and the thought of leading some nutjob around a bedroom on a lead is not my thing, thanks all the same.'

As Candy continued to rummage Jenny came and sat on the bed next to Violetta and gave her a nudge. 'What about you, Vi? I'm telling you it's easy money and I'll let you take over my website. It's all set up so all you'd have to do is tweak it a bit and change the payment settings and you'd be good to go. I reckon you'd be ace, and I swear, you don't even have to get down and dirty. It's totally hands-off.'

Violetta could feel herself blushing, and was slightly taken aback that Jenny thought she'd be good at it. 'It's okay, I'll pass. I don't think it's my thing and I wouldn't have the bottle. Is it not dangerous, you know, meeting strange men in hotel rooms?'

'No, not at all. They book through an agency and the guys are vetted then passed on to me. The locations are always classy, no seedy hotels or anything like that, which is why I charge a premium rate. It's all psychological, the more they pay, the more subservient they feel, like I'm telling them what I expect and they have to obey.'

Violetta was more curious than convinced. 'And you *never* have to do the deed?'

'Never. It's not about having sex with strangers, it's about feeding their fantasy of being dominated and all I have to do is play a part, sometimes one I invent and other times what the client specifies and believe me, that's an eye-opener. Have you ever seen a man in a nappy begging to have baby powder sprinkled on him? That's why the better you get at it, the quicker it's over, if you see what I mean.' Jenny gave Violetta a cheeky wink then went over to the end wardrobe and flung open the door.

'These are my alter egos... the many faces of Jenny or as I am professionally known, Alyssa. When I put one of these outfits on, I leave me behind and for an hour I become someone else, the scary lady who is more than happy to spank your arse or wrap you up in cling film and drip wax on your nipples. I really don't care as long as the payment hits my bank account before I even go into the room.' Closing the door Jenny started emptying her racks of shoes and chucking them on the bed as Violetta pondered.

'Hey, don't look so worried. I was only teasing but, if you fancy giving it a go let me know. I won't be giving the ladies at the Sally Army a heart attack just yet so the gear is here if you need it. You never know, if it all goes tits-up down under, I might want it back when I come home.'

At this Candy piped up, her face a picture of outrage. 'Don't tell me you're leaving it here. I live in fear of mum finding it and what about Dermot? He could wander in when you're gone and if he sees that lot it might give him ideas. As much as I'd like to give him a slap now and then that's taking it a bit far.'

In between fits of laughter, Jenny managed to speak. 'Oh just bloody tell him if he finds it. I don't care anymore if people know. I've done what I set out to do and earned the money for the trip and plenty more besides and I'm not ashamed of my job. I just can't be doing with gossips or people getting the wrong end of the stick... excuse the pun. Right, I'm going to the offie to get some wine while you two sort that lot out. Back in a bit.'

Once she'd gone, Violetta and Candy continued to pick over and fold clothes, the subject of domination closed, for the time being. It was later that night, and over the following week as Violetta slogged away at her day job, her desk piled high with manila folders, that her mind kept wandering to the wardrobe of clothes and the promise of some extra money. Which was why when she got home on the Friday night she plucked up the courage to ring Jenny and after a short conversation they arranged to meet the following day. They had two weeks before she headed to Oz and in that time, she was going to teach Violetta everything she needed to know.

In the three years that followed, before Darcy was born, Violetta continued her day job at the solicitors where her brain almost froze over and on the side, unbeknown to anyone apart from Candy, she began another career and Mistress Dina was created. Dominatrix to men with more cash than sense. She took time off, for the obvious reasons when she became pregnant but it was an intervention by Candy and a nudge from fate that once again brought about another change in direction.

Fortunately for Violetta, just as her maternity leave was coming to an end, so did her legal career. When the owner of her law firm was caught dating a woman young enough to be his granddaughter, despite his years of experience he was unable to untangle himself from a messy, toxic divorce. Throwing in the towel, he then folded the practice and buggered off to Spain with his nubile young lover.

The news was music to Violetta's ears because she'd already decided that being a solicitor wasn't really her thing, in fact, she hated it. Seeing her unemployed status and redundancy payout as a bonus, Violetta decided it was time to try something new and as luck had it, Candy came up with a great idea.

They'd been friends since secondary school. Both were fiercely loyal to one another, gatekeepers of epic secrets that would make their parents' hair curl, absolvers of their many failings, joyous in their occasional triumphs, and utterly avowed to the preservation of their friendship. That's why going into partnership together was a no-brainer.

Candy's dad was a baker and she was his apprentice and what she didn't know about bread was nobody's business. Her dad was ready to retire and hand over the reins to his daughter who had big ideas for the shop but needed a bit of a financial boost. Cue Violetta whose redundancy payout was sitting in the bank.

'It's the perfect solution. Quit writing wills and shuffling bits of paper, invest in the shop and help me revamp it. I want it to look like one of those gorgeous patisseries we saw in Paris selling artisan bread and speciality cakes.' Candy was animated, full of ideas and enthusiasm.

'And what the hell am I going to do? I can't even make a sponge from a packet mix, you know that.'

'You won't have to. I'll take care of the baking, you can run the café.'

'What café?'

'Seriously, how did you even manage to get your GCSEs, never mind go to uni? Keep up, gormless. We'll save a tiny space for a Parisian-style café with those wooden, curvy-backed chairs and little tables, and some outside too. We can sell the cakes and savouries, fancy coffee and real hot *chocolat*, remember the film, with the witchy woman?' Candy made a V with her fingers and jabbed towards Violetta who sent one back.

'Anyhow, it won't be a huge range of food, just what I make in the back while you run front of house. You'd be fab with the customers because you're a people person *and* you worked in the garden centre coffee shop for years. You'll ace it. And that's not even the best bit.' Candy was firing out ideas like a machine gun.

'Okay, go on, I'm intrigued.'

'You can work part-time at the shop and be with Darcy whenever you need to. We'll get someone else to cover the rest of the hours. And... it's the perfect cover so you can focus on your other job, the one that you're really good at. You could store all your equipment in the flat above the shop and not my spare room!'

As Violetta worked through the possibilities in her mind, the venture began to appeal more with every idea that pinged into her head and they had nothing to do with French tarts, well kind of, but not ones you could eat.

Her job at the solicitors had been a great cover but that was gone so, if she could work part-time at Candy's shop, and maybe expand her repertoire by investing in some new equipment, her family would still be none the wiser. Her mum might be pissed off about wasting her degree, not to mention the fact she'd paid off her student loan but if that was the case Violetta would soon be able to pay her back.

Candy's cheeks were flushed as she watched Violetta intently, twiddling fingers that were used to being busy, and were about to become even more so when she started making her fancy cakes.

One last question floated through her brain. *Violetta Appleton, are you really going to do this?* The answer was simple. *I most certainly am!*

Frantically clapping her hands, Violetta almost squealed her answer. 'Okay, when can we start? Me and you, partners. It's going to be brilliant.'

And it had been. For four years they had lived the dream. Yes, her mum had been dubious at first but once she'd listened to Violetta and Candy's pitch and seen their business plan, she had to admit it was a sound proposition, expanding on an already successful business.

It had all worked out just as they'd planned and time rolled by. The new-look bakery was a success and Violetta's secondary occupation remained a secret but things were about to change. The row of shops where the bakery stood was due to be demolished, part of a rejuvenation scheme. New premises were proving difficult to find. Then, out of the blue Candy made her big announcement. Actually it was more like dropping a nuclear bomb.

'You're going to what?' Hearing her own voice Violetta sounded as shocked as Candy looked nervous.

'We want to buy a barge and go travelling.'

'On a fucking barge! Are you mad? Where the hell are you going to go in it? Up and down the canal. Oh, I know, you could sail into the sunset on the River Bollin.' Violetta's sarcasm soon dried on her tongue when she spotted that Candy looked crestfallen and watery-eyed too, her voice trembling as she spoke.

'We've been thinking about it for ages now. Pipe dreams at first, to get us through the dreary days of lockdown but now Dermot has his redundancy money and seeing as you and I are stuck for new premises, this could be our now or never moment.

'You know I want to try for a baby and some time out, like a gap year from everything, might be just what me and Dermot need. It's been crap, you know that, Vi, and after all the lockdowns I'm tired and don't think I've got the energy to start all over again in a new place. I'm sorry but that's how I feel.'

Seeing Candy slump into the chair as she flicked away a tear brought Violetta to her senses, realising her oldest friend was reaching out and that she'd have been worrying about this conversation for days, probably weeks. And Candy was right. It had been a tough time but they'd scraped through and who was Violetta to stand in the way of her friend's mad dreams?

Going over to where she sat, Violetta knelt and grabbed Candy's hands. 'It's okay, mate, I get it and it's fine. You've always had my back and now it's time I had yours so if you want to bugger off on a barge, go for it. I want you to be happy, even if you are a complete lunatic.'

They had hugged and had a bit of a sob but the deal was done. They'd soon be closing the doors on the shop and Captain Candy Pugwash was off on her travels which left Violetta high and dry. No job, no cover story.

. . .

Appleton Farm, Cheshire. Present day

The turning to Appleton was up ahead. It was always the same when she went home, that feeling of peace as soon as she saw the sign, then the house set in the centre of the field, like a beacon. The big square windows were eyes, watching out for the family and the door in the centre offered safe haven. All you had to do was open it, go inside and there she would be. Their mum.

The many hours of pacing the carpet meant that Violetta had rehearsed most of what she was going to say when she saw her. She'd start by explaining about the bakery and how money would be a bit tight for a while, until she found a new job and the compensation money came in for the shop. Then she'd ask if there was a chance Rosina could find her some hours at the garden centre in the new year, anything would do. The thought of being back there, near her sister almost lifted Violetta's spirits as much as knowing that her mum wouldn't mind if she and Darcy came back home for a bit. If she could rent out her house it'd pay the mortgage and give her breathing space and at the same time, Darcy would love living at her grandma's. It was the perfect solution.

But it was the things that she couldn't mention that made her feel heartsick and the tears well in her eyes because as much as she wanted to get it all in the open, absolutely everything, no holds barred, she didn't have the bottle. It was the worst dilemma she'd ever been in. To expose a cheat she had to expose her own secret life. And now that cheat had a hold on her, or maybe it was a stalemate because he certainly wouldn't want everyone knowing what he got up to in his spare time. Either way she hated being compromised and that skin-crawling sensation of not being in control, ironic really under the circumstances, was never ever going to happen again.

Violetta had made up her mind and her days as Dina were over. She would email Jenny and ask her if she wanted her equipment back and if she declined it was all going down to the tip when they emptied the shop. And that would be it.

What happened in that hotel room had made her realise how easy it was for someone to blackmail her, threaten to tell her family, her child and all the parents at school what she did for a living. And even though for the most part she actually enjoyed what she did and wasn't ashamed at all, that didn't mean that the people she loved wouldn't be. Gossip was a pernicious thing, infecting the innocent and no way would she allow that to happen.

For now she was safe because the cheat would keep his counsel. She would have to learn to live with the guilt of what she knew and not die inside every time he looked at her. Most of all she hoped he would keep his promise not to look elsewhere for his thrills. What a position to be in, having to trust someone like that, who was so adept at putting on a face for the world, fooling everyone.

Finally, she had to make sure that nothing ruined The Big Christmas Weekend for their mum. It was doable but just in case, she decided to have a word with the big man upstairs. It'd been a while since she'd been in touch but he'd come through for her once before and performed a festive miracle so it was worth a try.

Pulling into the drive, Violetta turned off the engine and took a furtive look around and up at the windows. Nobody there. Then taking a deep breath, she closed her eyes and clasped her hands tightly on her lap and for the first time in twenty-one years, began to pray.

13

ROSINA

Gawsworth, Cheshire
Present day.

She couldn't remember the last time she'd rung in sick, and never over the busy Christmas period or worse, a Friday when the wages went out. There was no way she could face work, never mind hold it together for everyone in the office or, if they were short-handed, out front. Not a chance would she be able to fake a smile for the customers because she couldn't even do that for her own family, which was why she was hiding under her duvet, suffering from a pretend stomach bug. It was a sure-fire way to keep all of them at bay and Lou had been totally convinced when he came downstairs that morning to find her looking like death.

All night she'd been up, trawling the internet, looking for a solution, reading comments in forums and hoping the answer would lie in the responses posted by desperate people like herself, kidders kidding kidders, addicts soothing guilty consciences in order to salve their own. And Rosina knew that had she been able to get even ten pounds' worth of credit on any of the gambling sites, she'd have convinced herself that this was the lucky bet, this was the one that would solve all of her problems. That's how it had all started, after her gran died.

It wasn't an excuse, Rosina knew that, but her bereavement, the pain and loss was unbearable and she needed a distraction. She could even remember her first game. It was a Tuesday afternoon, her day off. The house was too quiet and normally she'd have been with her gran, doing a bit of shopping, lunch in the café at M&S, then home to watch a black-and-white film until the kids got in from school. Then she would drive her home after dinner. It was their thing, their day and Rosina ached for it. Tuesdays with Sylvia, just like the book about Morrie.

She'd been poring over photos on her phone and came across one of her and her gran both waving bingo cards. Granny Sylvia loved bingo and insisted they all played at Christmas where Max was the caller and everyone else dabbed their cards. She provided all the prizes too, from Poundland, another of her favourite haunts. Rosina had read somewhere that when someone dies you should look for signs, messages they send that sometimes you miss if you're not paying attention or as in her case, consumed by grief. It was while she sniffed and wiped her eyes that Rosina wondered if the photo was a sign from Sylvia and she was waving a bingo card in her face trying to tell her to bloody cheer up and stop snivelling, and have a bit of fun.

Tapping her phone screen, Rosina searched for online bingo sites and chose the one that she'd seen advertised on telly. It was so easy to open an account and she even got her first ten pounds free. Before she knew it, the twins bounded through the door, starving and wanting their after-school snack which curtailed the session in which she'd won sixty pounds. As she made sandwiches and half-listened to the twins chatter about what they did in science, all Rosina could think about was how time had flown while she was playing bingo and that she hadn't felt sad once. She also couldn't wait for everyone to go to bed so she could have another go.

The ease of online gambling opened up a new world for Rosina. She loved it and looked forward to any spare moment where she could play bingo or the slot machines. That was another of her gran's quirks, feeding the machines in the pub or arcade with spare coins and then clapping with glee at the rattle and clatter as her win dropped into the dispenser.

From the comfort of her sofa, a glass of wine by her side or in her office, with a cup of coffee and slice of cake from the café, Rosina saw her secret pastime as a treat, an escape, a bit of fun to break the monotony of life. It was also a tenuous link to her gran. She imagined her being thrilled when Rosina won, and telling her 'never mind' when – more often than not – she lost. It didn't matter at first, because there was always the chance to recoup your losses and she would simply dip into the housekeeping, and then their savings account. She was the one that took care of their finances. After all, that's what she did at work so Lou was more than happy for his wife to sort out all that boring stuff. The problem was that now and then he would check the balance if he went to the cash bank which is why Rosina decided to get another credit card in her name only.

The weird thing was that while she could remember her very first game of online bingo, she couldn't actually pinpoint when it all started getting out of control. Not just the losses, the craving, the inability to not think about her next bet, the lure of her phone that was full of online sites. She paid off one credit card with another, a sigh of relief and the problem was sorted. Five cards later she was in a fix because it was only the middle of the month and she had to make a hefty payment to the bank, who kept sending messages and trying to ring. That's why she stole the money. Her self-defence was that she'd been in a flap which then addled her brain and made her do something stupid, a spur-of-the-moment act. 'Borrowing' from the safe at work.

After stuffing the envelope into her bag on the Monday morning she watched every minute of the clock until she could nip to the bank on her lunch break. Once she'd deposited the cash using the fancy machine in the corner, perfect for avoiding eye contact with a cashier who would be able to see how red her account was, Rosina allowed relief to wash through her veins. It only took a few minutes to transfer the money and get the credit card company off her back. It took the same amount of time to have a cheeky whirl of the slot machines before she went back to work.

It was the payday loans that crippled her. Rosina saw it as the only option when a run of losses and big bets to try to clear them, mounted up. The repayments were astronomical but payday loans were so simple to arrange and they gave her breathing space to think and a bit spare to feed her addiction, because that's what it was. Although she knew it, she simply could not stop even though her life was becoming a huge lie. She lived in fear of missing the postman or Lou picking up the mail from the mat, of him deciding to log on to internet banking – which was why she changed the password. There was something else she feared even more; and that was not being able to bet. She needed to. She had to.

Rosina was £27,942.36 in debt. She had run out of lines of credit and if she didn't get her hands on more cash, Lou would find out. The night before Norman Carter came into the garden centre to buy a gift for his mum, Rosina had begged her gran for divine intervention. Lying in the dark as Lou slept peacefully by her side, she clasped her hands together and scrunched up her eyes in a last-ditch attempt for salvation.

Gran, you have to do something. I'm running out of options and seeing as you got me into this mess by dying on me, then sending me heavenly signs, I think it's only fair you sort it all out. Joking apart, Gran, I'm in trouble and the proverbial is going to hit the fan so please, have a word with the boss and ask him to help me out.

The following morning she happened to be passing through the store and recognised Norman instantly from school. They were all part of a group who she and Lou still saw occasionally at functions or in the local pub, not best mates any longer, more the type you wave to or share a few moments of banter. Knowing of his reputation and current profession, Rosina made a beeline towards him. She knew she was playing with fire as they sipped cappuccinos and went down memory lane. She was glossing over the fact that he was the school thug who'd done well for himself, while he glossed over the fact that his chain of pawn shops and debt-collecting business weren't exactly squeaky clean and above board. Everyone knew he was a loan shark and still a nasty piece of work, all wrapped up in his Armani suit.

She'd taken his business card when he offered it, and though she had squirmed when he suggested she gave him a call, Rosina assured him she would, and she did. The very next day.

'It's just a short-term problem that I need a quick solution to, no fuss. I realised after our chat yesterday that you might be able to help out and as you and I are old friends, I thought we could arrange something privately.' Rosina's face burned with humiliation, which was why she had to do this on the phone. The embarrassment was killing her as much as the stress of her predicament in general.

'And how much do you need to borrow?'

Swallowing down bile she grappled with a figure in her head, tempted to ask for the whole amount but that was astronomical so she settled for a month's wages: that would tide her over and balance the housekeeping books at least. 'Three thousand pounds.'

'And what is the money for, if you don't mind me asking?'

She'd already rehearsed what she was going to say. 'We're still catching up from when Lou was furloughed and I went a bit mad on Christmas presents for the kids so this will help until I get paid at the end of the month.'

'Why can't you just ask your mother? She's not short of a few quid.'

Sucking in her temper, feeling like she'd been slapped, Rosina forced a casual tone, hating herself for what she was about to say. 'Seriously, I'd rather stick pins in my eyes than have her know my business. That's why I'm asking you. You won't mention this to anyone we know, will you?'

'You'll still have to sign an agreement, but if you want to keep it between us you can rely on my discretion. As you say, we go way back. Leave it with me. I'll be in touch.'

Rosina knew she shouldn't have sounded too eager but she couldn't help herself. 'I need it soon, as quickly as possible so when will I have it, the money?'

'Why don't I pop down to the centre tomorrow, you can sign the paperwork and then I can arrange to have it in your account almost immediately. I'll see you at ten. In the café or would you prefer it if I popped into your office?'

Her mind raced. It had been a one-off and totally acceptable, chatting with an old friend in the café but if Norman came back people would be suspicious. 'What about the car park by the woodland trail. It's signposted on the road. I'd rather meet you there if it's okay? You know how people gossip.'

'That's fine, and yes I do. I'll meet you there at ten. See you tomorrow, Rosie.'

When the line disconnected, she shuddered and wondered if

she'd made a mistake but needs must and secrecy was of the utmost importance. The last thing she wanted was her mum seeing her with Norman and asking questions. All she had to do was meet him, sign the papers and the money would be in her account and then she could clear some of her debts. It had been such a simple solution, another quick fix, another huge mistake.

Hearing Tilly shout up that they were leaving, then the front door slam, Rosina listened to her daughters' voices as they walked down the path and off to school. Throwing back the duvet she rushed over to the window and pulled aside the curtains just in time to see the three of them turn the corner. The glass chilled her palm when she touched the window, suppressing the urge to call out to them, say she was sorry for not running them to school like always and that she hoped their dad hadn't made them the worst packed lunch ever. Instead, she stood there and sobbed.

She'd missed three payments and each time Norman had added more onto her debt. 'Interest,' he said. 'It's in the paperwork,' he said. And now what she owed had doubled and if she didn't meet him that afternoon with the full amount in cash, then he was going to tell Lou and her mum because, as he'd said when she finally rang him back, he knew exactly where to find both of them.

Stumbling back over to the bed Rosina threw herself onto the mattress, dragged the duvet over her head and closed her eyes. The urge to grab her phone and see if she could place a bet, or try the slots was crippling her. Maybe she could find some coins in the kitchen drawer and go down to the shop and buy a few lottery tickets – but the EuroMillions draw wasn't until Friday night and that was too late. Anyway, she'd wasted hundreds of pounds on the lottery already and she didn't have the energy to get dressed let alone go outside.

Don't touch your phone, don't touch your phone.

Rosina repeated the mantra, sucking in air, squashing down a surge of panic. Riddled with anxiety, exhausted from living on the edge, the shame and the guilt and the worry was just too much. And then for the first time, loud and clear, a voice screaming inside her head.

I don't want to be here anymore.

14

LEONORA

Lay-by on the A34
Present day

I t was pitch black and absolutely freezing outside the car but what could anyone expect at 5am on a December morning? And thank God for twenty-four-hour McDonalds and Google Maps for finding them a nice, isolated lay-by, perfect for a stupid o'clock rendezvous with the love of your life who was bleary-eyed and wearing whatever he'd rolled out of bed in, plus two sweaters and a beanie hat.

While they listened to the breakfast show, Joel kept the engine running as they ate their Big Mac breakfast, the steam from their breath and two large hot chocolates misting the windows, blocking out the world or, more to the point, the traffic that rumbled along the A34 towards the motorway.

This was how it had been for the past few weeks, snatched moments that somehow meant more than all the hours they'd spent together before he'd gone away. Ever since Joel had arrived back and sent her a text saying, *Can we meet?* and she'd replied *Yes* far too quickly, not actually caring how uncool that was. Then, after their first tenuous, friend-zone embrace, once they'd stopped trying to deny their feelings for one another and they'd kissed in the car park of the pub, clinging on like their lives depended on it, every single second they spent together had become precious, more exciting than the last. Even in a lay-by, not caring that you had brown sauce on your chin and you couldn't feel your toes.

'Is that heater actually doing anything or just making a racket? I mean it, next time we eat in mine because this is bloody ridiculous. And what is that funny smell?'

'I think it's my work boots, they got wet yesterday.' Joel leant over and pulled the fleece blanket around her body. 'There, that's better. Now stop moaning. I wanted to make it all cosy for our picnic. Look, how cute is that?' Joel pointed to the dashboard. 'I got it from the petrol station.' He flicked the tiny Christmas tree that was stuck to the dash with a sucker, the LED lights reflecting on the windscreen. 'And anyway, your car is too small: I get cramp. You know that from last time.' Joel winked at Leonora who gave his arm a thump.

'Well, just so you know there won't be any of that malarkey this morning. It's too cold and these thermals are staying on, okay!'

Joel stuck his bottom lip out as he opened his paper bag and pulled out a hash brown and beamed. 'It's okay, I'll munch on this instead.'

Another thump. 'You are so rude. Stop it.'

They ate in companionable silence, him dipping greasy potato into barbeque sauce, her sipping hot chocolate. Regardless of her grumbling about the cold, Leonora would have stayed in Joel's beat-up car forever if it meant she could be with him. *The things you do for love,* she thought as she wordlessly passed him her last hash brown.

'See, this is why I love you. Who else would sacrifice such a thing of beauty?'

'They're crap and you know it! I only get them because you like them.'

Joel ripped the lid from the ketchup pot as he replied. 'See, I rest my case. We are the perfect couple. Symbiotic, yin and yang, peas and carrots, Richard and Judy…'

'Stop, right now before I take it back. Richard and bloody Judy?'

Leonora couldn't help but laugh while she continued to drink her chocolate and Joel made another meal out of collecting all their wrappers and pots and serviettes, making out like he couldn't bear his car being a mess. Then once he'd scrunched the paper bag shut, he chucked it over his shoulder to join whatever hideous things were lurking on the back seat and floor of his trusty bone-shaker.

'You scruff!'

Ignoring her rebuke he took her hand and swivelled in his seat to face Leonora. 'So, dare I ask what you're doing tonight, after your shift? I can meet you if you want, get something to eat.'

She knew why he was asking and her heart ached for him because if the roles were reversed it would be killing her. No, she'd be dead from sheer jealousy and rage.

'Let's play it by ear. He'll be in touch soon, checking up on me as always and if we're lucky he'll be busy all day. He might even have something on with work then I'm off the hook. Otherwise, I'll have to see him.'

Leonora could imagine what was going on in Joel's mind and it was awful, but what could she do? 'Look, I know this is hard but I've swerved him for the best part of a week using work as an excuse and let's face it, my last period was the longest in the history of womankind but I swear if I give in and go round to his, that's all I'm giving in to. Do you understand?'

Joel let go of her hand and opened his arms, wrapping her in a hug as he sighed into the top of her bobble hat. 'Of course I understand and before you ask, yes, I trust you. I just can't bear you being anywhere near him and this might sound really sad but I'm getting bent out of shape with jealousy every time I think of him spending time with you over Christmas, opening presents, all that kind of stuff. I think it might be sending me a bit mad.'

Closing her eyes Leonora tried to blot out the image of a similar scenario but in hers she was ramming a giant turkey leg down Caspar's throat while her shocked family looked on, smiling a bit when she thought of Max, Tilly and the twins who would find that hilarious.

'You already are mad, we established that long ago but at least you'll be at your mum's and I bet she's chuffed to bits that you're home this year. It makes me happy that she's happy to have you there and I'll be thinking of you every minute, I promise.'

Joel gave her a squeeze. 'Mum's just as chuffed that we're back together even though it's killing her that it's a secret. She wants me to take you round to see her as soon as you're free.'

Leonora loved that his mum was happy for them even though she could've rammed the other imaginary turkey leg down Joel's throat when she found out he'd confided in his mum. But then again it was sweet that he was so happy and she'd forgiven him. Looking at the clock her heart dipped, knowing it was time to go so she'd be in Manchester for the start of her shift at six.

'I can't wait to see her again and I swear that will be soon. Just a bit longer and we will be together, I promise.' After waiting a few more seconds to let her words settle, she untangled herself from Joel's arms and said the dreaded words. 'I'm going to have to go. I'll text you when I'm in work and let you know what I'm doing later. Now give us a kiss, saucy lips, and for Christ's sake clean this stinky car out. I think something has died under the seats.'

Leonora was exhausted and it was only nine o'clock but her spirits lifted when she was welcomed into the break room with a smile and a wave from Sam who then beckoned her over, motioning to the chair beside him. It was the first time he'd ever requested her presence and as she took the weight off her feet, she got the feeling he'd been watching for her. She was right.

'I was hoping I'd catch you today because I'm not in tomorrow and I wanted a quiet word.'

Leonora blew on the froth of her cappuccino, her eyebrows raised. 'Oh-oh, am I in trouble? When my mum wants a quiet word that's usually what it means. So go on, what have I done?'

Sam chuckled. 'Nothing at all, Leo, but last night you looked so troubled and when you'd gone I felt bad that I didn't invite you in so we could talk more or even sit in the car to chat for a while.'

'Aw, that's so lovely of you, Sam, but I'm fine. I've got so much stuff trapped in my head it's driving me round the bend so it was therapeutic to blurt it out, but I'm sorry if I made you worry.' She spoke to his muddy-brown, kindly eyes that seemed to be looking right into her soul, checking if she was fibbing or not.

'Well as long as you are sure. I couldn't stop thinking about what you said, about your feelings for your other young man and your fiancé and I suppose it reminded me of something that happened to me a long time ago, before you were born.'

Leonora's interest was piqued and, aware of how private and shy Sam was, she turned her body slightly to face him, guarding her words and hopefully putting him at ease as she lowered her voice. 'Really... were you in love with someone else too?'

Sam nodded and his eyes had a faraway look, sad too. 'Yes, and that's what I wanted to tell you because I feel that even though they are decades apart, our situations are similar but I handled things very badly, so perhaps you may be able to avoid making the same mistake.'

'I see. So do you regret what you did, is that it?'

'No, I don't regret falling in love but I do regret not being honest and had I been braver, then maybe I wouldn't have hurt my wife as badly as I did. Had I the courage to sit her down and explain, tried to make her understand then there's a chance we could have worked things out, at least remained friends.'

Leonora's heart went out to him, touched that he cared enough to share his past so she reached out and placed her hand on his arm. 'Does it still bother you, that you hurt your wife?'

'Yes, it does because I hurt other people, too. It was like the pain I caused spread and once the news got out, gossipmongers had a field day.'

'Oh, I can imagine the gossip but I'm not too worried about that. I'm more nervous of how Caspar will react because he has connections to our family business. I honestly think if it wasn't for that and the time of year I'd have told him by now. In fact, I know I would. I can't bear the thought of him being there over Christmas, getting on my nerves and then he will be in all the flipping photos forever and my memory of us being together will be ruined, looking at his stupid face.' Leonora's foot began to tap which always happened when she was annoyed.

'The thing is, Leo, what concerns me more than photographs is that the longer your affair goes on, the more you deceive those around you. Then when the truth comes out the harder it is for everyone to comprehend and unfortunately, our good intentions no matter how misguided, can be misconstrued. I wouldn't want that for you, to be judged unfairly because from our chats and watching you around here with your colleagues, I've learned that you are a good person, Leo. Subterfuge isn't your forte and I sense that the deceit weighs heavy. It's a huge burden to bear.'

There it was again, Leonora could feel that tangible connection, two strangers with a common bond and she wondered if they had been meant to meet. 'You are so right. I have been sneaking around for a month, ever since me and Joel got back together and I hate it. And in a weird way it's making me despise Caspar more.

'It's as though I'm seeing him through different eyes and all the things that have always been there, stuff that I chose to ignore or put up with are blinding me now. I sometimes think he's suffocating me with his controlling ways and it makes me a bit panicky to imagine what he would be like if we got married, and I can assure you that is not going to happen.'

Sam patted her hand that still lay on his free arm. 'And the more you lie and avoid the inevitable the worse these feelings will get because deep down, it's not who you are or how you want to behave. Believe me, I know.'

It was such a relief, to talk to someone who understood at last. 'Everything you say is true. I'm sure you can imagine the lies I have told so that I can steal some time with Joel. Like this morning for instance, getting up at stupid o'clock so we could meet in a lay-by and share breakfast in his car before I came to work. Then I worry that Joel might be wondering if I can do this to Caspar, could I do it to him. Even though he swears he doesn't, it's there at the back of my mind that I'm a cheat, and there's no getting away from that. And I'm so knackered mentally, being careful not to slip up, and physically too, after swapping so many night shifts so I don't have to stay over at Caspar's. If it hadn't been for him going on a business trip for a week I swear I'd have gone mad but I'm pushing my luck now.'

Sam fell into thought for a moment, then asked a pertinent question. 'So Joel is definitely the one? Someone worth all this torment because you have to make sure that you're seeing things clearly. Not so besotted that it clouds your vision.'

'Definitely.' Leonora's response was firm and she believed it totally. 'We were in love before he left to work overseas and it was a huge mistake, us splitting up, and I was definitely on the rebound when I met Caspar, who with hindsight has railroaded me from the beginning. That really pisses me off more than anything. I should have listened to my gran. She didn't mince her words and had plenty to say about him I can tell you. She said he could get where water couldn't; oh, and his eyes were too close together, amongst many other things.'

Sam chuckled. 'She sounds like a real character and seemed to have been on the money where Caspar is concerned. So, we have established that you aren't wearing rose-coloured glasses and that with or without Joel in your life you wouldn't want to marry Caspar, which only leaves one question remaining.'

'Do I have my passport on standby so I can leave the country? Yes I do!'

At that Sam laughed, then became serious. 'Actually, I was going to ask who is more important to you, your family or Caspar?'

Leonora knew the answer immediately. 'My family always come first. And as much as Caspar isn't my favourite person I don't want to upset him but there's no way round that I suppose. I'm just going to have to suck it up, unless you have a better idea.'

'If I could go back in time I would do everything differently. I would have never married my wife for a start. We were so young, in our teens and she didn't deserve what I did. I wish I'd told the truth, set her free and, in the long run, myself.'

'Kind of like me and Caspar then, but it's not easy, is it?'

Sam shook his head. 'At the time, it seemed like such a terrible problem that it overwhelmed me. I thought it was the end of the world, unsolvable, a prison sentence. What I didn't understand is that in the grand scheme of my life, that it was really a small blip and something that I would look back on as a tiny period, a segment. Terrible and upsetting, but it didn't last forever and as I said, if I'd done things differently it would be easier to bear now, many years later.'

'I get it, I really do because that's how I feel. That this massive thing is taking over my life and it's ridiculous. I can make it stop like that.' She clicked her fingers. 'And that's what I'm going to do. Sod waiting. I need to tell him soon, today. Yep, I'm going to do it today, after work.'

Turning his head Sam checked the clock on the wall behind them. 'Looks like I'm out of time so I'd better go but you know where to find me if you need to talk more. Please understand that I'm not trying to interfere, or sway you. It was simply a feeling I had that I should say something and I hope you forgive this old fool if I make matters worse.'

'Hey, you are not an old fool and I feel blessed that we met, I really do because you have eased my mind, I swear.' Leonora removed her hand from his arm to allow him to stand, resisting the urge to hug him, suspecting it would be one gesture too far for her shy confidante.

'I'll see you next week then. I hope it goes well, Leo, I'll be thinking of you over the weekend.' Sam seemed to hesitate but said no more and after a nod, he turned towards the door.

For a second she thought he was going to give her his phone number, and she considered offering hers so she might let him know. But the opportunity was lost and as the door closed, she turned her thoughts to Caspar. Delving into her trouser pocket she pulled out her phone and began to type him a message, asking to meet up after work. She'd made up her mind and it was time to do what Sam hadn't done all those years before: the right thing.

15

CARMEN

Appleton Farm, Cheshire
Present day

Turning away from the window and the misty morning view of the frosty fields, Carmen got on with the task in hand, checking her list. She was in her mum's newly repainted bedroom that was currently Christmas Presents Central. On the floor was a giant gift bag for each member of her family and then three more containing treats for the garden centre staff plus the tombola and lucky dip prizes for their children.

Ticking off one more item, she allowed herself a self-satisfied smile and a bit of a chuckle at her own rather extreme behaviour. Like her suggestion that everyone wore Christmas jumpers at dinner. She thought it would be fun; everyone else told her where to go! At least they'd capitulated graciously when she insisted they were all under one roof on Christmas Eve morning, but they owed her, after spending so many years worrying where each of her girls were. She would fret all day, in fact it always began the week before, this niggling fear of things going wrong and then all her preparation and saving and wrapping and the excitement that had built up might be ruined by some cruel quirk of fate.

When the girls were little it wasn't too bad because from the minute school broke up for the holidays they'd be home with her. But as they'd got older and started to roam, Violetta especially, her teenage daughters had sent Carmen's blood pressure through the roof on more than one occasion. And now, her two eldest grandchildren were a constant worry, not because they were bad kids, more because they were growing up in an increasingly dangerous society. Even the local park was like a ghetto. That was why, just for once, she wanted not to worry and wake up with a full house of the most special people in the world.

She could see it all. The adults could have a deserved lie-in. Not her though. She'd be up at the crack to prepare a huge breakfast. After they'd gathered in the kitchen the children could watch Christmas films or play outside. Bern was going to roast chestnuts and make his special stuffing and Lou was in charge of the mulled wine that always fragranced the kitchen with wintery spices. The girls would help with lunch preparations like when they were young where every year – and this one would be no different – vegetable peelings on the table took Carmen straight back to that last Christmas in London.

There was no way she could avoid those memories so she let them wash over her whenever they came calling. Giving a nod to the past was sometimes painful but other times uplifting, but mostly a bit of both.

Droylsden, Manchester. 1970

When she and her mum arrived in Manchester to start the new year in a different home, school and city, it was as though her life had been put in a sack and shaken really hard. And her mum changed too. Gone was the happy-go-lucky young woman who saw good in everyone. She looked the same, hugged the same but her real smile was only for Carmen. For everyone else it looked like she was pretending, wary, mistrustful. It was as though she'd built a fort around herself and Carmen; and nobody else was allowed in.

Her mum's old school friend Angie was lovely. So was her name: it made Carmen think of strawberry Angel Delight, fluffy and colourful like their landlady. She was glamorous and funny and had lots of stories about what happened on the aeroplanes as they jetted across the world. And she didn't mind a bit that they had come to stay or a little kid followed her around like a puppy. Angie made life a bit more bearable especially because she spoke with a London accent whereas the kids at her new school constantly made fun of Carmen. Eventually though, they got used to her and she made friends, settled in and got on with it.

Two years passed quickly and still she'd not heard from her dad. No letters, no matter how many times she watched the postman walk up the path. The phone never rang no matter how much she willed it to. And her prayers weren't answered, no matter how many times she tried to get through to heaven.

Even though Carmen was mindful of how sad her mum had been and that her dad had done a very bad thing, it didn't stop her loving him. To be on the safe side she kept her hopes and wishes to herself. She consoled herself by believing he'd gone back to sea, sailing around Cape Horn, Good Hope, the Galápagos Islands, places she traced on the atlas she'd brought with her. Her mum had let it go, when she saw that Carmen had smuggled her dad's books out of the house and over the years there had developed an unspoken rule between them. It was best not to mention *him*, and then everything was okay.

Life was actually okay in Manchester and Carmen was

happy enough. Her mum got a job in a local supermarket and was always there when she got in from school or to watch her in school plays and sports day. But as soon as the nights drew in and winter wrapped itself around the city, the spectre of Christmas crept into her conscience. It was like marking time to Christmas Eve, the day when everything changed forever. While she joined in with all the festive fun at school, making her mum a glitter-fest card, wearing a new party dress, whispering in Santa's profoundly deaf ears, opening the windows of her advent calendar, there was always someone special on her mind.

Which was why on her third Christmas without *him*, during the church nativity where her mum had clapped like mad after she'd played 'Little Donkey' on the recorder, while the shepherds listened agog to the archangel, Carmen clasped her hands together and scrunched her eyes shut. Ignoring Molly Parker and her tinsel halo, she asked Baby Jesus, God and his angels if they'd please make everything okay. She didn't expect a miracle straight away; she would be patient but if there was a chance they could arrange a visit from her dad, or even a phone call, she'd be immensely grateful. And seeing as she was too big to go and sit on Santa's knee and, on the off-chance he did actually exist, would they pass on a message? She would happily trade all of her Christmas presents for the rest of her life, if her dad would come home on Christmas Eve. It would be the best present ever.

When another year passed and nothing happened, Carmen didn't give up. In fact, she'd never given up. Every year on Christmas Eve she would wait, be disappointed and then before she went to sleep ask again for next year.

Time ticked on. When Carmen went to secondary school her mum got a job in the cigarette factory, working shifts. Angie met an American lawyer on a transatlantic flight to New York and went to live stateside, as she put it when she wrote or rang every now and then.

They moved into a flat of their own and Carmen embraced being the daughter of an independent woman, a team of two. Her mum loved working at the cigarette factory and made lots of friends and even went out for the odd meal with one of the machine engineers. But no matter how much Carmen encouraged her Sylvia remained an avowed singleton. She still despised and mistrusted most men and was so set in her closed-minded ways that in all honesty Carmen didn't believe there was a man on earth that would put up with her. It was a shame, though, because when she stopped hating everyone who wasn't white, straight or Christian, her mum could actually be quite nice.

When she left school, Carmen got a job in a typing pool for an insurance company and it was at the Christmas party she met a handsome sales rep called Sebastian. It was at that point, as her head was turned by an older man who took her under his wing and made her feel special, that Carmen thought maybe her luck had changed. Even though her wish still hadn't been granted, someone upstairs had given her the next best thing.

Her mother hated Sebastian on sight and despaired of her daughter. 'You're making a huge mistake,' she said, and insisted Carmen went down to the Family Planning pronto before she made another. The advice came a bit too late and her mother's prophecy came true. Carmen was pregnant and engaged to a begrudging older man who'd had his wings well and truly clipped. The rest, was a very unfortunate history.

Appleton Farm, Cheshire. Present day

Carmen drew a line through *tombola* and *lucky dip*, thinking as she did how life was a bit like pulling a random ticket out of a barrel and hoping for a winner or rummaging round in sawdust trying to find the best prize. And it was bizarre, how history repeated itself. Not verbatim, but life had a way of drawing comparisons albeit with a tweak to the script.

Violetta had got pregnant to a stranger and her daughter would never know her dad. Cast in the image of her defiant grandmother, she was another avowed singleton who had a very dim view of men in general. And then, when she started her tattoo phase, Carmen wondered whether it was her granddad's genes sending a message down the line. At least she didn't get an anchor, or a compass and swallow because that really would have freaked Carmen and her mother out! Independent and unpredictable, Violetta was their little firecracker who stood out in a crowd and on photos. With her flame-red locks, piercings, body art and boho clothes, none of them would have her any other way and Darcy adored and looked up to her, just like Carmen had looked up to her mum. And one of the things she loved the most was that even though Violetta had sometimes thrown a grenade into the room with her exploits and announcements, Carmen preferred her openness and honesty to secrets and lies. What you saw was what you got with Violetta.

Rosina had always been the rock of the family and had showed little interest in following a career that would take her away from Appleton. So it had seemed like a natural progression that she would continue to be mother's helper down at the garden centre. It was a role that Rosina was born to, hard-working, organised, loyal and trustworthy, a natural successor once Carmen decided to let go of the reins and take it easier. And although Sylvia had kicked up a fuss about Sebastian, she had no qualms about Rosina marrying young. Everyone loved Lou and knew he was the perfect match, one of the good guys that Violetta and her gran insisted didn't exist.

And then there was Leonora who, devastated and cast adrift after being so badly hurt by Joel, had brushed herself down and got on with it. Knowing her daughter was in such distress was hard for Carmen to bear as she listened at the bedroom door while she cried herself to sleep. Wishing for someone to come back, wondering how to start again, place one foot in front of the other when morning came round again – Carmen had done both. Maybe Sylvia had too, not that she'd ever admit it. They'd all willed Leonora to get over Joel, not wanting anything to thwart her dreams and ambition. Out of all her children she was the most focused on her future and thankfully, settled at last in a happy relationship with Caspar which gave Carmen great comfort. As did knowing Rosina was content with her brood and had a lovely, decent man to take care of them all. Hopefully Violetta would one day find the same.

All in all, her daughters were good girls and in the grand scheme of things, growing up, teenage tantrums, outraged vicars and the beleaguered village bobby aside, they hadn't really brought any great trouble to her door. So with less than a week to go before The Big Christmas Weekend, Carmen dared to think the words *so far, so good.*

Folding the flap of her notepad she slid the biro through the wire hoops and went over to her dresser and took a moment to look at her rogues gallery. As always, her eyes and heart was drawn to the frame at the end, the one she'd placed well away from the photo of her dad, respecting her mum's feelings to the last.

It came and went, the waves of missing her, the need to remember, even if it meant walking straight into the storm. As she picked up the photo and touched her mum's face for some strange reason she sensed that one was brewing. Or was she so used to looking for portents that the habit was hard to break?

Maybe it was Rosina ringing in sick, or Bern's upcoming

meeting with his solicitor, or Leonora being evasive and Violetta just being Violetta. Or was this just her being her? No matter how hard she'd tried to curb her obsession that they were cursed, the thought still lingered but who could blame her?

Oh, Mum. I miss you so much. I hope you're happy now. Carmen sighed and took the photo over to the window, clasping it to her chest, lost in the memories of a day she would never forget.

Appleton Farm, Cheshire. October 2020

The ambulance was on its way, they could hear it coming along the road. The plaintive wail of the siren made the situation in the front bedroom of Appleton more real, and utterly terrifying. All her girls were gathered on Granny Sylvia's bed. She was so poorly and the paramedic who'd attended first was in no doubt she needed to go to hospital immediately. She would have to make the journey alone and that was killing Carmen as much as the sight of her frail mother gasping for breath.

'Mum, please keep the mask on. You need the oxygen, like the nice man told you.' She went to replace the plastic cover but Sylvia brushed her hand away.

'No, I want to tell you something...'

'Mum, not now please, save your energy. You can tell me tomorrow, okay. When they've made you better.' And even though she wanted the words to be true, Carmen could see how frail her mum was and tomorrow seemed a long way away.

'Mum, let Gran speak. Go on Gran, it's okay. Just take your time.' Rosina's voice was gentle as she smiled at Carmen and held Sylvia's hand.

Letting go of the mask Sylvia reached out for her daughter. 'You're a good girl and I love you very much. You know that, don't you?'

'Mum, of course I do and I love you too, we all do.' As hard as she tried to hold them back, tears escaped and Carmen forbade her face to crumple.

'And you mustn't worry about anything. What's done is done. Do you understand, Carmen?'

'Yes, Mum–'

Sylvia interrupted, her voice a whisper yet urgent. 'I want to tell you about your dad... before it's too late... I did it for you. He loved you, he won't have forgotten, you were his pearl, do you remember? He wanted you to know. I should have told you before... I'm sorry, Carmen. If you see him... tell him I forgive him.'

Carmen battled with despair and confusion. What did her mum mean about seeing her dad? And of course she remembered about the pearl. Then a more urgent thought: she had to let her mother know that she didn't blame her for anything.

Sylvia was exhausted and when her eyes closed and her hand went limp, Carmen thought she was going to faint until Rosina replaced the mask and the reviving oxygen brought a flicker of an eyelid and renewed hope. A hush fell on the room as each of them, alone with their thoughts, watched the rise and fall of Sylvia's chest. Reaching out to brush the wispy fronds of ice-white hair from her mum's face, Carmen tracked the peach-soft skin of her liver-spotted face.

When Sylvia's eyes slowly opened she focused on Carmen, who reassured her mum. 'I know you did everything for me, Mum, so please don't worry about all that. We were fine, just you and me. I love you so much, you have to know that. Mum, Mum, can you hear me?' Her eyes opened, a look of love, the slightest hint of a nod and then she drifted into unconsciousness.

The room was completely still when a faint tap on the door

preceded Bern's voice as he popped his head inside the room. 'The ambulance men are here. Can they come in?'

When they took Sylvia downstairs all three of her granddaughters were distraught and Carmen was barely holding it together. Though she was partly glad that her mum hadn't witnessed everyone's distress, the other half willed Sylvia to come round so they could have one more word before she went. The sight of the ambulance doors closing, that last glimpse of her mum would haunt Carmen forever. It had been much worse than the hours that followed, when they'd kept vigil in the kitchen, none of them sleeping, the clock on the mantel ticking like a heartbeat while Carmen prayed her mum's was doing the same.

And then that early morning call and the kind voice on the end of the phone telling them the worst news ever, that Sylvia was gone. If the world hadn't already been dark enough, it was as though someone had turned a switch and snuffed out the light.

It wasn't until after the meagre funeral, while she sat and watched her own grandchildren play in the garden that she wondered what her mum had meant, about seeing her dad and forgiveness. They were still reeling from the shock and awe of losing the true rock of their family because as Carmen said when she raised a glass to Sylvia, 'She showed me how to be, what hard work meant. Mum always put me first, us first, and our happiness was what she cared about most in this world.'

Was that what her mum was trying to say? That if she could forgive the man who had broken her heart, it was okay for Carmen to go and find him, see him again. Was that what she meant by telling her not to worry, and she understood? Or did she mean something else entirely?

She endured another awful Christmas and as the months passed, the notion that perhaps she should search for her dad became more frequent. So one year later, when she visited Sylvia's grave on the first anniversary of her passing, Carmen told the headstone what she was going to do.

'I think I worked out what you were trying to say, Mum, and I've decided I'm going to try and find Dad. I know if you were here it would have been hard for you, raking up the past and seeing him again and that wouldn't have been fair. Like a slap in the face. I always felt I owed you that loyalty, for looking after me so well, for your selflessness.

'My dad hurt you a lot, and you were hurting for me too and it's the most terrible thing, seeing those you love sad. I do get it, more than you know. I did when Sebastian died; before too, because he let me down so much. I don't think I can forgive him for the way he was. That's why, once again, I'm in awe of you so if I do find my dad, I'll tell him you what you said, I promise.

'I suppose we all do things we regret, or make decisions we can't alter, or take matters into our own hands because we believe it's for the greater good. You were such a stubborn bugger and set in your ways, the strongest woman I ever met and I was so proud to call you Mum. I always will be and I'll tell him all about you, how I never wanted for anything.

'But I'd like to see him again, find out what he did after he left and even if he was happy with Martha. Maybe they split up, they might have made a go of it. I could have siblings out there, who knows? One thing I do know is that I'll only ever have one mum and she was the best in the world.'

Picking up her basket and gardening tools Carmen took one last look at the headstone and then set off home, knowing in her heart that her mum would understand.

Appleton Farm, Cheshire. Present day

The sound of the front door slamming and a familiar voice

calling up the stairs took Carmen by surprise as did the tears that she wiped away quickly. Replacing the photo she called down that she would be there in a minute, then rushed to the bathroom to compose herself, at the same time curious and mildly concerned that Violetta had paid her a visit. If past experience was anything to go by an impromptu visit from her middle daughter would only mean one thing. Trouble.

16

VIOLETTA

Appleton Farm, Cheshire
Present day

Pushing open the front door Violetta called out, 'Mum, it's me, where are you?'

'Up here. Put the kettle on, love. I'll be down in a minute.'

Hooking her bag and coat onto the wooden stand Violetta spotted Bern's waxed jacket and wondered if he was there, and hoped that he wasn't.

Distracting herself from all that was on her mind she took a moment to indulge in her ritual, the one she carried out each time she came home. First, she ran her hand over the antique mahogany stand that had always been by the door, a sentry guarding the entrance, even on the day her parents first saw the house. How it never toppled over she couldn't fathom because it was constantly heaped with their school blazers and anoraks, hats and scarves that were haphazardly chucked onto the circle of hooks, dangling, clinging on.

Looking downwards to another original feature, she remembered how she and her sisters would throw their rucksacks onto the Victorian mosaic floor that stretched the length of the hall. It had stood the test of time, pounded by hundreds and hundreds of muddy footprints as they rushed to the kitchen for a snack and into the arms of their mum.

She stopped by the gilt mirror and took a second to tut at her pasty face that she'd tried to disguise with make-up. A red curl had escaped from her bobble hat that she left on, concealing the fact she hadn't washed her hair. The mirror hung above an armoire, so heavy it was impossible to move, a monstrous beast, long and wide enough to hide a dead body. Its intricately carved doors, an arts and craft theme of flowers and swirling stems, hid its cavernous cupboards that had once contained their wellies, shoes and boots.

Their house phone still stood on top but rarely rung these days. They'd gone through quite a few over the years as styles changed and this one was her favourite, a replica, black, 1950s with a circular dial that completely befuddled her nieces and nephews and Darcy too. Violetta and Rosina had spent many an hour there, chatting to their friends or sitting on the battered Queen Anne chair at the end, willing it to ring and some spotty boy from the village to be at the other end.

Comforting. That's what Appleton was. The rituals, the memories, the furniture and knick-knacks immediately relaxed her, reassured by the sights and sounds and smells of her childhood home.

Passing the huge lounge on the left she spotted the roaring fire surrounded by mismatched sofas and armchairs, some covered in throws to hide the tatty bits, a couple of new retro additions but mostly the furniture had remained the same since she was a teenager and the house had finally been restored.

In those days it had been the elder sisters' job to bring in coal and wood then fill the scuttles in each room. Violetta had loved it, never thinking of it as a chore and used to imagine she was accompanied by the ghost of a maid. She'd named her Mary and she would tut and huff if the fire wasn't set right or the grate wasn't cleaned properly.

On the right was the dining room, only really used for special occasions, bathed in morning sunlight that shone on the huge walnut table that was piled with festive bits and bobs that her mum would use on Christmas Day. Violetta sometimes imagined that if she travelled back through time this room would be the one that looked the same, with its high-backed velvet chairs and fancy chandelier that *nobody* but her mum was allowed to dust.

At the foot of the stairs was one of the pine trees that they'd decorated weeks before. The house had been alive that day, a proper Appleton memory. Bern and Lou had brought in the trees and what seemed like a hundred boxes down from Room 101 in the attic. The gold and red of the baubles; the fluffy tinsel that all the kids seemed bloody fascinated by and draped around their necks; Max lifting Darcy up so she could pop the angel on top; her mum making a giant pan of soup. That day, Violetta didn't have a care in the world. How a few days can change your life.

Again, Violetta shoved the things she didn't want to deal with to the back of her mind for a few more minutes, saving her tale of woe, desperate not to think about the other thing – him.

Going into the long, wide kitchen that ran along the back of the house, she filled the kettle then spooned coffee into mugs while she waited for her mum to come downstairs. Taking a glimpse outside, Arthur, Mitzi and Petra were racing around the back garden that was more like a small field, darting in and out of the pagoda, chasing leaves and each other. Right there and then she was envious of them, playing carefree.

She pulled out a chair and sat at the table, exhausted even though she'd done bugger all. Taking it in, her old home, eased her soul. The creamy kitchen walls that bowed in places were lined with oak shelves, weighed down with cookery books and Kilner jars that contained all manner of ingredients.

The long pine table with its mismatched chairs in the centre of the room was where everyone gathered. At mealtimes certain places were still reserved for the sisters. It was the law. Placing her palms on the tabletop, Violetta felt them merge with the grain, moulded over the years while she sat in her place, eating, doing homework, colouring in, laughing with her sisters.

At one end, opposite her mum's, a chair was pushed underneath. Now and then Violetta was sure that from the corner of her eye she'd spot her Granny Sylvia, drinking tea and reading the paper and, before she was banned, smoking a cigarette with an ashtray by her side.

The clock on the mantel chimed the half hour prompting Violetta to replay the day her mum gave them the task of working out how many times it had chimed since they'd moved in. The winner would get a bar of chocolate. With an answer of 24,820 Violetta won the prize and the number was lodged forever in her head.

The clock had been there when her parents bought the house and she'd often wondered how many more times it had chimed before they arrived. Apparently it was ticking so loudly when they walked into the room it sounded like a bomb. It used to drive her dad mad but her mum refused to throw it out, saying it was part of the house and therefore part of them.

Directly underneath, the black Aga was set into the chimney breast. It was her mum's pride and joy and ever since the day it was installed she'd told her girls that it was the heart of their home. The heat it emitted spread upwards through the pipes, like veins pumping hot water and warming every room in the house.

Like all of the memories and stories she'd been told about Appleton Farm, they were her treasures, the things she clung on to, touched, coveted because they made her who she was, the real Violetta, not the woman in the mask who'd messed up, again.

And while she held on tight to all of her snapshots of the past, one of them remained the most important, most special. It marked the day she told her mum about Darcy.

Appleton Farm, Cheshire. October 2014

At the time, if she'd wanted to blame anyone it would have been her best friend Candy who had organised a girls-only holiday to Croatia. But Candy hadn't got Violetta drunk to the point of being paralytic, so bad that she woke up the next morning inside a wooden dinghy on the beach, no knickers, no idea how she'd got there but with a vague recollection of what she'd done. Less so about who with.

Thirteen weeks later, her crazy fortnight break still a thing of legend, Violetta sat opposite her mum at the kitchen table and confessed that she was pregnant.

Always a beacon in the dark, the most unflappable of women, the only emotion her mum showed was an involuntary paling of the skin but otherwise she did a sterling job of keeping control of her facial muscles, giving nothing away. 'Okay. So what happens now?'

'I'm keeping it. And before you start to panic about money, I'll be fine. I've been able to save really hard, thanks to you paying my student loan off, so I'll have enough for a deposit on a place of my own soon. And I already know you're not going to throw me out into the snow for bringing shame on the family name.' Violetta smiled, never surer of anything, or appreciating the many benefits of living at home more than she did right then.

Her mum nodded. 'So I take it there's no point in us going round the houses and talking this through.' After swallowing down resignation with a sip of tea she rested into the pine chair and watched Violetta intently.

'Not really, no.' Everyone knew that once Violetta decided something she rarely changed her mind and she was glad that on this occasion her reputation preceded her.

'So you have it all worked out then?'

Violetta was winging it but tried not to let it show. 'Sort of. As much as I can anyway.'

'There's plenty of space here so as you said, you'll be fine. We'll get by. There's all the stuff from when you three were babies and Rosina's came along. We can give it all a dust down.'

'I'd like that. Our family heirlooms.'

A smile from her mother and then another expected question and offer. 'And do you intend to go back to work after? Me and your gran will help out with childcare like we did with Rosina's mini tribe, that's a given. I wouldn't want your dreams of being a hotshot solicitor to be shelved when there's no need.'

Violetta's heart dipped while her brain told her face not to let on. 'Oh yes. I want to be able to provide for the baby myself so I'll be going back to work as soon as I can but that's a way off yet. For now I have to get my head around being a mum. I'm sure you know that feeling.'

Her mum reached over, giving Violetta's hand a squeeze as she spoke. 'Oh I do and I think you'll be just fine, love. But I do need to ask the big question and I have a funny feeling I won't like the answer. You and I don't do beating about the bush, do we?'

Pre-empting what her mum was about to ask, Violetta took

the initiative, wanting to get it over with. 'No we don't. So in answer to your question I have no idea who the dad is. It was someone on holiday. A one-night stand, I suppose. He's called Gabe, no surname. Sorry, Mum, but that's the truth of it. And yes, I know, Gran's going to bloody love that when she finds out!'

'Never mind what your gran says and to be fair, I think she might surprise you. She has a habit of doing that once a decade. For now let's focus on you and that baby. The rest we'll make up as we go along. Right, let's start with some lunch. I have fresh sausage rolls in the Aga with your name on them.' Pushing back the chair she went to the oven and opened one of the three doors to release the heavenly aroma of warm pastry.

After the big announcement and a plate of sausage rolls, life simply jogged on. Violetta suspected that privately her mum may have had a weep. Disappointed tears over a stalled career and a very expensive degree. Not so much the daddy factor. Her mum wouldn't give a monkey's about that.

The family rallied as Violetta knew they would. A new baby was a reason to rejoice, to prepare, to look forward. She had never doubted her mum, not for one second. Just like Appleton Farm she was their sanctuary and with her, you would be safe.

Appleton Farm, Cheshire. Present day

Footsteps in the hallway preceded the arrival of the woman herself who immediately came over and planted a kiss on the top of Violetta's bobble hat and wrapped her in a long hug.

'Well, this is a very unexpected but pleasant surprise, I must say. To what do I owe the honour and why aren't you at work?' Letting go she headed over to the back door, chatting as she went.

'Don't tell me you're poorly too. Our Rosina has rung in sick which is very unusual, and she's not answering her phone either.

Have you heard from her?' Once she'd opened the door, without needing to be bidden three very waggy dogs raced inside, going suitably daft when they saw their guest and only when she'd greeted them all one by one, they abandoned her for a slurp of water and their bed by the stove.

'No, I haven't. She's probably asleep so leave her be. I hope she's better by Sunday though.'

The click of the kettle prompted her mum to finish the job Violetta had started and as she watched her fill the cups with water, she checked who was in the house before beginning her speech. 'Is Bern here? I saw his coat on the stand.'

'No, he's at work. He leaves coats all over the place. That'll be his dog-walking one. Right, here we go, have you eaten? I can make you some breakfast before I head down to the centre. I said I'd stand in if Rosina left them short-handed.' Placing the mugs on the table her mum pulled out her chair at the top.

'Sorry Mum, am I holding you up? I'll drop you off if you want when we've had this, save you walking.' Violetta felt slightly glad her mum had to go out, then reminded herself that she couldn't keep putting it off and if she didn't get it over with now, she'd only have to say it on Sunday and then her sisters would be there. She wanted to broach the subject of coming home in private; the other thing would unfortunately have to wait until after Christmas.

'Oh, it's fine, there's no rush. So, what's up? It's written all over your face that something is bothering you so come on, let's have it. Tell your old mum everything.'

Taking a sip of her coffee, Violetta winced at the irony of her mum's comment so before she lost momentum and nerve, she rolled her eyes and took a deep breath. 'I can't kid you, can I, Mum?'

'Nope, so, go on, what've you done this time?'

Placing her cup on the table, Violetta folded her arms and

let her palms connect with the grain, channelling confessions of the past while hoping that at the other end of the table Granny Sylvia had popped down from heaven, ignored house rules and lit a cig and was there to back her up, or call her a pain in the arse. The latter probably.

'Well, the thing is... it's looking like after the new year I'll be out of a job and if I get a bit tight for money, could me and Darcy come home, until I get myself straight?'

When her mum sighed, then smiled and reached out to wrap long fingers around hers, Violetta knew it was going to be okay. Some of it, anyway.

17

LEONORA

Selfridges, Manchester
Present day

When the screen lit up and she saw Caspar's name, Leonora looked for a quiet corner in Selfridges where she could speak to him in some kind of privacy. She was already annoyed that he'd read her messages and hadn't bothered to acknowledge them, so along with being tired from her shift, his stupid mind games were the last thing she needed. Or the attention of the creepy security guard who was eyeing her up.

'At last, he replies.' Leonora absent-mindedly flicked through the rail of Christmas jumpers that she had zero intention of buying but conscious of looking like a shoplifter, feigned interest in Santa and his pompom nose.

'Sorry, I was in a meeting and couldn't text back and anyway, you've got room to talk. I've forgotten what you look like, with or without clothes.'

Blood rushed to her face, the heat of anger making her cheeks burn. 'And what exactly is that supposed to mean?'

A sarcastic laugh at the other end of the line was followed by a very unhelpful remark. 'Well, let's face it, I might as well take holy orders because apart from not seeing you for a week, I can't remember the last time I had any action under the sheets.'

You selfish, self-obsessed get. Leonora was raging yet somehow managed to lower her voice as she moved on to the next rail containing glittery T-shirts. 'Why are you being like this? You know I was really rough with my you-know-what and Christmas is a mad, busy time at work so after last year's washout I'm glad to actually have a job. So don't start giving me a hard time, I'm not in the mood, okay?'

'Chill out, I was only joking. I miss you, that's all.'

Well I don't miss you! The irritation at such a simple statement only confirmed to Leonora that she had had enough and this ridiculous relationship – because as far as she was concerned that's what it was – should end. And the sooner the better.

'Well, I've finished work for the weekend so I was going to come over to yours later. What time will you be home?'

'Hallelujah! My fiancé finally has time for me, I'm honoured.'

Leonora bit her lip and inhaled patience, forbidding herself to respond for his sake and that of all the innocent shoppers around her. She heard a sigh, then his words that felt like he was doing her a massive honour.

'I have one more meeting so if you like I can swing by yours and stay over. I can be there in about an hour. If you set off now we should be there at the same time.'

'NO!' She hadn't meant to be so forceful and cringed when the security guard raised his eyebrows. 'I'll come to you. Mum's got Bern round tonight; she's making him a meal or something so let's leave them in peace.'

'We could go out to eat, then we won't be in their way. It's not like your house is tiny and anyway, I have plans for you... we need to make up for lost time.'

Just fuck off and take a sodding hint. Leonora's skin was crawling and she really was running out of patience. Maybe it was better to give him the hint, prepare him for the fall. Yes, that would be kinder than wham-bam, guess what, you're dumped.

'Look, Caspar. I think we need to have a chat, that's why I want to come to yours where we can speak in private.' The silence that followed told her he was taking her words on board so preparing for an interrogation she turned her back on the nosey security guard and moved to the corner of the store.

'Why, what do you want to talk about?' His voice was clipped. Laced with suspicion.

Deep breath, you can do this. 'Us. I want to talk about us.'

'And why would you want to do that? Is something wrong?'

'Actually there is. There's no easy way to say this but I've been thinking things over and I'd like a break.' Bloody hell. She'd said it. Her legs felt a bit shaky, her mouth had gone dry and the pulse in her temple kept time with her palpitating heart.

'Ah, right. A holiday. That's no problem. We can have a look online tonight. Where were you thinking?'

Are you fucking kidding me? 'No, Caspar. I don't mean I want to go on holiday. I meant a break in our relationship.' *Which you knew, so stop trying to be a smart-arse.*

'Sorry... have I missed something?' He sounded incredulous with a tinge of Caspar-style sarcasm.

'No, you've not missed anything. It's just that being apart so much these last few weeks has made me rethink stuff and...'

'Are you breaking up with me?' His shock was evident.

At his point Leonora bottled it and started to ramble. All the thoughts in her head came tumbling out one after the other. 'No, well, yes... sort of.'

Hearing nothing at the other end forced her on and imagining his wide-eyed expression made her desperate to fill the gap. 'The thing is, I'm feeling trapped and I am well aware you hate the shifts I work and it made me think that when I do open my own bistro which could be next year, I won't have a minute spare to plan a wedding or spend every waking moment with you which made me realise that it's not going to work, me and you, because you're too...'

'Too fucking what? Go on, say it. You've not had a problem dishing out the truth so far so don't hold back.'

Leonora looked around at the busy shoppers and the security man who was now speaking into his radio, eyes locked on her.

The nosey bastard.

Giving him a death stare, she turned away and caught a glimpse of herself in the mirror and asked the pale-faced girl who stared back a question. *Are you really going to break up with your fiancé in the woolly jumper department at Selfridges?*

Yes, I bloody well am!

'Caspar, you're just too controlling, and clingy and it really pisses me off that the only time you ask me about work is to find out who I've talked to and when I'll be free, and I don't want you to come to my house for Christmas either. I want it to be just us – family – and you're not family.'

Shit, did I really just say that?

'Are you dumping me, at Christmas?'

Leonora rolled her eyes and rubbed her forehead, exasperated. 'No, I'm breaking up with you on a Friday in December. Christmas has nothing to do with it and I'm not being held to ransom because of one day, okay!'

'No, it's not okay, Leo. We're getting married. What will your mum say? She's been planning it for ages and what about the garden centre, and my job? Your mum respects my advice and one day I'll be part of the team there. You know this, we've talked about it. You can't just cut me off like this. And I am part of the family, I'm your fiancé.'

It was right at that moment when Leonora really saw her and Caspar for what it was. He wasn't interested in her, not really. She was his foot in the door, an appendage, a side dish of fries, or onion rings, or–

'Are you listening to me, Leo?' His voice brought her back to earth with a bump.

'Yes, and I'm sorry, Caspar. I didn't mean to tell you like this. That's why I wanted to see you tonight, so I could tell you face to face.'

When he spoke his anger seemed to have abated and nice, cajoling Caspar had returned. She should have known he wouldn't take it lying down, it wasn't in his nature. He always had to have the last word.

'Listen, we can sort this. It's just a blip. You've been working too hard and I've been neglecting you, I can see that now so I'll come to yours later, pick you up and take you for a nice meal. My treat. I know, we'll go to that Michelin place and you can steal ideas for your restaurant.' When his fake laugh received no response he ploughed on. 'You just need a bit of pampering and a bottle of the best champagne while we talk things through, see where we can make changes. That's all it takes, compromise and understanding.'

'No, Caspar. See, you're doing it again, telling me how it's going to be, controlling me. And I'm not a child who you can bribe with treats so for once, do as your told. I've already said that I don't want you to come round and you totally ignored me so I suggest you give me some space for a few days and then maybe we can talk, on the phone. There will be things to sort out, like the money for the wedding – you'll want your half back.'

Silence.

Leonora waited for a response as she stared at the cold-hearted woman in the shop mirror, with her black plaits popping out from her bobble hat, huddled into a green parka with its big shoplifting pockets, a thought that made her glance at the security guard who was actually looking the other way now. Maybe he'd heard her conversation and realised that corners of shops weren't just for sticking things down your knickers, and that boyfriends weren't forever or for Christmas. Unless they were called Caspar who just wouldn't give up.

'Christ! Have you been planning this? Because it sounds like you have. I can't believe you're being so callous, Leo, please. At least give me a chance to put this right. I'm sorry but I won't take no for an answer. I'll be at your mum's in an hour. I'll meet you there, then we can sort this out. Look, I have to go. I'm late for a client. I love you, Leo, I really do. See you soon, okay.'

When the call disconnected, Leonora stood wide-mouthed, staring at her reflection and it was only when she realised that she looked stupid she snapped her mouth shut and herself back to reality as her temper flared. How dare he railroad her into a meeting at her own home! That's why he'd cut her off, so she couldn't object. Well, she wasn't having it. Swiping the screen she scrolled to his name and fired off a text. In capitals.

DO NOT COME TO MINE. I WON'T BE THERE. IT'S OVER. THERE IS NOTHING MORE TO SAY. STAY AWAY. I MEAN IT. I WILL BE IN TOUCH NEXT WEEK.

Emerging from the corner, Leonora made her way towards the exit and as she passed him by, received a nod and a kind smile from the security guard and in return, she gave him the thumbs up. 'Have a happy Christmas, mate. Sorry if I stressed you out.'

Seconds later she stepped onto the street and sucked in the city air, embracing the chill and the wonderful feeling of being free. Looking upwards at the blue sky and winter sun, she imagined Granny Sylvia looking down and giving her a wink, or maybe a round of applause for finally getting rid of Shiny Suit. And while Leonora embraced the relief she took a moment to take stock and give herself a few words of advice.

She'd had a lucky escape and as much as she knew that Joel was the one, she was going to take things slowly, at her pace, follow her dreams and, if he was the man she thought he was, he'd be with her every step of the way. A bit like Bern had been with her mum; walking side by side, supportive, wanting the best for one another; not taking, manipulating, controlling.

Somehow she knew she'd be okay with Joel and with that thought in mind she set off on her way. Taking the route back to her car via the Christmas market she dodged pedestrians and soaked up the festive atmosphere of the stalls selling seasonal bits and bobs. Her thoughts then strayed to Sam. She wished she had his phone number so she could tell him he was right, that being honest with Caspar was the way to go, even if she had missed out the Joel element. And maybe she could ask him what the hell she was going to tell her mum about the wedding and if it would be wrong to ring Joel right there and then and not sound excited when she told him they could finally be together. She knew Sam wouldn't have minded her asking for advice and not being able to made her feel odd.

Stopping by a stall selling mistletoe she read the sign, encouraging you to buy a sprig and make a wish and for the first time in a while a huge wave of sadness and longing swept in, consuming her right there on King Street. Trying to shake it off Leonora applied logic, telling herself it was merely a touch of stress-induced melancholy caused by dumping the stubborn boyfriend from hell.

The thing was, she missed Granny Sylvia so much it hurt. And knowing she couldn't change that was worse and in times like these she wouldn't have minded having a granddad. She would call in, have a brew and talk about what was going on in *Corrie* or what books they'd read. Because there was no doubt about it. If mistletoe wishes did come true she would ask for a granddad and one in particular. Leonora would choose Sam.

18

ROSINA

Appleton Farm, Cheshire
Present day

T he woodland trail car park was deserted, just as Rosina
had expected it to be. Not even a dog walker to spot her
sitting inside her people carrier and wonder why she was there,
alone on a freezing cold day, staring out the windscreen. She'd
surprised herself, actually managing to find her way, the state
she was in.

The Herculean task of dragging herself out of bed and
getting dressed was reminiscent of being drugged up on
pethidine during labour with Max. She'd been so spaced out it
was almost impossible to comprehend what the midwife was
telling her to do yet somehow her body did what was needed.

It had been exactly the same this morning as she'd lain on
the bed, watching the minutes of the bedside clock click over,
her meeting with Norman getting closer, the walls closing in
again and the whispers of her tormenters getting louder. She

knew she had to go; the alternative didn't bear thinking about. So through the fog in her head, a claggy, grey, dismal mist that made her muzzy and disorientated, she'd dragged off her pyjama bottoms and pulled on her jeans. Taking off the top was too much of an effort so instead she'd left it on and struggled into a jumper. She couldn't remember going down the stairs, putting on her coat or leaving the house and it was a miracle that her depleted brain still had the capacity to change gear and drive in a straight line.

The day was bright and sunny but as she'd rounded the bend then pulled off the main road and drove along the short track to the car park, Rosina felt the mood darken, descending into gloom as the shade of the barren trees cut out the light. The forest beyond the parking area was dense and in contrast to the spring and summer months when it teemed with families and hikers, in the winter, alone, it seemed a desolate place. She could hear the odd car as it sped by. The main road was notoriously fast and a cut-through used by locals and speed freaks taking advantage of a rural, camera-free zone.

And there she waited for Norman to arrive, staring into the woods beyond her car, ignoring the buzz of her phone, another text, probably her mum checking to see if she felt better.

Don't think about Mum. Don't think about any of them. Be strong.

Instead, her mind wandered to her cold toes, an uncomfortable yet welcome distraction. Somewhere along the way she'd forgotten to put on socks and it was left to her Ugg boots to fend off frostbite. The heater made her too hot and panicky when the thought of smoke, pumping from the exhaust as the engine fumes met the cold air took her mind down a dark path. It would be so much easier not to be there, a final solution, a way out.

It's a shame you didn't drive into a ditch, or a tree. You'd have done everyone a favour and solved all your problems at once.

The real shame was hers to bear. That she actually felt this way, drowning in this pathetic self-inflicted state of self-loathing and desperation.

But the kids need you. Imagine their horror, knowing you left them behind, what it would do to them? And Lou, poor Lou. And Mum, and Vi and Leo. You can't do that to them. You have to find a way to make this right.

So lost in her mind, clinging on to the saner voice in her head, Rosina didn't notice the car until it pulled up alongside hers and when she did a sea of bile rose from her empty stomach as simultaneously her heart contracted. Her whole body seemed to have clenched, muscles taut with anxiety as she removed her keys from the ignition, opened the car door and stepped outside.

After slipping her keys in her pocket next to her phone, she pushed both hands deep inside to hide the fact they were shaking. The cold air pinched her cheeks like a spiteful foe, making life, the day, being her, seem crueller. And for some strange reason as she walked across the rough stone of the car park, the feeling of bare feet inside her soft boots made Rosina feel exposed, unprepared and vulnerable.

You shouldn't have met him here; it's too quiet, you're too alone.

Well, that's what you deserve. It's all your fault, so deal with it.

Norman got out of his car, a sleek black Jaguar that reminded her of a predator ready to pounce. They met at the rear of both vehicles by which time her whole body convulsing and as much as she tried to avoid his stare, she had to face him, face up to it all.

His hands were also in his pockets as he swaggered towards her, cocksure as always, cold, blue piggy eyes staring out of his sunbed Bisto face. He got straight down to business. 'Do you have my money?'

Rosina had only one answer available to her. 'No, but I will get it. I told you, I just need more time.'

'For fuck's sake. Are you simple? I told you today was the day. Do you think I'm pissing about here? You do realise that I've given you more leeway than normal punters. I'd usually send a couple of lads to collect but you wanted the personal touch and I've honoured that. Pity you haven't done me the same courtesy.'

'I'm sorry, Norman, I really am but you will get it. I'm going to ask my mum to lend it to me, this weekend.'

'Err, sorry, have I missed something here? Didn't you say you wanted to keep Mummy out of it?' The smirk and exaggerated, confused expression that accompanied his sarcasm said he didn't believe her.

'Yes, I did but my back's against the wall and I've no alternative so please, give me a couple of days. That's all I ask.' Rosina could hear the whine in her voice and the lie, because even though she knew it was the only solution she still didn't know if she had the guts to face her mum, let alone Lou.

'Na, no can do.'

'Please, Norman. One more chance. Give me till Monday.' Pathetic, she sounded pathetic and loathed herself even more for begging.

Norman tutted, then turned and began to pace, making a meal out of thinking it through. He was loving keeping her dangling, she could tell. At least he hadn't said no. Stopping abruptly he turned to face her and as he shook his head, let out an exasperated sigh. He was wearing the kind of expression you'd use on a naughty child who'd pushed their luck but was getting one more chance. Rosina's heart skipped a beat.

'Okay then, you've got till Monday on one condition.'

Inside her pockets Rosina balled her fists. *Yes, thank God.* 'Okay, whatever you want. Thank you, Norman.'

Norman smiled and took a step forward and held out his right palm. 'Car keys, hand them over.'

Rosina's response came out as a squeak. 'What?'

'I want your car keys, as insurance. That way if you don't pay up on Monday, I can flog it. Either way I won't lose out. Don't worry, I won't leave you stranded in the middle of nowhere. I'll drop you off at home and get one of the lads to pick the car up later. Now give.' He beckoned impatiently with his fingers and stepped forward, almost backing Rosina against the boot of her car.

Raising her palms she attempted to stop him from getting any closer, her trembling hands only a centimetre from his chest. He was so close she could see sunbed goggle circles under his eyes while cold puffs of his breath skimmed her face. 'No. No, you can't take my car. What will I tell Lou?'

'Not my problem, love. Not my problem.'

'Please, Norman. Be reasonable. If I give you my car then I might as well tell Lou and you know that's what I'm trying to avoid... look, you know where I live so if I don't get the money by Monday then fine, I give in, come and take the car, tell Lou, tell the whole of sodding Gawsworth but I beg you, one more chance, please.'

His piggy eyes were cold and uncaring. She saw not a flicker of compassion or understanding on a face set in stone so when a smirk slid across his fake tan skin, it made her skin crawl. And when in one slick move his body was pushing against hers while his hand roamed the front of her jacket, slowly tracking her body, Rosina thought she was going to pass out, stunned and rendered mute.

Pressing his weight against Rosina, he leant closer, his lips touching her cheek then her neck. 'How about I give you a choice. You could give me a down payment right now, while there's nobody about. Let's call it a show of faith, a bit of goodwill. Or I take your car. It's up to you, of course – but now I come to think about it. I prefer option one.'

He had her trapped. His hand began to grope between her legs, the other hand pushed inside her coat, trying to find her zip. This was really happening, he really meant it. She had to make him stop.

'No!'

He flicked open the top button of her jeans and pushed his other hand under her pyjama top. 'I don't think you have a choice really, do you?'

'I said NO!' Raising her knee, catching him square between his legs, Rosina pushed him away as he howled and grasped his crotch. But rather than tame him, the pain he was evidently in seemed to fuel Norman's rage, grabbing her coat with his other hand as she struggled to free herself, punching and twisting, kicking his shins.

Norman held on tight. 'You fucking bitch. You are going to be so fucking sorry you did that, you slag.' Lunging, Norman pushed Rosina off balance and they both crashed to the floor, landing between the cars as she scrambled forward on her front, trying to get to the driver's door.

When she felt his hands grab her left leg, she twisted and screamed. 'Get off, get off, you fucking pervert.' The terror inside echoed in her ears, rage and the recklessness of despair fuelling her instinct. Fight or flight.

DO BOTH! DO IT NOW!

Raising her right knee and then with all her might, with everything she had left, Rosina powered her leg forward, her boot smashing into Norman's face making contact with his nose. And another, for luck.

The howl of a wounded man, then her left leg being freed

spurred her into action. In a second she was on her feet but so was Norman, a trickle of blood escaping from his nose and knowing she'd never open her door in time Rosina obeyed the voice in her head.

RUN! GET TO THE ROAD. FLAG SOMEONE DOWN OR JUST KEEP RUNNING.

NOW, GO NOW.

She ran.

Staggering to his feet, Norman growled a threat. 'Don't think you'll get away. You're fucked, Rosina. One way or another, you are fucked.'

Oh God, he's mad, he's going to kill me. I'll never see the kids again. Lou, I'm sorry, I'm sorry.

As she raced ahead, for once she had something in her favour. She was nimble where he was lumbering, he was dazed while she was alert, wired, and even though her fear matched his rage she was still a few metres in front. If she could get to the road, into the open, he might tire, or she could hide, yes, that would work too. The end of the track was only two strides away, and as she raced across the tarmac and into the sun, she saw that the road in each direction was deserted so made the decision to hide, take cover in the trees and undergrowth and wait until he gave up, or a car came by.

Taking a look behind her she saw him, half running, half staggering but still determined, mad as hell and about to cross the road as she thrashed her way through the bushes that lined the route. And then a sound, the roar of an engine as it took the bend, then the screech of brakes and a thud, silence, and then two more thuds.

What the hell?

Stopping in her tracks, Rosina turned and crouched, then crawled forward still hidden from view. The sight that met her – Norman's body sprawled on the road, blood oozing from his head, the car that had hit him parked at an angle – made her clamp her hands over her mouth, trapping in the horror of the scene.

Oh God, he's dead, he must be dead.

And then a sound, a car door opening and the legs of what she could tell was a man stood over Norman's body. He was wearing black trousers that she followed upwards to his white shirt, arms hanging by his side. It was only as she got to his head that the light dawned and Rosina realised who it was, suddenly recognising the car. The urge to call his name, shout for help was smothered by a lightning flash of sense.

No, what would I say? He can't know you're here. Don't move. Breathe, nice and steady. Think. You have to get back to the car. He'll ring the police, then they'll find his car, your car. How can you get past him?

Rosina didn't have to wait long for an answer because he began to walk back to his car, but faster than he'd approached the body and for a second she presumed he was going for his phone, to ring the police but when she heard the door slam and the engine start, the shock of what was happening really hit.

He's driving off. Oh my God, he's driving off.

Her horrified brain zapped a message to her quivering hands that grappled in her pocket, trying to grab her phone. Yanking it out Rosina jabbed the camera icon on the screen and tried to hold it still, clicking, clicking, clicking as she watched from her hideout. The car reversed a touch then drove around Norman before moving off at speed, fleeing the scene. The last photo she took was of his number plate.

Rosina was weak, her legs felt funny as her mud-splattered body sagged against a tree while she fought to comprehend the ramifications of what she'd seen and also, what it meant for her.

Norman was dead, so for now he couldn't collect his debt and her secret was safe, as long as she could get back to her car and away from the area without being seen. Which meant she had to move fast, before another car came along. But that meant passing Norman.

Just do it, just run, don't look, focus on the track, look ahead not down, think of your family, think of getting away with it. Get up, get up now.

Standing, Rosina listened for a car. Nothing. Darting forward she pushed aside bushes that had concealed her then checked to her right and saw that there were no vehicles in sight, she couldn't see around the bend so on legs like Bambi, slightly wobbly but raring to go, she sprinted across the road and obeying her brain, didn't look at Norman, just straight ahead.

Seconds later she was in her car, starting the engine and thanking Bern for suggesting they had a one-way system when they designed the trail car park. It enabled her to exit further along the road, leaving the body of Norman and her guilt behind her.

She glanced in her rear-view mirror only once to make sure nobody had found him and before she met any oncoming traffic, took the first turning on her left, off the main road and alongside the forest.

Taking deep breaths to calm herself, Rosina forced herself to concentrate. She had to get to her kids. They would be home from school, probably in the kitchen raiding the fridge, making a mess but she didn't care. All she had to do was sneak in, shout hi as she ran up the stairs. Take a quick shower, put on clean clothes, stick the muddy jeans and jacket that was stained with Norman's groping fingerprints in the washer. Act normal. As normal as anyone could when they'd been propositioned, almost raped, threatened, chased, then to top it off, witnessed a hit-and-run.

She could do it. She'd been faking it for months, living a lie and now she had a reprieve, a breathing space to think things through, come up with another plan. As she drove towards home her heart rate began to settle while her mind refused to rest, keeping up a frantic pace, going over and over what had happened.

Okay, so she could push one problem to the back of the queue but another remained, stood firm, stubbornly refusing to budge until it had been heard. Rosina had one hell of a dilemma on her hands. How could she expose a hit-and-run killer without exposing herself? Telling the truth, pointing the finger at a man who was part of her family, a man who had behaved in such a callous way and left another for dead?

Rosina couldn't let someone she loved live a lie; she knew how that felt and no way could she bear another burden, keep another secret. But she might have to, to save herself. What the hell was she going to do?

19

CARMEN

Appleton Farm, Cheshire
Present day

Lifting the lid of the pan, Carmen gave the curry another stir then covered it again, smiling at Mitzi who sniffed at the aroma of cardamom and star anise, two amongst an array of Indian spices that had all gone into Bern's favourite curry.

Moving over to the table she occupied herself with kneading the naan bread, no coriander. Bern hated it and said it tasted like soap. He would be there anytime and she was looking forward to spending an evening at the kitchen table, eating a meal, listening to the radio. Maybe later they would play cards in the lounge or read by the fire. That was her favourite thing to do, relax with a glass of wine, a good book and one of her favourite operas playing softly in the background. Especially when she looked up and Bern was there too.

It wasn't as though it was a new thing, him spending the night, and soon they'd be together every evening, and morning.

However, his imminent permanency lit up her heart, and that made her want it even more. She had never really been alone in the house because even after Rosina and Violetta moved out, she always had her mum and Leonora for company and more often than not, one or more of the grandchildren for a sleepover. That was why she'd never felt that having a man in the house was a necessity, or the lack of one a loss. It was how it was. Her and Bern rumbling along for years.

The girls, even Violetta who had for so long clung to a false image of her dad, treated Bern like a stepfather. He was part of the family, a kind, funny bear of a man who had always been there for them. He'd taught the girls to drive, round and round the garden centre car park when it was closed, doing three-point turns and emergency stops, chugging up and down the lane practising gear changes or in Leonora's case, kangarooing back and forth, giving Bern whiplash.

Sometimes, things had a way of coming together and even though they both prided themselves on being self-sufficient, valuing their own space, it had been during lockdown that suddenly that space became too wide. When you really needed the security of someone's arms, a hug, normality, it had been snatched away, prohibited.

To know that Bern was a short walk away and alone in his house was heartbreaking, frustrating too. And as much as the temptation to sneak over there and break the rules was overwhelming, that terrible fear of infecting someone you loved, spreading a germ around your family had, quite frankly, terrified Carmen. The nights she had lain in bed and tormented herself with scenarios mirroring the ones she'd seen on the news reduced her to tears. In the end she'd stopped watching, unable to bear seeing the daily stats and hearing the sombre tone of the newsreader.

And that was another reason why she and Bern were

throwing caution to the wind and living for the moment because never again, whatever the world threw at them, would they endure it in separate homes even if they did end up driving each other round the bend. She'd rather go mad with Bern than rattle around a huge house alone.

Covering the naan with a tea towel she left them to prove and not wanting to dwell further, banished thoughts of the past and focused on what was going on in the here and now.

Checking the clock on the mantel she gave a tut. *Where is he?*

Going over to the window she peered out into the wintery night. Nothing, just the fairy lights in the garden and in the distance the soft glow from the lamp post that marked the entrance to Appleton. No sign of headlights coming along the lane to the house. Carmen hoped one set would belong to Leonora's car and that she'd changed her mind about staying out.

Needing a few minutes to rest her feet she turned towards her armchair that was nestled in the corner by the chimney breast, giving Arthur's ears a tickle before scooping up Petra and plonking her on her knee. The other two never seemed to mind that the little dachshund was the attention-seeker of the tribe. They were best friends and inseparable yet each had their own quirky ways.

At night the three dogs always slept together, snuggled in a giant basket that stood between the armchair and the Aga although during the day, Mitzi preferred the battered sofa which she regarded as hers. Humans had no place there. Arthur liked to stretch, usually upside down in his basket, making the most of his space. Petra was the lapdog and loved a cuddle so as always, Carmen was happy to indulge her.

Stroking the soft fur of her dachshund while Mitzi and Arthur snored, warmed by the oven that was baking bhajis, Carmen looked at her dogs one by one and smiled. They were just like humans, all of them had their own personalities, foibles and yes, they all liked their space. A bit like her three daughters who, it had to be said, were acting peculiar of late. Maybe she'd been so busy with her Christmas arrangements that she'd not noticed but now she thought about it, each of them seemed preoccupied.

It really had been a funny old day. For a start, Leonora had gone AWOL. She knew Carmen was making curry and was looking forward to relaxing after a long week – she'd said so that morning in a text. It was sent at 5.45am, probably before she started her early shift.

Can't wait for curry night. Going shopping after work. Looking forward to a big chill. I'm shattered. Should see you about six. Love you x

Leonora would probably invite Caspar but as always, Carmen secretly hoped he wouldn't turn up. Yes, it was wrong that she pretended to like him but she'd had to put up with her mum tutting and finding fault with everything about Sebastian. So she'd tried hard to break the mould and go with the flow where her daughter's choice of partner was concerned.

Carmen had never admitted it but she actually agreed with her mum's erudite summation of Caspar and sometimes wondered what Leonora saw in him. Yes, he was extremely handsome, a bit gangly, like a thoroughbred horse, all over the place, unable to rest, shiny coat, immaculately groomed, fast out of the gate, driven, determined to finish first.

Her mum had repeatedly warned her to watch him, saying he was after getting his feet under the table at the garden centre. Carmen suspected the same but that was never going to happen. That business was hers, and for the girls and Caspar was in for a rude awakening if he thought he could manoeuvre himself into position once he married Leonora.

Something was definitely up though. She'd been disappointed when Leonora texted again that afternoon to say she wouldn't be home for dinner and was staying in town with a friend.

Sorry Mum. Change of plan. Been invited out by some friends from work. Last-minute Crimbo knees-up. Will stay over. Please save me LOTS of curry. I'll text you in the morning.

Love you x

Carmen didn't think anything of it because Leonora had stayed with friends loads of times and gone straight to work. However, when she heard the roar of an engine racing up the drive and stones scattering when it screeched to a halt, then the doorbell ringing like there was an emergency, her own alarm bells rang. Opening the door to Caspar she was about to tell him off for driving so fast when he beat her to it.

'Is Leonora here?'

Carmen scanned the drive to confirm the obvious. If her car was absent, she was too. 'No, she texted to say she was staying out tonight. Has she not told you?'

Completely ignoring Carmen, he asked a question of his own. 'Did she say who she was with, where they were going?' His face was quite pale with a smudge of pink across his cheeks and she wasn't too sure if it was caused by the cold air or anger. Wary, Carmen was vague in her reply. 'No, just that it was a friend from work. Why, is something wrong?'

'No, no, nothing's wrong. Just a case of crossed wires. I thought we were meeting here but she must have meant in Manchester. My mistake. I'll head there now, see if I can track her down. Sorry to have disturbed you, Carmen.' And with that he turned and marched back to his car.

Feeling Arthur by her side reminded her about Caspar's driving. 'Oh, and Caspar, please don't drive into the garden so fast. Remember the dogs are about and it's the countryside, not Brands Hatch.'

But Caspar wasn't listening. After slamming his car door and totally ignoring her request he reversed, scattered more stones and sped off like the devil and the ghost of Granny Sylvia were on his tail.

Furious, Carmen had gone straight inside and tried to ring Leonora but her phone was switched off so she'd send a text instead, letting her know what had happened and asking her to ring. She was still waiting.

Carmen was so cross about the way Caspar had behaved and resolved to have words with him the next time she saw him. And, she'd had to go out with the rake and smooth over the stones to remove the tyre tracks, which was when she noticed the side of her car had been pebble-dashed. She would get Lou to have a look at it. He'd know if it needed a respray or not and if it did, Caspar would be paying!

Thinking of Lou made her smile. Thank heaven he was nothing like flash Caspar. At least Rosina had ended up with a good man, someone who would look after her and the children properly. He was such a gentle soul, hard-working and perfect for her daughter. Even her mum had not found fault with Lou, or the fact that he and Rosina were childhood sweethearts and wanted to be married at nineteen, a year older than when she'd married Sebastian. In Granny Sylvia's eyes Lou and Rosina could do no wrong and she'd been pleased as punch at their wedding and a linchpin when all four of Rosina's babies came along.

They'd been such happy days, when the house was full of

toddlers and babies and all their paraphernalia and Granny Sylvia had come into her own, running the family crèche while she and Rosina ran the garden centre, and Lou went off to work at the garage. Carmen had loved it, them all living under one roof and Appleton had come good, providing shelter for everyone when they needed it. A young family saving for a place of their own, a mad granny, a widow and her daughters.

Carmen knew why her mum was so keen on Lou, and why Rosina had grabbed her first love with both hands. It was because in her own way, Rosina wanted proof of the fairy-tale marriage. For love to be real and true, to be with a man who would never let her down and adore her as much as she adored him. In Lou she saw that. He was the opposite of her father. The disappointing wife beater who she'd always despised.

Thinking of Lou, and the spectre of Sebastian brought Carmen's thoughts to Violetta. She wished her middle daughter would find someone to love, a proper relationship not the casual dates she said she went on. Sometimes she suspected her daughter was fibbing, making out she was fine and going out for dinner with men she said fell short, weren't her type and bored her to death. That's why she was happier alone.

If only she could meet a nice chap, perhaps someone like Bern or Lou, certainly not Caspar. Surely there was a suitable man out there, one who would love Violetta and Darcy too. They'd discussed it earlier, when her weary-looking middle child had called in unexpectedly, red-eyed and anxious, with things on her mind.

It had hurt Carmen, not that she showed it, when earlier, Violetta had unburdened herself and amongst other things had told her about Darcy's Christmas wish for a daddy. In an instant all those prayers and wishes she'd made came flooding back.

'Honestly, Mum, I couldn't believe it when she said that. I

was gutted, especially because she was basing her dream daddy on Kyra's father who is a total, utter pillock.'

'Why, what's wrong with him?'

Violetta huffed. 'Just believe me, he's a prat and fake as fuck.'

'Oh, I see. Well, I'll have to take your word for that but he always seems so nice at school events and his wife is lovely too.' Seeing Violetta's look of disdain, Carmen changed tack.

'But I do see it from Darcy's point of view and in her innocence not only was she being honest, she was thinking of you too. I used to wish my dad would come home but that was solely for me. I never wanted another dad, just the one I'd left behind. I didn't really consider that my mum might be lonely.'

'Yeah, but that's because Gran was an out-and-out man-hater and you probably knew she wouldn't entertain another bloke in her life, so why ask for one? And Darcy doesn't mention her real dad that much, thank God. Until now she's just accepted that it's the two of us. That's why it was such a massive shock. I thought we were okay as we were.'

Carmen stood and went to put the kettle on again, feeling the need for a cup of sweet tea, her mum's go-to solution for most things.

'Well, my mum probably thought I was okay, but that's because I never told her. I knew she hated my dad for what he did and I remembered her crying in bed at night when she thought I was asleep.'

'Aw, poor Gran. I remember her as being so tough. I can't imagine her as a young mum and being sad.'

'I know, love, but that's the front she put on for everyone. She changed when we came to Manchester. I suppose that's one of the reasons I kept my thoughts to myself. She had to provide for us both and the last thing she needed was me causing problems. I wanted to protect her feelings and as I got older, I respected her so much for being a single parent, and I also respected her wish that we didn't talk about my dad. It's how it's always been, or was.'

For a second, Carmen wondered if she should tell Violetta about her plans to find her dad, then decided it was the wrong time and she'd wait until Sunday when all her girls were together.

Violetta frowned. 'So do you think Darcy wants to talk about her real dad?'

'Perhaps. She's never mentioned him to me and you know she talks me to death about everything so I'd be surprised if she kept something like that to herself. You did the right thing, Violetta, being honest when she asked the first time so that's probably why she's being honest with you in return.' Carmen filled the teapot with boiling water as she spoke, remembering how Violetta used to ask so many questions and sometimes, share angry words.

'Mum, can I ask you something?'

Taking the teapot over to the table Carmen gave her stock reply. 'Always.'

'Be honest when you answer this, but did I hurt your feelings when I used to bang on about Dad all the time?'

Pouring the tea into the waiting mugs, Carmen kept the faith and wondered if Violetta had read her mind. 'Yes, in a way you did because a bit like Darcy, no matter how hard I tried you always wanted him back. But I got that, how could I not? My dad had an affair with another woman and chose her over me. I was lucky though. There was always a chance he would come and find me.'

'It must have driven you mad though, hearing me build him up to be a big hero while you, Rosina and Gran knew what he was really like and still you shielded me from the truth. Allowed me my fantasy dad.'

Keeping herself occupied helped Carmen rein in her

emotions and accompanying thoughts about Sebastian. After spooning two sugars into Violetta's tea and then pouring in the milk – just a drop, strong and sweet, how she liked it – Carmen answered.

'How could I deny you that? You were so young and even though he was a terrible husband to me, he was still your daddy and you were entitled to your memories. Like I told you when Rosina blurted out the truth, he was two separate people, the daddy that you loved and the man who let me down. That's why even now, I don't mind that you talk about him. So stop worrying.'

'I hate men sometimes. In fact, I hate them a lot of the time.'

The simple, shocking statement stopped Carmen mid-pour, and she replaced the jug of milk, focusing her attention on Violetta who was on the verge of tears.

'Oh, love, what's wrong? Come on, tell your old Mum.' At which point Violetta broke down, sobbing like there was no tomorrow which prompted Carmen to race to the sink and grab the kitchen roll, then shoot over to the table to comfort her daughter.

Once Violetta had cried it out and calmed down, it turned out that her distress was nothing to do with men, but everything to do with her future.

It had been a lot to get her head around. Violetta dropped her bombshell about the bakery but Carmen had immediately promised her safe haven and in the New Year, a job at the garden centre to tide her over.

She pondered mentioning that Bern was moving in too, and also wondered how he would feel about Violetta and Darcy coming home. Having set Violetta's mind at rest over money and work she decided to leave the Bern announcement until Sunday. What she couldn't shake off was the feeling that the Darcy business had really rattled Violetta. Bloody Kyra and her perfect bloody dad.

Later, when Violetta dropped her off at the garden centre, Carmen reminded her puffy-eyed daughter that just because people put on the appearance of being a happy family, it didn't mean that behind closed doors life was hunky-dory.

'Just don't go beating yourself up, love, and remember, anyone can put on a show and make out they are wonderful but it may not be the truth, the real them. Loads of women think they've bagged themselves a prize guy when in reality he's a total pillock. And women are no better, we all have our secrets and believe me, none of us are perfect.'

In response, Violetta had managed a weak smile as she waved Carmen off. 'I know, thanks Mum. For everything. I'll see you on Sunday. I'll explain it all to Rosie and Leo over lunch so let's keep it between us till then, okay.'

Carmen nodded and after a quick wave, Violetta was gone.

The rattle of the back door sent Mitzi and Arthur bounding over, tails wagging like crazy as Bern entered the kitchen. Placing Petra on the floor so she could join in, Carmen went over to the table and after sprinkling water over the naan, popped them in the Aga.

Once the cacophony died down and the dogs returned to their resting places, Petra choosing the warmth of Arthur's belly to cuddle, Carmen got a word in. 'I thought you'd got lost. I didn't hear the car; have you walked?'

'Sorry, love. Yes, had a bit of engine trouble but it's all sorted now. Something smells good.'

Carmen watched as he slipped off his boots and padded over to the table in his woolly socks. Not wanting to hear about the ins and outs of his mechanical problems, she asked instead about his trip to the solicitor. 'Is everything all sorted with the house?'

Bern nodded and began setting the table. 'Yep, all done and dusted. It was simple really, just signed a few papers and then I was on my way. Got all togged up in my fancy pants for nowt.'

'Oh, good, about the solicitors, not the pants. Are you sure you're okay? You look miles away.'

'I'm fine, I promise. Bloody starving though, so get a wiggle on.'

Carmen laughed. 'Coming right up, your Highness. It's been all go here today, I can tell you. First Rosina rang in sick, then Violetta turned up for a heart to heart, and there's something going on with Leonora and Caspar too. Sit yourself down and I'll tell you all about it.'

Saying nothing and doing as he was told, Bern pulled out his chair and sat, looking concerned as he waited for Carmen to take hers at the top of the table. Seeing his expression she smiled. 'Don't look so worried, love. At least you're not in trouble, not this time anyway.' She gave him a wink and his hand a quick squeeze, letting him know that it was okay. She had it all under control, as always.

20

VIOLETTA

Gawsworth Church, Cheshire
Present day

V ioletta placed the bouquet of flowers on her father's grave and stepped back, linking her arm through Rosina's and Leonora's, each of them silently lost in their own thoughts. It was another glorious winter day and the three sisters were braving a strong easterly wind that blew everyone's hair over their faces and nipped at Violetta's ankles in the space between the hem of her jeans and the top of her boots.

The graveyard was busy with people making their sombre pilgrimages and Violetta wondered if they were like them, the ones who turned up for birthdays, Father's Day and Christmas because they felt they had to, appeasing guilt for not coming more often. She was sure that some of the visitors who milled about took great comfort from tending graves and having a few words with the dear departed. She didn't. And as time went by and the more she became wiser to the world, disenchanted by it and her memories, Violetta found she was losing patience with the ritual.

Leonora gave her sister's arm a squeeze. 'Are you okay, Vi?'

'I don't miss him anymore, you know.' A gasp from Leonora didn't ebb the tide. 'And if he was here I'd want to ask him why he was so awful to Mum and Rosie. In fact, I'm starting to think this is all a bit fake and we should stop coming.'

'Vi! What's got into you?' Leonora's head nearly span off her neck.

Violetta shrugged. 'Well, let's face it. You never met him, Rosie can't stand him and right at this moment in time I am running out of patience for twatty men who treat women like shit, and he was one of them.'

The jerk of her head in the direction of the grave indicated her anger that for some reason had converted into tears that were stinging her eyes, making her glad of the biting wind. She would blame that if the others noticed.

Leonora, always the peacemaker, turned to Rosina and gave her a nudge. 'Rosie, tell her she shouldn't feel like this,' then looking back to Violetta, 'you're entitled to your own memories of him, Vi, no matter how we feel about him. Isn't that right, Rosie?'

Rosina shrugged. 'She's right though. And as much as I don't want to stand over someone's grave and slag them off, I really don't have anything nice to say about him so perhaps we should go and see Gran. We've done our duty here.'

'I agree. Come on. Let's go and have a chat with Sylvia. I can tell her how totally fucking shit my life is right now! Give her something to roll her eyes at.' And with that Violetta tugged at Leonora's arm and led the way, not giving her time to object.

The three of them traipsed through the graveyard towards where their gran lay *'as far away from that bastard as possible.'* The words on her very detailed handwritten list of instructions had been carried out to the letter. All apart from playing 'Another One Bites the Dust' by Queen. Their mum had put her foot down about that which was a shame because the sisters had cried tears of laughter when she'd read it out.

They followed the path in silence, broken by Violetta's phone pinging inside her pocket, a sound that she totally ignored. All Saturday she'd had texts from him. One after the other.

You'd best keep your mouth shut. One word and I'll make sure everyone knows what you do. Imagine what the parents will say about you – schoolyard fodder. What would your daughter think? Poor little Darcy. Your mother will disown you.

In the end she'd switched her phone off and the only reason she'd turned it back on was because Darcy was at Rosina's with her cousins. She liked to be contactable in case there was a problem so couldn't even put the bloody thing on mute.

Violetta couldn't wait to get to her mum's. She'd brought Darcy's uniform so they could stay over. Then she could sink a bottle of wine and drown her sorrows, block out the world and the vile creature who was sending the text messages.

It was Rosina's turn to do the honours with the flowers and Violetta watched as she placed the bouquet in the vase next to the one their mum always used that was already laden with flowers. Next, Leonora stepped forward and put the poinsettia in the middle. Their gran loved them and it was a tribute from her grandchildren who had all written their name in the card that dangled from the stem. It was as Leonora took her place in the middle that Violetta noticed that Rosina was in a bad way, silently sobbing into tissue, her body literally shaking.

She and Leonora both tried to comfort their sister. Violetta took the lead. 'Hey, Rosie, come on, stop this. Gran would go mad if she saw you in this state. What on earth is the matter?'

Still Rosina couldn't speak so Leonora had a go, rubbing her sister's back as she spoke words of comfort, attempting to jolly her out of it. 'Don't bail on us, we need you to tell us one of your funny Gran stories. I know, do the one about her pinching a pair of specs every time she went in the pound shop.'

'Or when she took Leo to Blackpool but got on the wrong train and they ended up in Birmingham and didn't get home till midnight because she decided to go shopping and to Wetherspoons instead.' Violetta nodded at Leonora, giving her a cue.

'And I cried all the way back because I'd not been to the fair or got any rock. And when the taxi dropped us off Mum went totally mental at Gran in the garden because she thought we'd been abducted and made Bern call the police, who were on their way over.'

Finally, at this, Rosina began to half laugh, half sob but at least she could speak. 'I'm sorry for losing it, I just miss her so much and I wish she was here to help me...'

'What do you mean, "help me"? Do you mean with the girls because you know all you have to do is ask and me or Leo will do our bit, we always have.'

'It's not the girls. It's me. I'm such a mess and I can't cope anymore and being here... it's too much. It's just too much.'

Leonora made the decision that was on Violetta's tongue. 'Okay, I think we should go home and get a warm drink and then we can talk about whatever is bothering you. Come on, let's get you to the car, we'll be home in two ticks. Mum will know what to do.'

When Rosina began to sob again, they could only look at each other with surprised eyes as they steered their broken sister along the path and away from the churchyard.

Rosina

Rosina sat in the back of the car as they made the short way home through the village, holding tissue over her mouth and cursing herself for losing it.

Stop it, stop it right now before you blurt it all out. Keep it together or you'll totally ruin the day. Sort yourself out.

It had all been too much though. Starting with the events of Friday and the longest night in the history of the universe where she lay in bed, feigning illness, waiting for the police to knock on the door. She'd been convinced that someone would have seen her and reported her reg – but they hadn't, not yet anyway.

It had been on the local news the following morning, that a man had been killed in a hit-and-run and police were asking for help with their enquiries. No name had been given but just hearing the words dripping poison from the radio brought Rosina out in a sweat that had Lou placing his palm on her forehead and suggesting she spent another day in bed. And that was exactly where she'd spent all of Saturday while the girls brought her mugs of tea and toast that she couldn't swallow.

Every now and then Lou had popped his head in and even though she assured him it was just a bug, he looked at her with concern and her guilty conscience screamed that he didn't believe her. He was right. She was a liar.

Sleep evaded her. It came in fits and starts and when she did nod off she was plagued by dreams, messed-up, mixed-up horror stories starring a zombie that peeled himself off the road and chased her through the woods, running, never giving up, into the garden centre, in and out of the polytunnels that sagged around her body, the plastic covering her face, suffocating her. In the end she'd gone downstairs and watched the BBC, only the BBC, because there were no adverts, no late-night temptations for poker games or betting sites. See, she could do it if she tried. There was hope.

It had only been the kids, their excitement at being allowed into the garden centre once it closed later that day, an annual tradition where they got to play in the grotto and have as many rides on the Santa Train as they liked. Then it was back to Appleton for a giant takeaway, marking one more sleep before Christmas week began. How could she let them down? And her mum wanted some time with her and her sisters, apparently she had something important to talk to them about so Rosina had to go.

Pulling up outside the house they all bundled out and while her sisters fussed and asked if she was okay, Rosina assured them she was fine, overtired from work, a bit under the weather and hadn't been sleeping, that's why she'd lost it a bit when they went to see Granny Sylvia. They seemed to believe her and as she sucked in a deep breath, she congratulated herself on being the most deceitful sister and daughter anyone would not wish for. She was getting so good at winging it, buying time, kidding herself and because of all of these, Rosina felt nothing but shame.

Leonora

Leonora lingered in the hallway that was like a sensory time bomb, combining all the elements of Christmas that she had come to expect from their family home. First of all, it smelt divine as she inhaled the scent of cinnamon and pine and next, there was a festive treat for the eyes courtesy of the tree decorated with half a garden centre and handmade heirlooms from when they were children. Ears next, and they hung their coats on the stand to the strains of a familiar song on one of the CDs her mum refused to throw out, even though it was scratched and only played half of 'The Little Drummer Boy' before skipping to 'A Space Man Came Travelling'. Leonora knew the running order of both *Now It's Christmas* CDs.

While Rosina nipped to the loo, no doubt to sort out her face, Leonora surreptitiously checked her phone and grimaced when she saw the missed calls and texts from Caspar. Jeez, that man really would not take no for an answer. She'd scraped through Saturday without him bugging her mum, begging her to intervene and speak to her 'recalcitrant' youngest daughter. That was the actual word he'd used in a text to Leonora. She'd had to look it up, confirming again that he was an utterly condescending pillock. Fingers crossed, she could stall him a bit longer and if he dared turn up there, he'd be the sorriest man in Cheshire.

The first thing she did when she got back to her car that Friday afternoon was delete his photo from the contacts on her phone and now he was just a name, no smarmy face popping up and that in itself was so liberating. Then, she drove to Joel's brother's house, stopping at the first supermarket she came to where she bought enough ingredients to feed the street. She had that Friday feeling. It was the first Friday where she and Joel could spend the whole evening together and wake up in the same bed and she did not feel one ounce of guilt.

The next thing on her list was to change her phone number or block Caspar completely. She'd already done that on Facebook and Instagram. But first she wanted to tell her mum about their break-up in private which was scheduled for later that night, once they had the girls-only lunch and the Chinese banquet or whatever the kids decided on. She had planned to mention it to her sisters on the way back from the churchyard, knowing they'd keep shtum, but Rosina's meltdown had taken precedence and now it was her mum's time.

Leonora was actually very curious about what her mum wanted to tell them but then again, it was probably something really boring, and bound to be to do with the garden centre.

Violetta was already in the kitchen when she arrived to what could only be described as a top-class spread that Leonora would have been proud of herself. 'Mum, this looks fab... I think you've excelled yourself this time.'

Pulling out her chair she took a seat at the table and shouted to her sister, 'Rosie, hurry up or I'll eat all the salmon sandwiches.'

Coming over to the table, her mum kissed the top of Leonora's head and whispered, 'Violetta has just explained about Rosina so don't worry, I'll keep my eye on her for the rest of the week.'

Hearing footsteps in the corridor as Rosina appeared in the doorway, Carmen clapped her hands. 'And here she is at last, no show without Punch. Right, sit down and let's get this party started. Violetta, you can do the honours with the champagne. I thought I'd treat us and then once we've eaten, I'll tell you my news.'

The sound of Rosina pulling out her chair was joined by the pop of a cork and as glasses were filled, Leonora took a moment to glance around the table.

Violetta was sipping her drink, trying not to giggle at her mum's detailed description of every single sandwich filling and every single cake. Rosina fiddled with her napkin and looked miles away but at least she'd stopped crying and their mother, the great and wonderful Carmen was in her element, loving having her biggest chicks gathered around.

Allowing herself a quick thought of Joel, she enjoyed the tickle of excitement that flickered in her chest, and now she'd dealt with Caspar, she also enjoyed being the sister with a big secret. She had a right old tale to tell about her rekindled affair with Joel – but only when the time was right. They'd all be so surprised, she knew that, shocked she'd kept something important to herself because they'd always shared so much. It was usually Vi who dropped teatime bombshells and Rosina never put a foot wrong so today, she would be centre stage with her news. The tapping of a spoon on pine drew her back to what was going on around the table where her mum was making a little toast, to daughters, sisters, family and the future.

21

CARMEN

There was definitely something wrong with Rosina. After polishing off the champagne, Violetta was knocking back the white wine like her life depended on it, and as for Leonora, for want of a better word she looked slightly smug. It was all very odd and not how Carmen had envisaged her special lunch because she'd spent most of it watching her daughters like hawks. Did they really think she wouldn't notice the signs?

Violetta was staying over, a sure sign she intended to get merry... or was she drowning her sorrows? That was understandable. After all, her business was about to fold but there was something else. She seemed edgy and hadn't stopped checking her phone that never stopped bloody buzzing.

And yes, Leonora had that dreamy look of a teenager which made her suspect she and Caspar had made up after their little tiff, or whatever it was on Friday. Her suspicious mind was on red alert and she wondered if Caspar's flap had something to do with, dare she even think it, grandchild number six? If that was the case it would put the mockers on a big wedding, unless they intended to do it quickly or postpone again, which wouldn't be a problem. She decided once she'd told the girls her first bit of news she'd drop the hint about getting back to planning the wedding. The Bern thing was more of an encore and could wait.

It was Rosina who was really bothering Carmen. She was behaving like she did at her gran's wake, miles away. Lost in thought then being dragged into the present to exchange pleasantries but within moments she was gone again, eyes misted over, detached from everyone in the room. It could be visiting the churchyard that had brought back memories and from what Violetta had hurriedly explained, it sounded like work was getting on top of her. The only thing she couldn't fathom was why Rosina hadn't said something.

Carmen had always been there to lend a hand. Looking after a home with four kids in it was a challenge, especially when the twins arrived. Nevertheless, with a bit of help here and there Rosina had got through teething, toddler tantrums and teenage strops. Now they were older, the grandkids looked after themselves more and more and as for work, Rosina could run the garden centre with her eyes shut. So why was she so stressed? This was another conundrum she intended to solve by the end of the day but first, maybe she could distract all three of them with her announcement.

Petra was seated on her lap, snout resting on the table, transfixed by a lone egg and cress triangle that had her name on it. Tapping the table to bring order, Carmen got down to it.

'Right, I think it's time I told you my bit of news. Well, it's an idea really and I wanted your thoughts on it.'

Violetta piped up first. 'I knew it. You're going to start a reindeer farm, seeing as you've gone Christmas bonkers! Will you do sledge rides? Ooh, we could get huskies and a giant snow machine.'

Leonora tapped her sister's arm. 'Stop being sarky, Vi. Go on Mum, what is it?'

Taking a breath, Carmen told them her plan. 'I want to track down my dad.'

All three sisters gasped and before they could bombard her with questions she held up her hand, signalling they should wait. 'I always respected Mum's wishes and feelings, knowing how much it would hurt her if I searched for him and brought him back into our lives. He was a taboo subject, you know that, but for the past few years I've had a sense of time running out. He'd be in his seventies now, seventy-six to be precise, that's if he's still alive so now Mum isn't here and I can't upset her, I think it's the right time to try and find him.'

Violetta spoke first. 'I think it's a brilliant idea, Mum, so go for it. And I'm sure Gran would want you to do this. Maybe she even suspected you would once she was gone. Did she ever say anything to you? You know, give you her blessing?'

'No, nothing. Not directly, apart from what she said the last time we spoke but I don't want to talk about that today, it's too painful. I'd rather focus on the future.'

'We understand, don't we?' Leonora looked around the table and received nods from her sisters. 'So, where are you going to start?'

'I'm going to use a special agency that deals specifically with this kind of thing. I've already been in touch and I'm going to send them his details in the new year, not that I have much to go on, really. Only the two photos and a marriage certificate. Mum must have taken it so she could apply for a divorce but she never got round to it. I'm hoping there weren't too many George Samuel Wilsons who were born in South Shields in 1945. He could be anywhere now though. As you know, he was in the merchant navy and I always imagined that when Mum left him, he'd have gone back to sea so he might have settled abroad for all I know.'

Rosina reached over and took Carmen's hand. 'You have to do what's right for you, Mum. We all toed the line for Gran and as much as she was set in her ways I truly believe she will understand that you need to do this. I once tried to talk to her about Granddad and she point-blank refused to discuss it so no wonder you're a bit limited in the information department. At least you know where he was living in London. So with a bit of luck there will be a paper trail, merchant navy employment records for a start. I think you've got a really good chance of finding him, you know.'

'Do you? I hope so. I have to prepare myself for the fact he might have passed away but even then, I'd like to know what happened to him after we left. It's tormented me for years.'

When Violetta leant over and placed her hand on top of Rosina's, Leonora quickly followed suit. 'And we will be there every step of the way. I'd love to meet my granddad, you know. I bet he's just like you. I wonder what he'll look like now.'

Leonora piped up. 'I reckon he'll have changed loads from the photos upstairs and because they are a bit grainy and black and white, it's hard to imagine how he'd have changed. All you know is he had dark hair... What colour were his eyes?'

'They were very dark brown, and his hair was curly, blacky-brown like yours and Rosina's. I always remember it slicked back though, with Brylcreem and a quiff. Violetta has my grandma's hair apparently, so Mum said. I wish I had more photos but your gran left all the ones of her and my dad behind and the few I have of her family are faded so like Leonora said, it's hard to imagine my grandma's red hair, or my dad's navy uniform. I suppose that's what it is. I want to see him in colour, in real life, like the dad in my dreams with red-and-blue tattoos on his arm.'

'I bet that's where I get my love of ink from – Granddad. Ooh, if we find him we can compare tattoos and I could get one like his.' Violetta was animated, pouring herself another glass of wine as she spoke.

'Well that's fine, as long as it's not an anchor on your chest, or a swallow on your neck, okay!' Carmen loved that the girls were on board and was touched by their support. Her heart also went out to Violetta who, she suspected, would welcome her granddad with open arms: her need for a male role model had never waned. Which reminded Carmen about her suspicions regarding Leonora so she took the opportunity to mention the wedding, hoping it might drop a hint or reveal a clue.

'And, if all goes well and we find your granddad, we could invite him to your wedding, Leonora, which we need to start planning in the New Year. At last, I can get my notebook out again.'

All eyes were now focused on Leonora who it had to be said looked like a rabbit in the headlights as they all waited for her response which, when it came, wasn't quite what any of them expected.

'Sorry, Mum, that's not going to happen.'

It was as though the room and everyone in it held their breath, over on the sofa even Mitzi's ears pricked up and Arthur stopped mid-snore. Petra kept her eyes on the sandwich.

Once Carmen gathered her wits, she asked the obvious question. 'What do you mean? Why wouldn't it happen?' *She's pregnant, I knew it.*

Leonora looked calmly at each of them one by one, and then replied, 'Because I'm not getting married to Caspar. I broke up with him on Friday so while it's confession time, I might as well tell you that me and Joel are back together and in love. So, I'm sorry, Mum, no big white wedding. It's off, for good.'

Everyone around the table was stunned and simply stared at Leonora. Knowing at times like this there was only one thing to do and hearing Granny Sylvia's voice loud and clear, Carmen placed Petra on the floor, gave her the sandwich she'd been mesmerised by then went over to the Aga. It was time to put the kettle on. They all needed a cup of hot, sweet tea.

22

LEONORA

It was becoming a habit, blurting things out, and she hadn't meant to rain on her mum's parade about finding their granddad. However, all said and done, at least she'd got it over with. And so far nobody seemed very upset that Caspar was history. Or, that 'the one who'd broken her heart' was back on the scene.

When her mum returned from putting the kettle on, her default trauma setting, she had very flushed cheeks that could have been due to the wine or the non-wedding news. 'So when were you actually going to tell us about Caspar and how long has it been going on with Joel? I didn't even know he was back.'

'I was going to tell Vi and Rosie when we were out earlier, then Rosie got upset so I changed my mind and I didn't want to spend all of our nice lunch talking about knobhead so I was saving it till tonight. You know, after we've put our Vi to bed.' Leonora winked and expected her sister to find her jibe funny but was met with a blank expression. Vi was clearly unamused.

Soldiering on, Leonora decided to get it all off her chest. 'Okay, so Joel came back a month ago and we met up more or less straight away. Without going into the gory details, we basically knew it had been a mistake to split up. We starting seeing each other in secret whenever I could escape from Caspar. And yes, I know it's cheating and that's wrong but we couldn't help it. It's as simple as that and I certainly don't regret it.'

Her mum still looked confused. 'But you and Caspar seemed happy together. You never fall out or anything like that so I don't understand why all of a sudden you don't love him anymore. Or am I being naïve?'

'Nail on head, Mother. You're the only one who thinks he's okay when we all know he's a total pillock. Sorry Leo, but he is.' Violetta grabbed her glass and took a gulp of her wine.

Leonora laughed. 'No need to apologise, Vi. I agree. The thing is, Mum, we've been coasting along for ages. Lockdown, despite its horrors, actually gave me breathing space because I was already having second thoughts. I've been stupid I know and I should have called it a day after Gran died but it was a case of finding the right moment and not causing a drama. Then Joel came back and I just knew it really was over.'

'Oh, I see. I wish you'd told me how you felt though. That you were unhappy with him and actually, Violetta, I've had my reservations for a while but I kept them to myself because I didn't want to be the parent who interfered. I wish I'd said something now.'

Leonora could see her mum felt guilty. 'Mum, it's fine. I suppose at first I mixed up his concern with control. I was flattered and liked the attention he gave me. His proposal took me completely by surprise but it wasn't the worst offer I've ever had and at the time I was quite into him. I think over lockdown he started to bug me, calling here all the time, never giving me any space. It was like he was checking up on me which got on my nerves, especially when he knew where I was every day. Here, with you or down at the garden centre helping out.

'Then, when I went back to work, I realised how liberated I felt and literally couldn't wait to get there. It was a way of avoiding him and deep down I knew that was wrong. Joel coming home was the catalyst, the kick up the arse that I needed. My master plan was to get Christmas over with, endure being around him for a bit longer so it didn't ruin the Big Weekend, then I was going to tell him.'

'So why did you change your mind all of a sudden, if you were so worried about Mum's feelings?' Violetta sounded pissed off which took Leonora by surprise.

'He got on my nerves and I just blurted it out, in Selfridges to be precise. And for your information, miss narky-knickers-who's-had-too-much-to-drink, I'm still thinking about Mum because he's been texting me non-stop and I'm worried he's going to be a pain in the arse where the business is concerned. He's our accountant remember, and it might be awkward for Rosie too. So don't try and make out I've not thought all this through because I have. I've blocked him everywhere so he can't contact me and fingers crossed he's got the message. Anyway, it's done now so whatever he does, we'll just have to deal with it.'

When Violetta slammed her hands down on the tabletop then threw her head back, a loud 'HA' echoing around the kitchen caused all three dogs to bark. Everyone had her attention, stunned looks focusing directly on her angry face.

'Yes, Leo, we will all have to deal with it now, won't we! Seriously, sometimes you are *so* fucking selfish.'

Leonora felt her face burn red. '*Me*? Vi, what's wrong? Why am I selfish? What do you mean?'

'I mean that because of you hitching up with that fucking weirdo Caspar, and bringing him into all of our lives and then ditching him the minute lover boy comes back we – *me* in particular – are in the shit.'

If Leonora thought her face was red, in comparison her

sister's was deathly pale while angry green eyes stared her out. It was their mum's intervention that solved the puzzle.

'Violetta, what do you mean? Why does Leonora breaking up with Caspar affect you? What's going on?'

When Violetta's body sagged, whatever pent-up anger had been boiling her blood seemed to evaporate. She rested her elbows on the table and placed her face in her hands as Rosina, who hadn't said a word throughout, tentatively patted her back. When she finally looked up, their flame-haired sister concentrated her gaze on their mum while Leonora swallowed down nerves, knowing whatever Violetta was going to say, it wasn't going to be good.

'Because there are things that you don't know about me, none of you do, but Caspar does and while Leo and him were a thing my secret was safe. His too. I thought it was odd, that I started getting nasty messages from an unknown number on Friday. I knew who it was, though, but at first I thought he was drunk. I can only surmise at that point, he was hoping to win you back and wanted to make sure I didn't tell you the truth about him. Unfortunately now he knows Leo means it, he won't care if she finds out which leaves me wide open to blackmail which, going by the message I received first thing, is about to happen. He wants to meet me, his exact words were, *It's time we had another little chat.* I reckon if I don't do as he says, he's going to tell everyone.'

Leonora's brain felt like it was going to pop. 'Tell everyone what?'

Violetta looked up and across the table, straight into her sister's eyes. 'What I really do for a living.'

Nobody spoke, the only sound in the room was the clock on the mantelpiece ticking. And then Carmen. 'And what do you do, Violetta?'

Leonora gulped down nerves and watched her sister as she answered their mum.

'I'm so sorry, Mum, Leo, for what I'm going to tell you. And you too, Rosie. Please don't hate me, all I ask is you hear me out first.'

The clock struck three, making them all jump and then Violetta finally told the truth.

23

VIOLETTA

Tears pumped from Leonora's eyes as she rocked her sister and made shushing noises, stroking her hair, begging her to stop crying while their mum looked on, utterly shocked and uncharacteristically quiet.

She'd rushed around the table as soon as she'd heard Violetta's confession. 'Vi, shush now, please stop. It's okay, we will sort this, I promise, and I don't care about what you do. I swear I don't.'

Rosina was busying herself with cups and the teapot, her face ashen and in between spooning tea leaves, wiped away her tears, constantly looking back at her sisters and mum with wide-eyed concern.

When Carmen stood and moved around the table she seated herself next to Violetta and placed a gentle hand on her back while her voice was firm as she spoke. 'Violetta, stop now, that's enough. Come on, look at me.'

Doing as she was told, Violetta slowly pulled away from Leonora and turned to face her mum who took her hands in hers and rubbed them like she used to do when she'd fallen over on the path.

'Now you listen to me, young lady. I am not ashamed of you so you can wipe that thought straight out of your head this instant. Yes, I am shocked, just like your sisters are, but not in the way you think. It's more that for all this time you've been leading a double life and that's a biggie to get my head around. As for the rest, like Leo says, we will sort it out. I promise. Right, let's all calm down and talk this through. No point in panicking just yet, he's probably just calling your bluff. Now, drink some tea, or would you like some coffee?'

Accepting squares of kitchen roll from Rosina, Violetta nodded, the swell of relief on hearing her mum's words almost setting her off again. Feeling a kiss being planted on her head, she blew her nose while her mum returned to her seat at the end of the table. Rosina took her place by Violetta's side, still quiet, probably trying to digest what she'd heard.

Violetta watched as her mum lifted the teapot. 'Tea is fine, thanks Mum, and Rosie, and you, too, Leo. I'm so sorry for snapping at you and I wish you didn't have to find out what he's like the way you did.'

Leonora poured herself some wine, shaking her head as she spoke. 'I'm actually glad I know the truth. He's an out-and-out weirdo and I've had a lucky escape, and from what you said when he realised it was you in the hotel room, rather than being shit scared, it gave him a kick. God, I hate him so much.'

'Oh yeah. He thought it was funny. I can see him now, fixing a drink from the mini bar then he lay there on the bed more or less naked, telling me how it was going to be. He reversed the roles in an instant. There was no way I could tell you without exposing myself, and he said if I did tell you then he'd make sure everyone at Darcy's school, the garden centre, the village, everyone everywhere would know what I did.'

Her mum huffed loudly.

Violetta carried on. 'To be honest, I'm not ashamed of what I do. It's a service I provide. I do appreciate that others and even you three might think differently but no way on this earth was I going to bring shame on you or my daughter. That's why I had to agree.'

Leonora had switched to tea, vigorously stirring in sugar as she spoke, a deep frown splitting her forehead. 'He is such a sleaze and, as always, loves being in control, doesn't he? Never in all my life have I hated someone as much as I hate him right now. I feel like going over to his place and punching his head in.'

'Darling, I think the sugar has dissolved now.' Carmen smiled and nodded at Leonora's cup as she spoke. 'What if he's bluffing? I could just as easily have a word with Edward at the accountants. He and I go back a long way and I'm sure once he realises what that little toad is like he'll give him a stern talking to or, better, his marching orders.'

Violetta's heart melted at her mum's innocence and frankly, totally rubbish idea. 'But to get Caspar in trouble, you'd have to explain about me. Do you want your old friend knowing that? And you can't sack someone for the things they do in their personal life, I'm sure of that. Rosie, is that true?'

Rosina had been listening to everything but saying little, however, she spoke up to confirm Violetta's theory. 'Yes, you'd be wide open to being sued I reckon and just because you've known Edward for years doesn't mean he won't blab at the golf club. You'd be wasting your time, Mum. The best you could hope for is that Edward takes him off our account. You could say you're uncomfortable with it now he and Leo aren't together. That's totally understandable I reckon.'

'Well, I'll do that then. I'm sorry, I'm not thinking straight because I'm angry. There's still a slim chance that once he's got over being dumped he'll calm down. Right now he's hurt and kicking out. If you like I will ring him myself and tell him that we all know about what you do and it's no big deal. That might do the trick.'

Leonora rolled her eyes at Violetta, then tried to get through to their mum. 'You're not getting it, are you? He will be so pissed off that he's not going to wriggle his way into our family and, as Gran always said, the business, that he will want revenge. That's what he's like and if he enjoys getting his kicks the way Vi described, Lord only knows what his nasty mind is capable of. He will probably spread rumours for the fun of it. He's still in control.'

Carmen slumped back in her chair. 'Oh, yes, I see what you mean.'

Violetta could see the worry that was spreading across her mum's face. It mirrored what was going on in her heart. This was exactly what she'd been dreading and had spent a whole week churning over and over in her head. At least now she could to talk it through with her family and the relief was immense.

'Do you know what I'm scared of the most? If he starts spreading rumours at school. It's so easy to do in anonymous messages like the ones he's been sending me. He could tell the head. I'll have parents whispering behind my back and all it takes is for one of the older kids to hear and say something to Darcy. Or that fucking smart-arse Kyra. How could I look my daughter in the eye if she asks me questions? I'll die of shame, I know I will.'

Leonora still looked mad as hell. 'What exactly do the texts say?'

Taking her phone from her back pocket, Violetta opened the app and turned the screen so they could all see. 'This is his last one. It's a screenshot of my online ad. Obviously it hasn't got my real name on it and you can't see my face, but the message below is clear.'

I think this should be your new Facebook profile, or I could do a review for the garden centre. Oops, sorry, looks like I posted a photo by mistake. I'll be in touch.

'See, he means business. Scroll through, they're all there.' Violetta passed over her phone and looked on as Leonora began reading the messages.

After a few seconds she offered it to Rosie who shook her head so instead, she leant over and gave it to her mum who frowned at the screen. 'Blackmail is a crime. I think we should ring the police.'

Violetta knew that was a no-go. 'But the texts aren't from his phone – he's obviously got a spare. I couldn't prove it was him.'

'So what are we going to do?' asked Carmen. 'It looks like we have two options. We either sit here and wait for him to strike or, I speak to him and see if I can persuade him to play nice. He's greedy and money mad, so we might have to give him what he wants.'

The hairs on Violetta's neck stood on end. 'Mum, *no!* I can see what you're thinking and you are not paying him off.'

Leonora agreed immediately. 'Vi's right. You can't trust someone like him. It's a terrible idea and asking for more trouble down the line. It could never end.'

Carmen was vehement. 'But we have to protect Darcy. I don't care about the bloody garden centre. So what if the customers hear a bit of tittle-tattle, or the vicar and half the village are shocked to the core. They can all sod off and mind their own business but what I won't have is my granddaughter's schooldays ruined by cruel kids and gossipy parents so somehow, we have to stop him.'

Then out of the blue came a tremulous voice. 'I know how to stop him.'

You could have heard a pin drop when all heads turned

towards Rosina who wasn't actually looking at them, just staring straight ahead. Her face had gone from alabaster to rose pink and there was a sheen of perspiration on her forehead. Her body looked rigid, her hands were clasped tightly in front of her on the table. She looked serene, trance-like.

It was Violetta who spoke first and broke the spell. 'What do you mean, Rosie? How can you stop him?'

Still not looking their way Rosina answered, her voice surer, and clear. 'Because I saw him kill someone. He knocked them down in his car and then drove away... and could someone get me a glass of water because I think I'm going to fai...'

When Rosina's body crumpled and her head hit the table, her mother screamed as Violetta and Leonora sprang from their chairs, all of them wearing horrified expressions. While Leonora gently called Rosina's name and tried to revive her, Violetta held Carmen tight, both their bodies trembling.

Amidst the chaos and while she willed Rosina to wake up, Violetta felt the phone in her back pocket buzz and for the first time in what seemed like forever, she wasn't scared of what the message would say.

24

ROSINA

When she came round she was lying on the sofa. She had no idea how she'd got there or why everyone was staring at her. Then it hit. She'd told them about Caspar. It was as though she couldn't hold it in. Any of it. She had felt so weary and heavy, and sick of people like Norman and Caspar, men who reminded her of her father. Ruining people's lives with their bullying, controlling ways. She couldn't let Vi suffer, or little Darcy. Enough was enough. That's why she'd said it and actually it had been quite easy and for a moment she'd experienced immense relief, like a whoosh of everything pent-up leaving her body.

Then she woke up, on Mitzi's sofa.

Leonora was seated on the floor by her side, holding her hand as Violetta stepped forward and passed her a glass of water. 'Sip this, Rosie, it'll make you feel better.'

Doing as she was told, Rosina took the glass, grateful for the cool liquid and a moment to compose herself.

Violetta pushed Rosina's legs to the side and squashed onto the end of the sofa. 'You gave us such a fright, Rosie. Have you been eating properly? I'd noticed you'd lost weight but you're actually gaunt now. It was like lifting a feather when me and Leo brought you over here. You're not poorly, are you?'

'No, I promise I'm not.' Rosina gave her sister a weak smile but still hadn't found the courage to look in her mum's direction so when she spoke, it was unavoidable. For the first time ever Rosina couldn't read her mum's face.

'So what's wrong, Rosina? Take your time but I'm worried. We all are and I've never seen you like this. You said you saw an accident. Was it the one on the road by the trail car park? Did you see what happened?'

She managed a nod, and couldn't fathom if her mum was annoyed with her or merely confused. 'Yes, I saw it all. It was Caspar who knocked the man over. Then he drove away.'

'Oh dear God!' Leonora let go of Rosina's hand and covered her mouth, her eyes round with shock.

Violetta. 'So it was a hit-and-run?'

'Yes.'

'The sick bastard!' Violetta sounded disgusted while Leonora looked like she was in shock.

And then her mother asked the dreaded question that Rosina knew would blow their world apart. 'So were you driving past? And why didn't you tell the police? Why haven't you said something before now? I don't understand what's going on, Rosina.'

Leonora had gathered her wits. 'Mum, give her time. You can tell she's traumatised by what she saw. It's okay, Rosie, it wasn't your fault. Lots of people panic when they see stuff like that so don't be worrying about the police, they'll understand why you didn't ring them.'

Rosina shook her head, knowing what she was about to say would further add to their confusion but she had to take it steady, not just blurt it all out in one hysterical go. 'It's not what any of you think and if you thought Vi's confession was a shock, wait till you hear the mess I'm in.'

Her inquisitors looked from one to the other but it was her mum that Rosina was most concerned about. When her face softened, the voice that sliced through the hush was calm and measured, no panic, no drama, no fear. 'Just tell us, Rosina. Whatever it is, we will stick together as a family. I will sort it out, I promise.'

'You make it all sound so simple, Mum. You always do and I wish I'd come to you earlier because now I have the death of a man on my conscience. And if that wasn't bad enough, my shame, the secret I've been keeping actually caused it. So before I tell you, I want you to know I'm sorry. More sorry than you will ever know.'

When nobody spoke – and who could blame them after a speech like that – Rosina took their shocked silence as her cue and before she was interrupted took a lungful of Appleton air, gripped the glass of water, and then told them all the truth.

Leonora had made coffee then called them over to the table while Rosina stood over the sink, splashing her face with cold water to de-puff her swollen eyes. It was done. All out in the open. Every sordid detail of the sad life she'd been living for months. And to give her family credit, none of them had keeled over from the shock of finding out their sister was an addict and in terrible debt, never mind being an accessory to a fatal road accident. After drying her face with the tea towel she turned to face them, her stoical sisters and steel-faced mother.

Resigned to a further grilling, she went over to the table and took her seat while they waited quietly and patiently for Violetta to return from the loo. When she did, her first words were an attempt to lighten the mood; it was her go-to tension reliever.

'Right, I'm back. I hope I didn't miss anything... like Mum confessing to being a serial killer and burying the bodies under the garden centre, and that Bern used to be called Bernice and Gran was a spy in the war.'

Leonora chuckled as she passed around mugs of coffee. 'Vi, what are you like!' Taking a sip, she looked along the table to her mum who was ominously silent. 'What are we going to do, Mum? About everything. I feel like ringing Caspar up right now and telling him what a sicko he is.'

Rosina remained silent. She was depleted in every way, too exhausted to speak or think so she let the others do it for her.

Carmen rubbed her forehead as she replied, her tone telling them all who was in control of the situation. 'For a start we need to be sensible and very cautious. None of us will speak to Caspar. Not until we have a plan.'

Leonora was aghast. '*A plan?* What do you mean? The first thing we should do is tell the police what he did. He can't get away with what he did to that man.'

To this, Carmen asked a question of her own. 'You mean the man who tried to blackmail and rape your sister? A man that has probably made many people's lives a complete misery with his inflated interest rates, feeding on their desperation to make a fortune. And what do you think he would have done if he'd caught up to Rosina? Beat her up, dragged her into the forest and raped her, taken her car keys? I'm sorry, Leonora, but I'm having trouble dredging up an ounce of sympathy for someone like that.'

Leonora lifted her palms in surrender. 'Well, I suppose when you put it like that. I was just thinking of his family, if he has one. Surely they will be upset and want justice.'

Rosina knew the answer to that. 'He hasn't got family, no

kids. It's common knowledge that he lives fast and loose, always bragging about his young girlfriends and jet-set lifestyle. He fancied himself as one of the Cheshire set but I'm not sure if that was the case. That's not the issue, though, is it. The issue is doing the right thing, whatever that is.'

Violetta piped up next with plenty to say on the subject. 'Well, I'm sure it will come as no surprise to any of you that I have zero sympathy for either of them. Caspar has been cheating on Leo ever since they met. He told me in his fake-name emails that he'd been seeing doms and escorts for years and I'm sorry, Leo, unlike me, escorts get their hands dirty, so to speak.'

Carmen sighed. 'Dear Lord, you have such a way with words, Violetta.'

Shrugging, Violetta continued with her analysis. 'And as for that fucking loan shark, if he wasn't dead I'd kick him in the bollocks for what he tried to do to Rosie, never mind trying to take her car too. He's a scumbag and people like him feed on despair and get a thrill out of thinking they have power over someone. They disgust me and I'd be more than happy to spit on his grave.'

Leonora gave her sister a sideways glance. 'Jeez, Vi. Say it like it is, why don't you?'

Violetta gave another shrug as her mum agreed. 'You're right, about both of them but let's focus on practicalities first. Starting with you. Our main aim is to prevent Caspar from blabbing about your ex-career and most of all, Darcy being upset. Are you really giving it up, do you mean it?'

This was met by furious nodding from Violetta. 'One hundred per cent. No way am I risking this ever happening again. It was a massive wake-up call and after I left here on Friday I went home and deleted all my social media accounts,

Dina's I mean. I shut her down. I promise you, she's gone for good. And I did the same with my own, just in case.'

Violetta took a gulp of her coffee, two red spots appearing on her cheeks as her green eyes flashed emerald which told Rosina her sister was telling the truth.

Carmen gave a nod. 'Good.' Then she addressed Rosina and Leonora. 'You two won't know this but Violetta's bakery is closing which means she might struggle financially for a while, until she decides what to do going forward. So she's going to come and live here with Darcy and let out her house to cover the mortgage. Rosina, I'd like you to take her on at the garden centre. Violetta has a little nest egg saved but I would prefer her not to dip into that. Let's face it, she's earned it the hard way.' Raising an eyebrow Carmen gave the hint of a smirk.

They all managed a chuckle at that, even Rosina. 'Of course, just let me know when you want to start. There'll be loads to do in the January sales. I'll sort it and it will be nice having you there and here, too, like the old days.'

She could feel emotion swelling so was glad when Leonora interrupted to ask a serious question of her own. 'How are we going to keep Caspar quiet though? I can't bear the fact he works for the people who look after our accounts. I feel invaded, don't you, Mum?'

All eyes were on their mum. 'Because as Rosina so rightly said earlier, she knows how to stop him. He thought he held all the cards but now, we do. He has killed a man and left the scene of a crime. I'm not sure what the penalty is for that but he could be looking at prison, never mind the scandal and, he's missed a very important factor in all this.'

'What?' Violetta frowned.

'Well, for a start, who the hell gave him the right to threaten you in the first place? He should realise it works both ways. We could tell all his colleagues and clients a thing or two about how he gets his kicks between meetings. What a very professional, positive mental image they'll have of the chap who's come to audit their books. I'm sorry, girls, but I am absolutely livid that two of you have been held to ransom by men like these. How dare they make you feel low, and you, Leonora, having to put up with a slimy control freak! As far as I'm concerned they can all just piss off.'

Leonora was open-mouthed, so was Violetta and it took Rosina to speak on their behalf after listening in silence to the conversation. 'Who the hell are you and what have you done with our mother?'

When they all convulsed into laughter, it took a moment or two to regain composure. Then Rosina noticed her mum's gaze and serious expression. The room fell silent.

'And now we have to sort out your problem, Rosina.'

Rosina's stomach turned. She had no idea how the hell they could solve any of it, but rather than interrupt she listened and accepted Violetta's hand when it reached across the table.

'As far as I am aware, if you witness a crime, nobody is legally obliged to report it to the police. It's more of a moral obligation to help bring someone to justice. Which means you won't get into any trouble for not telling the police what you saw.'

Leonora chipped in. 'But that also means Caspar is going to get away with what he did.'

'Oh no. You mark my words, he is not going to get away with it and he will pay for what he's done to that man and you and Violetta, with his silence. But I will deal with him so let's focus on your sister for now.'

Rosina swallowed down nerves as she listened, feeling like a teenager again but not caring if she was grounded forever, as long as her mum sorted it all out.

'Right, Rosina. First of all we're going to clear your debts.'

'But Mum–' She found herself silenced by the simple raising of a palm and her mother's glare.

'We can do this today. It will take seconds. As soon as possible you and I will have a proper chat about what's been going on in that head of yours to get you in this situation. From what I've read, it's not always as simple as a cheeky game of bingo getting out of hand.'

Rosina couldn't speak so when Violetta piped up, her gentle words prompted the tears she'd been holding back. 'Mum's right. It's been a big day and we are all wiped out, but you do need to talk to Mum, and maybe think about getting some counselling, after New Year. I'll come with you if you want but in the meantime if you struggle, tell one of us. It's killing me knowing you've been going through all this alone, Rosie, so please, promise me you'll ask for help.'

Rosina could only nod as she felt Violetta's fingers twining around hers and being locked together that way reminded her of when they were little. Huddled in the bottom bunk, shivering in the cold as she'd tried to distract Violetta from the monster she thought lived in the wardrobe, when the real monster was downstairs, shouting at their mum.

Maybe it was time to let her little sister take care of her for a change because she was so tired of being mother hen. And then two thoughts occurred, like a thunderclap that made her wince. 'What about what I owe Norman? The loan was between us, as far as I know. And Lou... Oh God, what am I going to tell him? I can't keep a secret like this from my husband. Not for the rest of our lives but I feel so ashamed. I can't tell you how low I feel about myself right now. This is why I've been going mad with worry. The thought of you all finding out.'

Suddenly two more sets of hands slid across the table, covering hers and Violetta's. It was her mum who answered the question.

'We'll wait and see what happens with the loan. Maybe someone will come knocking, maybe they won't. I suspect that little arrangement was designed to avoid the taxman and this agreement you signed was a way of extracting more money; but either way, unless someone turns up here with it, nobody will be getting paid. We can cross that bridge another time. As for Lou. That's entirely your call. What has been discussed around this table is between us and us alone.'

Two nodding heads gave the signal for her mum to continue. 'If Violetta is okay with Lou knowing her part, again, that's her call. If not, you'll have to keep her secret and just tell him your story. If I know your husband as I think I do, he will support you all the way. And you're right, Rosina. Carrying a secret like this through a marriage won't be easy so I suggest you tell him the truth.'

Leonora agreed. 'There's been enough secrecy to last us a lifetime and as Vi said, we'll be here for you Rosie, like always.'

Violetta was next. 'And I want you to tell Lou about me. As I said I'm not ashamed of my old job. This is my body and I'll do what I want with it. I know Lou is a good man, and Bern too, and I don't want either of you to have secrets from the men you love. It's outsiders that scared me, people who would have a field day gossiping and making stuff up. So, Mum and Rosie, you have my permission to tell them, it's fine.'

Rosina turned to her side and gave Violetta a hug. 'Thank you, Vi.'

Their Mum then used her stern voice, the one none of them really took any notice of anyway. 'Honestly, you three with your mysteries! I don't know what's got into you all. If you'd have just come to me and told me what was going on I'm sure all of this could have been avoided. So from now on, *no more secrets*! Or else.'

Violetta freed herself from Rosina's embrace. 'Well, if you must know, mother, I blame you for everything.'

'Me! Why?' She rested a hand on her chest and looked shocked.

'It's obvious. And I think I speak for Leo and Rosie too. You are perfect, always have been, so how could we tell you we'd messed up so badly?'

'Don't be daft. I've always been very understanding of your cock-ups, no matter what you did.' Her mum looked affronted.

Rosina backed Violetta up. 'No, seriously, Mum. I get why Leo didn't want to tell you about Joel, who I'm very chuffed about, by the way.' She winked at Leonora who beamed and gave her one back.

'And again with Vi, who I must say has done a sterling job of pulling the wool over our eyes for so long and in my opinion missed her way and should be a secret agent.' At that, they all laughed as she grabbed her mum's hand and then became serious. 'But this Christmas is for you and none of us wanted to spoil all your plans because if anyone deserves their perfect day, or weekend or however long you want it to go on for, you do.'

Violetta spoke next. 'Rosie's right. You've never ever let us down and for as long as we can remember you've been the best mum and grandma. And I know you never talk about it much, but you put what happened when you were little behind you, and focused on us, always giving us the best Christmas Day you could so now it's our turn to make it special for you.'

Leonora agreed. 'And that's why in our own messed-up ways, without knowing we all had secrets, too, nobody wanted to be the one who ruined it. You're ace, Mum. You really are the best example anyone could wish for, it's as simple as that.' Leonora's voice cracked on her final word, and when her mum spoke hers was slightly croaky too.

'Well, those were lovely words and thank you for trying to

protect me but you shouldn't put me on a pedestal, you know. I'm not perfect, I'm really not and I've made mistakes and done things that have kept me awake at night so in future, please remember that. We all have our secrets.'

Rosina tutted. 'Well, I find that very hard to believe. In my eyes you're our rock.'

Carmen smiled. 'Actually, I think the true rock of our family was the person who is missing from the table right now. Your gran was the strongest, most honourable woman I know and okay, she had her views that could make us cringe sometimes but she put me first always, and then you three when she came to live with us and honestly, without her help I wouldn't have been able to build the business. She's where we get our strength from, she was the glue, the one who kept us all together and I miss her so much.'

Rosina remembered that her gran always told them it was okay to cry, let it all out and then get on with it, so they did. They shared a moment of quiet, all four overcome by emotion. The clock ticked and from the corner of her tear-filled eye, Rosina imagined her gran, sitting at the end of the table, smiling as she flicked her lighter. It was probably her imagination but she could have sworn there was a hint of cigarette smoke in the air, and someone whispering in her ear.

I was listening, Rosie, my love. And I always will.

25

CARMEN

Violetta, in her inimitable way, was the one who brought them all back to earth with an unsurprising statement. 'Ladies, I need another drink! And not a mug of sweet tea, either.'

'Well, why break the habit of a lifetime?' Leonora was wiping her eyes with her sleeves, giving Rosina a wry smile as she spoke.

'Hey... don't knock it. I have three able-bodied babysitters at my beck and call and after the week I've had I'm going to make the most of it. And being able to conk out in my old room cuddled up to Darcy. That mattress is still the most comfy one in the world.'

At this Carmen smiled. She loved the fact that when they stayed, Violetta and Darcy still slept in the same bedroom that had Violetta's name plate on the door. She also loved how her three daughters had stuck together over the last couple of hours and rallied, their usual banter creeping back into what had been a heavy set of conversations.

It would probably take a while for her to truly digest everything she'd heard and out of the three confessions,

Leonora's had troubled her the least while Rosina's and Violetta's had almost given her heart failure.

Not that she had let it show. First rule of being a mum is wearing an impassive expression while your children tell you something you really don't want to know – like the time a letter went home to all the Year 3 parents about stealing food; and at bedtime, Leonora admitted it was her who'd taken Philip Bolton's orange Kit Kat from his lunchbox and eaten it in the toilets. Show even a flicker before they've confessed, they will clam up; and if you overreact, they will never tell you anything ever again! It was the law.

In all honesty, she'd been that shocked during Violetta's outburst that she couldn't even think straight, let alone speak. So whatever expression she'd portrayed during that, and then Rosina's astounding revelation wasn't actually down to acting, more being totally and utterly dumbfounded.

It was seeing her daughters' distress that had really and truly rocked her. And that alone brought such a rush of white-hot rage that it wiped out all traces of shock, clearing her head and allowing her to think straight. They were relying on her. She had to pull herself together and fast. And if it hadn't been for her ridiculous hankering for a happy-ever-after Christmas, they'd have been able to nip some of it in the bud even sooner.

And there was something else that bothered her. Their insistence that she was perfect, beyond reproach. Was that why they felt unable to confide in her? She hoped not. God only knew she wasn't perfect yet no matter how many times she'd told them, they wouldn't have it.

Then again, through her own rose-coloured specs she remembered her mother, the great Granny Sylvia, as being beyond reproach when they all knew she could also be a complete nightmare. Refusing to eat her Kentucky Fried chicken when she found out it was halal, turning off her favourite soaps if one of the characters turned out to be gay and then thinking Nigel Farage was the answer to all her prayers.

It was an easy thing to do, turn a blind eye to a parent's mistakes and forgive them. Like she'd forgiven her mum for taking them away from London and a place her dad could easily have found them, or rang them on the phone. And then there was belief and trust that what a parent says is true, and does things for the best. She'd believed her mum when she said her dad had run away with Martha but what if he'd changed his mind and decided he loved them more? He might have wanted to come back. In the end Carmen chose right over wrong. She'd been there when Martha came round to tell them what her dad had done. He'd been bad, going off with another lady and that was that.

It was the same with her own children. Rosina had witnessed her father's behaviour first-hand, and Violetta and Leonora had taken everyone's word that it was true. Yet still, after all these years none of them had ever questioned her role in it all. None of them had been cross with a silly young girl who had thought she knew best and tried to trap a man not once, but twice with a baby. It was she who had insisted they stayed at Appleton, a place Sebastian hated. It had driven him away and made him bitter so that he sought solace in drink and women he met on his travels. That was no excuse for the way he'd treated her but then again did she have an excuse for the things she'd done?

'Mum, earth to Mum.' Leonora clinked two glasses together in a further attempt to attract Carmen's attention. 'Would you like a glass of wine? You were miles away then.'

'Yes, that would be lovely. And then we need to get ready. The others will be here soon and heaven help us if we're not raring to go. And Bern can't wait to be in charge of the train... Ooh, which reminds me.'

Violetta stopped mid-pour. 'Reminds you of what?'

'That I had two things to tell you but somehow... Oh yes, it was Leonora's news about Joel that diverted us and then all hell broke loose. Anyway, I have something else I'd like to tell you, apart from looking for my dad.' Carmen took one of the glasses of wine and a fortifying sip, noticing as she did that all three daughters had her in their sights and were waiting.

'Well, and I know we've taken our time about it, but Bern is moving in here, to Appleton, with me.' There, she'd said it and had no idea why she felt so hot and bothered because they were used to seeing him there, had been for years. Maybe it was the silence around the table that unnerved her. 'Somebody please say something! Put me out of my misery for goodness' sake.'

Violetta did just that with a round of applause and a *woohoo*, followed by her sisters. 'At bloody last! What's brought all this on? Oh, oh. I know. You've got Berny-Bernice pregnant, haven't you, Mum?'

Carmen couldn't help laugh at Violetta's ridiculous question and took it in good part, she had no other option really. 'No, I haven't got Bern pregnant, you monster. Sometimes I wonder where your mind goes, I really do.'

Leonora threw her head back and laughed. 'I think that's a conversation for another day, don't you? When Mum's out of the room because I am *dying* to know what you got up to, Vi. Aren't you, Rosie?'

Rosina had declined wine and was drinking water, saying she preferred to keep a clear head in case she got overemotional again. 'I'm not really sure... well, actually, yes. Is it like that book? *Fifty Shades* of rubbish.'

Violetta tutted. 'Kind of... Anyway, *I* want to know all about Joel and when we get to see him again. We always liked him, didn't we?'

Around the table heads nodded which prompted Carmen to

make a suggestion. 'Why don't you ask him to call round later. He can have some takeaway or if he's free, meet us down at the garden centre. He's more than welcome.'

Leonora looked thrilled, and then cautious. 'Really? Are you sure? It's not too soon, you know, after dumping Caspar?'

'Are you mad? Don't start acting like Miss Prim and Proper when you've been jumping his bones…'

'Violetta! Do you have to be so brutally frank all of the time?' Carmen gave her 'the look' then turned to Leonora. 'It's fine. Just invite him, and Caspar is history so off you go. I can see you're eager to ring him.'

Pushing back her chair Leonora blew her mum a kiss then shot from the room as Rosina asked another Caspar-related question. 'So, are you going to deal with him, Mum, or should Vi do it?'

Carmen replied, 'I'll do it. I'm looking forward to putting that man in his place. I'll ring him first thing and set up a meeting and in the meantime, Violetta, you should just ignore him, or block his number. I'll suggest that Leonora does too.'

'Are you sure you can handle him on your own? I'd rather come along in case he gets cocky and I have a few things I'd like to say to him when you've finished.' Violetta drained her glass and slammed it on the table.

'I will be perfectly fine and the last thing we need is you being arrested for GBH so, let's forget about him now and enjoy the rest of the evening.' Carmen knew only too well what Violetta was like when she lost her temper. She hoped that her daughter had never entertained a client on a day she was in one of her moods. Quite shocked by her own train of thought and really not wanting to go there, she quickly erased it from her mind and smiled, seeing Leonora enter the kitchen. 'So, what did he say?'

Leonora was animated, her face flushed with happiness.

'He's going to meet us at the centre later. I think he's a bit nervous if I'm honest but glad everything is out in the open.'

'So, all that's left is to tease the life out of Bern when he gets here... bless his cotton socks. He doesn't know what he's let himself in for, does he? Does he know me and Darcy are coming back?' Violetta filled her glass, smiling mischievously.

'Oh, leave him alone, Vi. You are such a tease. And yes he does. I told him on Friday and he was very pleased. It's going to be lovely having you here and I am so looking forward to seeing Darcy every day.' That was the icing on the cake, having the littlest grandchild to stay.

'And she will love wrapping you around her finger every day too.'

Leonora then turned her attention to Rosina who was very quiet. 'Are you okay, Rosie?'

'I'm just a bit nervous about telling Lou, that's all.'

Carmen's heart went out to her. 'Would it help if I was there, when you told him?'

Rosina shook her head. 'No thanks, Mum. It's something I need to do myself. I just need to pick a quiet time and then I'll get it done with, well before next weekend, don't worry.'

Carmen then remembered something. 'Okay, and when we've finished our drinks you and I can go and sort this transfer out. I'd rather do it straight away then it's one thing off your mind.'

Again, Rosina looked crestfallen and Carmen knew it was going to be a long road for her eldest. Clearing her debts was just the start of a journey and it would take time to heal whatever wounds resulted in her telling Lou, and for the guilt and shame she so clearly felt to ease.

Leonora took the attention from Rosina with a question for Violetta. 'So, what's going on with Candy? Will you miss working at the bakery? I used to love coming to see you there. It was a cool place, a real French vibe.'

'Oh, basically she's going on a voyage of discovery on a barge, down the Manchester Ship Canal with Dermot where they hope to rock the boat and make lots of babies.' Violetta was getting merry and giggled at her own joke.

'I wish I'd not asked now.' Leonora looked confused.

'And I won't really miss the bakery. It was more a way of looking legit than anything but I did love chatting with the customers. That was my favourite bit really, and I knew most of them by name and what they liked.' Violetta looked a bit wistful until Leonora popped her bubble.

'I bet you did. I can see it now. Good morning, would you like a *hot cross bum*, sir? Or some *whipped* cream on top of your hot chocolate, and maybe I could interest you in a lovely *Queen of Tarts* and ooh, ooh... this is the best, wait for it... perhaps one of my specialties, sir, making your *sausage roll*.' Both she and Violetta were in hysterics and Rosina had cheered up, too, when they heard the front door slam and voices heading their way.

The dogs went crazy and raced off up the hall and above the racket, stifling her own giggles, Carmen called order. 'Right, that's enough. You two are terrible once you start.'

Leonora placed a finger over her lips while Violetta zipped hers and threw away the key. Before Carmen could say another word the kitchen was invaded by grandchildren and the dogs, followed by Lou and Bern.

Immediately bombarded by hugs, Darcy asked why they weren't ready while Ella and Lola were raiding the crisp cupboard and Max and Tilly rummaged in the drawer for takeaway menus. Carmen took a deep breath and tried to take in the scene of total mayhem. Not for the first time in her life, she felt shattered before the evening had even begun while at the same time, dramas and revelations aside, knew without a doubt that she wouldn't have it any other way.

Their mini family drama had been dealt with, so hopefully that meant no more big surprises, unless they were the type delivered by Santa and left under the tree. She was almost there. Five days to go until The Big Christmas Weekend and she couldn't wait.

26

CASPAR

Nature Trail car park, Appleton

U nder the circumstances it wasn't the ideal meeting place but there was no way he wasn't going to agree when Carmen had texted him. The word that came to mind when he read her message was 'bingo'. Even though it was slightly cryptic he knew exactly what her text meant although her choice of venue could have been better. Coincidence, that's all it was. And it looked like he'd got away with killing the nutter who'd run into the road.

From what he'd heard on the local news, the police were following a number of lines of enquiry and one of his colleagues had insinuated that the dead man was a bit of a rogue and probably had gangland connections. That's why he was meeting in a remote car park. He'd even suggested the killers might have dragged the body on the road after they'd killed him, to cover their tracks. All this ridiculous gossip was music to Caspar's ears.

With a self-satisfied grin, he checked the clock and saw he

was on time for the rendezvous. He couldn't wait to hear what Carmen had to say but as he'd lain in bed the night before, had imagined most of it. He couldn't see her pleading with him to keep her skanky daughter's secret. From what he knew of his ex-mother-in-law-to-be she wasn't the type. He had her down as more of a tough cookie negotiator who was prepared to offer a nice pay-off in return for his silence. That would suit him right down to the ground, plus a good word in his boss's ear and, better still, once he mentioned the little nugget he'd recently discovered in the books, he'd be able to turn the screw just a little bit more.

Dear oh dear, Carmen. What naughty little girls you have.

It was a pity he didn't have anything on his boring-as-fuck ex-fiancée. Then again, he shouldn't be too greedy. One way or another he was going to make them all pay. Two years he'd wasted, cosying up to mother superior and faking it with her daughter and he couldn't even bear thinking of that old hag Sylvia. Pursing her cat's-arse lips as she puffed away on her ciggies and giving him the evil eye. He despised that woman, even her accent grated and the way she held counsel at the end of the kitchen table like some all-seeing matriarch. He'd been so glad when she finally pegged it. He'd even thanked covid for giving him the perfect excuse not to attend the funeral or to have to comfort his fiancée whose grief was worse than a soggy, snotty hanky and Christ, she went through a few of those!

The entrance to the car park was up ahead and as he took the bend, it was impossible not to wince at the memory of hitting a man side-on and have his rag-doll body bounce on and off your bonnet. At least he didn't hit the windscreen but he'd triggered the airbags and made a dent in the paintwork that was now being sorted at a backstreet garage in Manchester. It was too risky sending it to a local repair shop or even one in Macclesfield. The big city was a safer bet. The only downside was having to borrow his mother's electric runabout. He'd parked well away from work that morning. Mondays were bad enough without being ridiculed by everyone in the office.

Pulling along the track, his skull connecting with the roof of the tiny Kia as he hit the potholes, Caspar spotted a car and there leaning on the bonnet, was Carmen.

Eager or what? She must be worried. Bless her.

Pulling up beside her Range Rover, Caspar turned off the engine. He didn't feel remotely nervous which gave him a kick. He was holding all the cards and was going to enjoy the game. Getting out, he instantly felt the bite of cold air in contrast to the stuffy, squashed interior of the warm car. It was bracing and gave him a spring in his step as he made his way towards Carmen who remained where she was, bundled up in her Barbour jacket, her jeaned legs crossed at the ankles, which were covered by stout walking boots. She looked casual, not only in her dress but demeanour, too, and for a teeny moment, it unnerved him. Only a second though.

'So, Carmen. To what do I owe the pleasure?' He had rehearsed this bit and was determined to open the show.

Carmen stood. Her hands remained in her pockets as she took a couple of paces then turned to face him, her back to the lane. 'Let's get one thing straight, Caspar. This is not a pleasure. Being in your company is quite the opposite, I assure you.'

He didn't like her sarcastic tone or smirk either. It got his back up. 'Well, excuse me for being confused, Carmen, but if that's the case, why are we here? I have better things to be doing on a Monday morning, you know.'

'What, like harassing my daughters?'

It was his turn to smirk. 'Ah, now we're getting to it. So, Violetta – or should I call her Dina? – has gone crying to Mummy. And now Mummy is here to make it all better. Am I correct?'

'You could say that.'

He laughed and shook his head. 'I knew it. Well, I'm sure it was a shock when you found out what your slutty daughter gets up to behind your back and I'm thinking the last thing you want is anyone getting wind of that... especially little Darcy. Let's face it, nobody wants to know their mummy does that for a living.'

'Nobody is going to find out about it, Caspar, I assure you of that.'

'Oh good, then we are definitely on the same track. And while I'm here, there's something you should know about Rosina too.' He was going to enjoy this. Wiping the smug look off her face and destroying the trust she had in her perfect, eldest daughter.

'Oh no, what could that be? Do tell.'

She sounded mad as hell, although credit to her, she was holding her nerve, not giving too much away which also pissed him off because he wanted to really shock her, see the hurt in her face.

Here goes.

'Well, because I am *so* damn good at my job, I notice the things that others don't. For example, the discrepancies in your daughter's bookkeeping and money moving out of your accounts and then back in again. Unfortunately, it looks like Rosina has had her fingers in the till. You don't have much luck with daughters, do you, Carmen?'

Again, she showed no reaction as she responded. 'I'm fully aware that Rosina has borrowed money from the business account and with my blessing. It was a private family matter and I am well within my rights, as is she, to use the funds. So what exactly is your point?'

This deflated him slightly and he suspected she was bluffing but he'd lost the moral high ground so retreated and focused on Violetta instead. 'Well there you go then. Mystery solved but, what are we going to do about Miss Whiplash? We still need to discuss how her dirty little secret is going to stay hidden.'

A loud tut. 'Keep up, Caspar. I've already told you that nobody is going to find out about Violetta, nobody at all.'

'That remains to be seen.' This wasn't going as he imagined and by now she should have been appealing to his better nature before offering him a sweetener. Instead, she was paying attention to his mother's car, a quizzical look on her face.

'I didn't have you down as an electric car kind of man, Caspar. Have you traded your boy-racer model in or is this your spare?'

Thinking it was a fairly reasonable but off-subject question, he answered. 'It's my mother's. Mine's gone in for an MOT.'

A sarcastic tone was evident in her reply. 'Oh, I see. So, it wasn't damaged then? You know, on Friday when you knocked that man down on the road up there and left him for dead when you drove off?'

Caspar's stomach turned and for a minute he thought he was going to pass out. He couldn't speak or think. Carmen did that for him.

'Mmm, now I wonder if I should ring the police and give them the reg of your car, and mention that you were in the area around the time the dead man was found. Perhaps they'd pay you a visit *and* contact the garage where your car is. You know, check whether it really is having an MOT; or a quick repair job after someone's body smashed into it?' She paused and then asked with mock concern, 'Oh no. You look a little pale, Caspar, are you okay?'

She knows. Fuck, she knows, but how?

Caspar's mind was in full screaming panic mode.

There was nobody on the road. So she must have been walking in the woods with her smelly dogs and seen what I did. How though? She'd been at the house just before so that means it was somebody else.

I'm fucked. I could go to prison. I can't go to prison. It'll kill mother. Keep calm, it's still her word against mine though.

Caspar took a gamble. 'You're bluffing. You have no real proof.'

Hope suddenly dissipated when she pulled out her phone and tapped the screen, then he felt his own vibrate. Taking it from his coat he opened the photo message.

Yes, I am well and truly totally fucked.

'What do you want?'

A smile from the winner. 'That's more like it.'

She removed her hands from her pockets and eyed him, a cold glint in her eye. 'This is what is going to happen. We will keep your secret if you keep Violetta's. It's as simple as that. And you need to remember, Caspar, that while you are looking down your nose at my daughter, you're the one who had... shall we say, certain fetishes and quirks which no doubt you would prefer to keep to yourself. Deary me, what would your mother say, or your fellow accountants, or your boss if they knew what you really got up to in your lunchtime?'

Caspar quailed, struck mute by the thought of the ridicule he'd endure. He'd been so sure he had it all sussed and as he listened to Carmen's words, she confirmed how wrong he was.

'So, now the past is done with, let me tell you about the future. You will never contact any member of my family again. You will look for another job, in another town, well away from here. Tell them you fancy a new challenge, a change of scenery. I don't care. Just go. Start again. You'll be fine.'

He opened his mouth to protest and was silenced by the raising of a hand and her pointed finger. 'I won't have your grimy fingers anywhere near my business and I never wish to see your face again. You have one month. If you don't do as I say I will ring the police and tell them what I saw when I was walking in the woods.'

Desperation at losing his job and his liberty forced him to speak. 'You'll get in trouble, for not reporting a crime.'

'Wrong. You're an accountant not a solicitor so stick to what you know or google it, like I did. And anyway, I was in shock, conflicted, maybe a bit scared of you. Whatever I say or however you look at it, Caspar, you are the one who killed a man so it's your call. Is it worth it? The scandal of leaving someone to die versus outing Violetta and yourself in the process.'

He watched, stunned as she turned and headed to the driver's door of her car where she stopped. 'So, do we have a deal?'

The look on her face was one of supremacy and in that moment he wondered how he'd not seen it before, the steel behind the eyes of a woman everyone revered. The cuddly grandmother whose family adored her, who treated her employees with kindness and respect, a stalwart of the community, local businesswoman of the year many times over, and an ice-cold, calculating bitch who'd just kicked him right in the bollocks. Carmen the Chameleon.

'I'm waiting, Caspar. I haven't got all day and you have a resignation letter to write.'

He knew when he was beat so nodded. 'We have a deal.'

And that was that. Without saying a word she opened the door and got into her car and within seconds, was driving towards the exit, back to her nice cosy life and imperfect family. Opening the door of the Kia he folded himself inside and as he started the engine caught a glimpse of his reflection in the rear-view mirror and spoke to the loser who'd been well and truly slapped into place.

'And a merry fucking Christmas to you too!'

27

LEONORA

Manchester city centre

T he break room had never been so full and Leonora and Sam were squashed into a corner, him clutching his raffle tickets. She hadn't seen him all week as they'd been on alternate shifts so in between draws she'd tried to bring him up to date with the Caspar saga without being overheard.

Anyone who could spare a few minutes had popped in to watch Bev, their manager, make the draw. The atmosphere was buoyant and as each number was drawn a loud cheer went up. Leonora suspected that most people, her included, were on a high and looking forward to a lull in the craziness of Christmas, now that the hotel was slowly quietening down as guests and diners headed home for festivities. She was also looking forward to a few days off and the party later that evening at the garden centre, and then the luxury of a lie-in on Christmas Eve.

Now that her mum had sorted everything out with Caspar, and Rosina had told Lou the truth it was as though everyone could breathe again. Lou was a diamond, he really was, and once he got over the shock had vowed to support his wife. Violetta literally couldn't wait to get her house listed with a lettings agency and move back to Appleton and it made Leonora smile, knowing that their badass sister was actually a home bird with a squashy centre. She hid it well but not from everyone. They hadn't told Darcy yet, simply because none of them could bear the thought of her pestering so it was going to be a big surprise in the new year.

Poor Joel had been so nervous when he turned up at the centre. But the kids waved at him from the train and after a few minutes it really was as though he'd never been away. He was still going to spend Christmas Day with his family and then Boxing Day at Appleton. Leonora felt a flutter of excitement when she thought of the other plans they had made over the past few days and it was as though all the hoo-ha had somehow been meant to be. It had given her and Violetta a kick up the bum in more ways than one.

It had occurred to her that now she was free of the Caspar burden and ready to make a fresh start, then why not stop dilly-dallying and take an even bolder step. After talking her idea through with her mum, they were going to get started on renovating the mill and open her own bistro. And that's where Violetta came in. She could still see the look on her sister's face when she and her mum pitched their idea.

They were once more seated around the kitchen table where Violetta looked slightly wary after being summoned for a pow-wow.

'So, this is what we were thinking. There's no point in me giving up my job until the mill has been fully refurbished, I mean, what can I do apart from boss the builders about and make them brews? I might as well keep earning and learning, as Mum always says. But I would need a project manager to oversee everything, you know, like on *Grand Designs*. You always said you'd be great at that job and stay on budget, and not have to sell vital organs to pay for designer taps.'

Violetta nodded. 'Yeah, that's true, but I'm not sure where you're going with this.'

'Don't be gormless, Vi. We want you to be the project manager and see the refurb through from start to finish. You can still work down at the garden centre with Rosina but you'll be on hand to nip up to the mill when we have deliveries et cetera and make sure it's all on schedule and budget. We both think you'd be brilliant at it.'

A huge smile appeared on Violetta's face. 'Really! Oh my, I would love to do that. I can't believe you'd trust me with such a massive project.'

Carmen tutted. 'Of course we trust you and that's not all. Your sister has had another idea.'

All eyes focused on Leonora. 'You remember I said how much I loved coming to your little café and you said you loved meeting and interacting with the customers.'

'Yes, that was the part I enjoyed, getting to know them and having a bit of banter, why?'

'Because when the mill opens I'll need a maître d', and I quite fancy it being a woman. And that woman is you!'

Violetta's hand flew to her chest. 'Me?'

'Yes, you. How about it? Team Appleton. You out front chatting to the customers, making them feel welcome, being the face of the mill while I slave away in the back. I think it'd be perfect, don't you?'

Violetta didn't answer straight away and when she did her lip wobbled and Leonora thought she'd finally broken the ice maiden. Then she managed to rein it in and answered in a very shaky voice. 'I think it would be perfect, too, so yes, yes please.'

Somebody had just won the cinema tickets with number eight and the only two prizes left were the bottle of green liqueur that Leonora hated and the huge wicker hamper. Hearing twenty, everyone cheered as the recipient of the vilest drink ever made went to claim their prize and turning to Sam, and over the noise, she carried on with her story. 'So thanks to your advice and me basically losing my temper in Selfridges, I told him it was over.'

'And how did he take it?'

'Not well. He was a pain in the backside for a few days, texting and making a nuisance of himself. But put it this way: once my mum gave him the hard word he backed off and I think he'll leave me alone now.' She didn't want to tell him their family business. It wasn't necessary. Looking at his raffle tickets she spotted he was left with twenty-four and twelve. 'That's my mum's birthday. She always says that the most special little girls are born on the twelfth and she's right.'

Sam smiled. 'Well, fingers crossed. It's the hamper next.'

There was a lot of dramatic hand-wiggling inside the box as Bev pulled out the ticket. 'And the winning number is...' She unfolded it slowly. 'Number... twelve.'

'Oh my God, Sam, it's you! You won.' Leonora clapped like he was winning an Oscar as her rather bashful and surprised friend went up to claim his prize that was so huge he had to leave it on the table and return to his seat.

The draw concluded, the room slowly began to empty and, as always, their conversation was brought to a close. Leonora had to go back to work as did Sam but she knew he'd never be able to carry the prize home on the bus. 'I'll give you a lift when we finish. It'll probably take two of us to carry it to the car anyway. I reckon that lot will see you through to the new year and beyond.'

'Thank you, Leo, I'd appreciate that and you're right. It'll save us a pretty penny over the next couple of weeks. I might share it with our neighbours, though, if we have too much.'

They both made their way back to the kitchen and as Sam was congratulated by more of their colleagues she was touched by his generosity and made a pact with herself that when they came back to work, she would take more time to get to know him properly. Perhaps find out more about his 'better half' and his life, but gently. He was such a shy, private person so he might not appreciate it but she *so* wanted to know if he had family because he'd never mentioned any. It made her feel sad to think of such a lovely man not having children. He'd make the best dad and granddad, that was for certain.

As she pushed open the door to the kitchen, the cacophony of pans and orders being shouted dragged her straight back into lunch service. Waving to Sam, she said she'd see him at two and after he gave her the thumbs up, he and Leonora went their separate ways.

Turning into Sam's street Leonora looked for a parking space along the row of terraces. She'd dropped the pastry chef on the way, too, and they'd all passed the time chatting about how busy they'd been and how dreadful the traffic was. When a car pulled out a few doors down from Sam's she nipped in the space and as she did, received a surprise invitation.

'I was wondering if you'd like to come in for a cup of tea and some Christmas cake. To say thank you for all the lifts you've given me these past few weeks. We never get a chance to talk properly at work or in the car and there's someone I'd like you to meet.'

Leonora was touched and rather thrilled to get to see inside his house. Her nosiness knew no bounds. 'Of course. I'd love that.'

Once they'd got the hamper out of the boot they carried it up the short path and Sam let them in. After shuffling along the narrow hall he backed into the small lounge where they deposited it on the sofa, both with a sigh. The room was neat and tidy, very cosy but a bit on the chilly side which prompted Sam to switch on the fire, the bars of orange quickly flickering into life.

Unbuttoning his overcoat he gave her a smile. 'Right. That should warm the place up. It looks like we're home alone so I'll put the kettle on, make yourself comfortable. I'll be back in a tick.'

Leaving Leonora alone he turned to the right and she listened to the sound of cutlery clinking against crockery as she pondered the photographs on the wall, and as she did, a little bit of Sam's puzzle clicked into place. Moving from one to the other she pieced together a visual history for her new friend, looking closely at the faces of who she suspected were his parents, maybe brothers and sisters and a photo of a ship, the name on its stern very familiar to her.

When Sam came into the room her head turned and she pointed at one of the photos. 'I recognise the name of this ship.'

He came over and stood by her side and smiled. 'Ah yes. The *HMT Empire Windrush*. My uncle sailed on it from Jamaica back in 1948. He docked in Tilbury, the first group of settlers from my hometown, Kingston. They were so full of hope, my uncle was anyway. He inspired me to follow him when I was old enough.'

Leonora was fascinated. 'I've read about this and seen it on the news. You were so brave, leaving your family behind to start a new life so far away from home. I never realised you were from Jamaica but now I come to think about it, I can hear it in your accent, ever so faintly. Maybe because you speak so nicely it's not so noticeable. What did you do over there?'

'I had hoped to be a teacher but my family didn't have the money to pay for my education. I never lost my love of learning, though, and broadened my horizons the best I could with books, which is what brought us together.' He smiled at Leonora.

Moving along she pointed to a family photo. 'Are these your parents and is that you, the tall one at the back? Goodness, you are so handsome.'

'Yes, that's my mother and father and two sisters, with me at the back, the only son who was such a disappointment.' The sadness in Sam's voice was unmistakable.

'Oh no, why? I can't imagine you disappointing anyone, Sam.' Leonora could see the wistful look in his eye and wondered if she'd gone a bit too far, after all, this was the first time he'd opened up about his private life but he answered immediately.

'My father was a preacher and a strict man, so let's say our relationship was troubled, whereas my mother was an angel and I adored her. Sadly she was caught in between two men at odds with each other and it caused her great pain and sorrow. It was one of the reasons I left.'

Leonora swallowed down the lump that was clogging her throat and was just about to ask why, when the sound of a key in the lock interrupted their conversation and Sam smiled before calling out,

'In here. And we have a visitor so no swearing.' Sam smiled again and winked at Leonora who was thrilled at last to meet his better half and after hearing what he'd just said, hoped even more that she was a nice lady.

All eyes on the door as a figure entered the room. Her heart flipped and she tried hard not to show surprise when a tall, stocky man walked into the lounge, unzipping his jacket and giving her a warm smile.

Sam made the introductions. 'Leo, this is my partner George. He has a fondness for berating people with expletives which is why I warned him you were here.' Sam gave her a wink.

Shaking the hand that was offered Leonora knew immediately that George was a nice man because his dark-brown eyes were kind, a genuine smile of welcome lit up his face and when he spoke, there was a northern lilt.

'Lovely to meet you, pet. Now, has this lazy bugger put the kettle on? He always makes a start but never quite manages to put the tea in the pot.' He unwound his scarf to reveal a small swallow tattoo on his neck.

'Lovely to meet you, too, George. I was just looking at Sam's photos and hearing all about his voyage and yes, I do believe he's put the kettle on but how far he got is anyone's guess.'

George shook his head. 'Give us a minute and we'll bring it through. Come on, Sam, get Leo some of that cake I made and I'll do the tea.'

They bustled off, leaving Leonora alone. She took a seat on the end of the sofa that was placed against the longest wall, squashing in beside the hamper. Taking in the cosy room she admired the large seascape that was hung on the chimney breast. The walls were decorated with tasteful flock wallpaper, the matching curtains still open against the fading December light and while she waited, she imagined a life for Sam and George.

She pictured them sitting in their armchairs on either side of the fire. Sam reading and maybe George too. There were books lining the shelves, oddly enough the same as her mum had at home. *Robinson Crusoe, Anne of Green Gables, Adventures of Huckleberry Finn, The Old Man and the Sea.* When she spotted the record player on the sideboard under the window, she added music to their list of enjoyments. By its side was a neat row of vinyl records, albums from the looks of them and she instantly recognised the cover at the end, *La Bohème* by Puccini: her mum had the exact same one at home. Fancy that.

She was about to get up and have a nosey at the others, fully expecting there to be some Beatles classics in there when Sam and George returned, the latter placing a tray on the coffee table in the middle of the room before they both took their seats. George on the left of the fire, Sam on the right. It made her smile, their synchronicity. They were like bookends and both seemed rather chuffed to have a guest.

George spoke first as Sam leant forward and began pouring the tea from a huge pot decorated in a Japanese ukiyo-e print. 'Sam tells me you live over Macclesfield way and that we once visited your family garden centre. We love garden centres, don't we?' He looked to Sam who nodded as he poured. 'And historic buildings like the one close by, we did both in the same day.'

Leonora could see that George was a natural chatterbox and very comfortable with strangers compared to Sam who was more reserved. She imagined being sat next to George at lunch and knew without a doubt she'd have heard his life history by the time she'd eaten her yoghurt.

'Gawsworth Hall, yes, that's literally five minutes from our place. We used to go there when we were kids, me and my two sisters. There's a churchyard close by where we dared each other to walk through at night.' She was going to say *and my goth sister's favourite place to get smashed,* but thought better of it.

'Yes, I remember you have sisters? See, there are so many things other than books we haven't talked about properly but we are always in such a rush at work, always something to do and a clock to watch.' Sam passed her a cup and saucer. 'Be careful, it's hot, I'll let you add your own milk and sugar.'

Doing just that she answered Sam's question. 'Yes, Rosie is the eldest and Vi is the middle sister, I'm the youngest. We're actually named after leading ladies from the opera. Rosina, Violetta and Leonora. It was my mum's idea apparently. She's named after an opera, too, Carmen. I saw your records so I expect you'll recognise them.'

When she looked up she noticed that Sam had stopped mid-pass and George was looking rather taken aback, one hand hovering as it waited to receive his cup and saucer. Worried that she'd offended them in some way Leonora placed the spoon back on the tray and asked if anything was wrong.

George appeared to have lost his voice so Sam spoke instead. 'You say your mum is called Carmen?'

'Yes, why?' There was definitely something wrong because the air was pure static.

'May I ask what your mum's surname is? I mean her maiden name.' George's voice was a whisper.

'Appleton, that's her married name but she was a Wilson before, Carmen Wilson.'

When Sam quickly placed the cup on the table then stood and rushed to George's side, placing an arm around his shoulders as if to steady him, Leonora asked the obvious question. 'What's wrong? Have I said something to upset you?'

George didn't speak at first, instead he gave a short cough and after Sam patted his shoulder in an encouraging manner, he spoke. 'Yes, pet. I think I do know your mum.'

For some reason Leonora had goosebumps and the hairs on her neck prickled. 'Really, how?'

His voice was a little bolder when he answered. 'Well, if I'm not mistaken, I'm her dad. And that means I'm your granddad.'

Leonora could feel her mouth making the shape of an O and her eyes were locked in position, her brain going like the clappers as it tried to compute what she'd just heard. Finally it worked it all out. 'Oh my... Are you Geordie? *My* granddad Geordie?'

And it was those words, one name that sealed the deal because when George heard her say it he crumbled, so did Leonora and it was left to Sam, who was equally emotional, to mop up their tears.

28

GEORDIE

Never in all his wild imaginings of the day he would find his daughter, had Geordie seen it played out this way. Right there in front of him, kneeling by his side on the floor was his youngest granddaughter and she was holding his hand. His own flesh and blood and he could feel her, see her, hold her. When she'd rushed across the room to embrace him he'd closed his eyes and let the moment wash over him, committing every second to memory. And now, after the emotion, amidst such a tremendous shock, all three of them were coming to terms with the reality of the situation.

Leonora spoke first. 'I just can't take it all in, can you? Me and Sam have been working together and we never knew we were connected like this. And all this time you've been living thirty minutes away from us, from Mum. And you came to the garden centre too. You could have passed each other by. Oh my word. This is going to blow her mind, you know. And yours, because she told us only last week, on Sunday, that she's going to start looking for you. I need to ring her, or should I wait? What should I do? My head's mashed–'

Sam interrupted. 'I think we all need to take a breath first, before we do anything. This has been a huge shock for all of us.'

Geordie nodded but had so much to ask, say. 'Did she? Well this is even more of a coincidence because I'd decided to do the same thing. I simply can't believe this is happening. I really can't take it in.' To know that Carmen was going to look for him brought such joy to his heart. 'Will you tell me about her, please. Have you got a photo? You don't know how much I've longed to see what she looks like now. You have a look of her, the same colour hair, like mine used to be before I went grey, wasn't it, Sam? Dark brown like Leo's.' When he looked to Sam he nodded.

'Of course I'll tell you. Let me get my phone: I'll show you some photos of all of us. You have five great-grandchildren too... can you believe that!' Leonora reached for her bag and dragged it across the floor and pulled out her phone, tapping on an album that said 'Famalam' then turned the screen toward him. 'There she is. That's your Carmen.'

Geordie frantically brushed away the tears so he could see properly and gazed upon the face of his little girl all grown up. He wanted to touch the screen and for his fingers to go right inside so he could touch her, make sure she was real. Her hair was still as dark as he remembered and she was slight too, like her mum. But the smile! It lit up the screen and his heart was so happy it made him giddy. He'd not been that for a long time.

'She's a bonny lass, all right. Look, Sam.' He turned the phone so he could see and watched the look that passed over his face. They'd talked about it so much, the two of them, trying to find Carmen and he knew Sam would be happy too.

Leonora touched the screen. 'If you swipe like this, I'll tell you who they all are.'

Doing as he was told, one by one, the faces of his family appeared. As he looked on in total wonderment, his lovely granddaughter – how odd that sounded but so perfectly amazing – told him the story of their lives.

Leonora was back on the sofa, sipping coffee that Sam had made after the tea went stone cold. 'I think I've told you everything but I'm sure you'll have lots more questions so if you think of any, just ask.'

'No, you've done a grand job of filling in the gap and that was some gap, wasn't it. I am sorry about Sylvia though. Even though we parted on bad terms I kind of hoped that after all these years we might be able to put that behind us. It's too late now and that makes me incredibly sad.' It was true. He and Sam had hoped that with age had come wisdom and forgiveness but when Leonora grimaced, he realised it might not be the case.

'The thing is you never could tell with Gran. She was one of a kind and set like stone in her ways so I'm not sure how she would have reacted but before she died she did say something to Mum that might give you comfort. It was the thing that encouraged her to look for you. Mum had always respected Gran's feelings so it was kind of like permission, I think.'

Geordie steeled himself. 'What did she say?'

Leonora replied, 'She said something on the lines of wanting to tell Mum about you, before it was too late. She said she did it for Mum and if she saw you again to tell you she forgave you.'

Sucking in a lungful of air to steady himself, Geordie glanced at Sam who gave a nod and smiled. It was what they had both hoped for and Sylvia's message meant as much to Sam as it did to him. It was Leonora's turn to ask a question and it wasn't totally unexpected.

'So can you tell me about how you two met, and what happened to Martha, the lady that Gran said you ran away with? That's all we know. She wouldn't talk about it and neither did Mum, mainly because there wasn't much she could say.

'Mum said that you were having an affair with a woman

called Martha, who came round on Christmas Eve and confronted you and told Gran everything. Then you left and chose Martha so Gran brought Mum here, to Manchester. What I don't understand is where you two met and what happened to Martha. Did you split up?'

Geordie sighed and looked towards Sam who said exactly what he expected. 'I think Leonora needs to hear the full story, don't you? And then she will understand.'

Nodding, he then turned to his wide-eyed granddaughter and told her his story, a telling that was long overdue.

29

GEORDIE AND SAM

Tilbury, London
1969

They met at the docks where Sam worked in the warehouses, loading and unloading cargo onto the vessels that were moored there. Geordie was married to Sylvia, and Sam was married to Martha. They lived on the same street and travelled on the same bus home one night and it was here, one summer evening in June, on a half-empty top deck that was thick with cigarette fumes that they struck up a conversation.

They chatted about work and where Geordie, who was home on a week's leave had sailed to and from. At the time he was working the North Sea route, shorter trips so he could be with his family. The days of voyages to his favourite place on earth, Japan and the land of the rising sun, were a thing of the past. The sea was his life and as long as he could still sail and come home to his little girl, that was all he cared about. Geordie was twenty-four and got married at eighteen in a bit of a rush when his girlfriend found out she was pregnant.

Sam was twenty, newly married and living in a shared house with his wife and her two sisters and their husbands. It was far from ideal. Even though they'd been promised the good life when they all set sail from Jamaica, the reality was that they were shunned by many, people who thought they were there to steal their jobs. Signs on doors of pubs and shops, even boarding houses, telling them they weren't wanted left them in no doubt and this reality had come as an immense shock.

That night, from the outside looking in they were just two young blokes sharing their stories on a bus. On the inside the attraction was there, right from the start and their truth, the one Sam's father tried to beat out of him in Jamaica, begging God to banish it from his son's wicked, perverted soul, was hard to deny.

Geordie had always battled with what he knew to be his truth. And he hadn't been alone in his fight. There were other sailors who also travelled the globe, denying their feelings and who they really were. The threat of prosecution had always hung in the air as had the stigma of homosexuality and even the changing of the law two years before they met hadn't changed attitudes. It was too soon so Geordie hid behind his family life and the aura of respectability that a wife and child gave a man like him.

It was much the same for Sam who had escaped his father and left behind his distraught mother who, even though she'd been heartbroken on the day he'd said goodbye, knew letting her son go was for the best. He'd met Martha not long after he arrived. She was a seamstress and worked in one of the factories near to the docks that made overalls. She was a vibrant, confident young woman who dressed in bright colours that matched her personality, all the colours of the Caribbean. The Jamaican community stuck together and missing his home, his mother and sisters, Sam had warmed to Martha and her loud but welcoming family who took him as their own.

During his week's leave, Geordie and Sam would meet in the park and chat while Carmen played on the swings, or they would stop on the street and pass a few minutes on the way back from the corner shop. The attraction grew. When Geordie said goodbye to his daughter and went back to sea, his heart was always heavy. When he said goodbye to Sam as they met in the alleyway that ran along the back of the row of terraces, it felt like lead.

And so their tentative romance began, spread over the summer months when Geordie came home on leave, right through the winter when the cover of darkness allowed them furtive meetings in cold doorways. The slight touch of a hand, the longing for a kiss, became too much to bear. It was one of Martha's sisters who saw them and blew their world apart. They'd taken a chance and it all went wrong. Christmas Eve, in a dingy alleyway by the bins was where they shared their first embrace and in that wonderful moment, as their lips met, they knew that what they felt wasn't wrong. However, for Sam, who at twenty was still underage, anything more would be illegal.

While Geordie sat in the parlour, smoking his cigarettes and reading the paper, and his wife peeled potatoes in the kitchen as she chatted to Beryl from next door, and his little girl watched the clock and waited for Father Christmas, seven doors down all hell was breaking loose.

When Martha barged through the door, demanding he told his wife what he'd done, it wasn't that he'd been having an affair with another woman, it was that he'd fallen in love with another man. Sam. No more playing happy families.

Sylvia was distraught, horrified, repulsed, betrayed, enraged. That night as they argued in their bedroom she went through a gamut of emotions. Jealousy, hate, desperation. Could they make it work? Could she wipe from her mind what he'd done? Could she bear the shame if it got out? If Martha's screeching accusations were anything to go by, half the street would have heard and gossip would spread like a fire throughout the terraces.

The thing was, as Geordie watched her pace and cry and pull at her hair in temper, he realised that it was no longer down to Sylvia, her forgiveness or understanding. He couldn't live a lie anymore. He couldn't fake it and in his heart he knew that neither could she. When he told her this, that it was over and that he would go and when she'd calmed down they would talk it through, the barrier between him and his wife went up. It was the final insult, the ultimate betrayal.

It had almost killed him, when Carmen came to the top of the stairs and asked him where he was going, if he was coming back. That night, when he closed the front door on his little girl and heard her fists battering the wood on the other side, had haunted him for the rest of his life.

He'd hoped Sylvia would come back and that they could talk it through sensibly, make arrangements for Carmen but it wasn't to be. During their final conversation, as he stood in her sister's hallway, they'd made a deal. She promised not to make Carmen hate him, to keep his secret as long as he stayed away and let them get on with their lives. Geordie had agreed for the sake of his daughter, making a pact with the devil-woman.

While Geordie was able to take a room in a boarding house on that most awful of Christmas Eves, Sam wasn't so fortunate. He'd also left home that night and found shelter at a local church, sleeping amongst the homeless of Tilbury, wandering the streets during the day and returning in the evening. There, he'd lain awake amongst the great unwashed of the parish, listening to their coughs and nightmares as their sins and demons haunted their dreams. Just like his own fears tormented every waking hour.

Sam hadn't been to work. He was starving and running out of money but didn't dare face his brother-in-law who worked at the same shipping company. He was petrified that Martha or one of her family would report him to the police yet he longed to see Geordie so, knowing the day he was due back on his ship, he hid close by the dockyard and waited in the early morning light.

Finally, just over a week since they'd last seen each other, a few days before New Year, as Geordie headed towards the dock he heard his name being called and a face he'd longed to see stepped out of the shadows. It didn't take long for them to decide what to do.

Geordie had already taken his meagre belongings from the house back to his lodgings and given his keys back to the landlord. Next, he withdrew all his money from the bank and bought an old banger which he loaded with, amongst other things, his record player, books, photographs and vinyl records and then as arranged, met Sam at the ring road out of London. They travelled north together, towards the docks at Salford. The Manchester Ship Canal was a thriving port, well away from anyone they knew in a city where they could blend in, stay under the radar and start a new life together.

And that was where they'd remained ever since, living separately at first and then once they'd found courage, and acceptance and tolerance within society, it slowly made them feel more comfortable and they moved in together. They bought a little house and lived a peaceful life in a city they now called home and ironically, only a few miles from the daughter that Geordie had never stopped loving.

❄

Leonora had listened to Geordie and Sam as they told their tale between them and now it was her chance to ask questions.

'So, pet. There you have it. The truth about how we ended up here and by some kind of miracle you came into our lives. If there's anything you want to ask us, feel free.' Geordie relaxed into his armchair, exhausted from the telling of their story and Sam looked much the same.

'No, I don't think there is. You explained it all so clearly. But one thing that has occurred to me is about Gran. Her attitudes to so many things kind of makes sense now. She was so set in her ways, a bit of a tough cookie who didn't stand for any messing and, if I'm totally honest, completely intolerant of most things and people. We always made allowances or laughed it off, putting it down to her age and coming from a certain era, or maybe her tough East End upbringing. Now I see it differently. She was taking her rage and hurt and disappointment out on anyone who reminded her of you and Sam.'

Hearing this left Geordie intrigued and rather shocked. No matter how hard he tried to picture Sylvia as Leonora had described, or had seen in the photos on her phone, he remembered her differently. To him she would always be the petite young woman who dyed her hair blonde because she idolised Marilyn Monroe. And even though she appeared bold and brash, she was always perfectly made up and turned out. Right up until that Christmas Eve she'd always been so sweet, mild and gentle with a kind heart. The knowledge that his actions might have altered her so dramatically pained him deeply.

'Did Sylvia remarry?' Geordie wished for the answer to be yes.

The shake of Leonora's head told him it hadn't been granted. 'No. She kind of dedicated her life to us, me, my mum and my sisters. While Mum got on with building the garden centre Gran looked after us, like our second mum, I suppose. We were her everything.'

Geordie was despondent even amidst his joy. 'It still makes me sad, though, that I hurt her so badly that she never gave love another chance and at the same time, kept her promise to me. She didn't turn Carmen against me or try to poison her mind. She stuck to the story about Martha and even though it was a lie, I'm grateful for that.'

Leonora nodded. 'That's what she was like. Resilient, I suppose.'

Geordie agreed. 'It must have been hard for Sylvia, leaving her home, friends and family behind but she was ashamed I suppose, of me and her marriage failing and people are such terrible gossips and she will have wanted to spare Carmen any more hurt. So, just like she forgave me, I forgive her, too, because at the end of the day it was my actions that caused it all and I have to take responsibility for that.' Geordie meant every word and as soon as he saw Carmen he would explain it all and try to make it right, if he could.

'Granddad, you mustn't worry about that now.' Leonora paused and her face lit up, as if something had occurred to her. 'Granddad... how ace does that sound? I've never said it before – and even better, you're both my granddads and after all this time I have two! That's so cool.' At this Sam and Geordie laughed, the mirth was a tonic to the seriousness of the conversation as she continued.

'What's more important is that you both found it in your hearts to forgive each other and because Gran loved Mum so much, she'd be glad I found you. I have a feeling that deep down she knew Mum needed to track you down but she'd dug her heels in for so long that she couldn't or wouldn't back down. That's why she gave Mum her blessing before she died: it set her free.'

Sam spoke next and addressed Leonora. 'So, now do you see what I meant the other day when I told you I'd made mistakes and wished I'd been honest from the start. I should never have married Martha. It was wrong and I wish I'd been given the chance to explain because it would have saved so many people a great deal of heartache. It's so hard, getting to our age and looking back on our errors then not being able to rectify them. I didn't want you to be in the same boat.'

'I do see. It all makes sense now, and your advice was the best and for many reasons I'm glad I took it. I still think it's sad. That people who loved each other were so fearful and I wish it could have been different for you both. I totally understand why you did what you did, I want you to know that.'

A look of understanding passed between all of them and even though he'd just met her, Geordie was so very proud of his granddaughter who clapped her hands together and asked another question. 'And now, we have another biggie on our hands. How do I tell Mum that I've found you? Should I ring her and explain?'

Before Geordie could answer, Sam interrupted and as always, had wise words. 'I think we should take a few minutes to consider our options and also your mother's feelings. You said she's hosting a party tonight, am I right?'

'Yes, for all the garden centre staff and half the village, knowing Mum. She's been planning it for yonks.'

Geordie realised where Sam was going with his question. 'Well, in that case I don't think we should spoil that, do you? I cannot wait to see her, or even speak on the phone but it will be a shock when you tell her and I think she needs to focus on her guests, don't you?'

Leonora's shoulders sagged. 'I suppose so, but I can't keep it to myself all night, it will kill me, I swear. As soon as I realised it was you I wanted to ring her but we were so wrapped up in your story I had to know what happened, and so will she. What do you think I should do then?'

Sam had the answer. 'Why don't you tell her after the party. Let her enjoy the evening and then once everyone is gone you can explain. That way it will give her time to absorb it all, because I'm sure George and I will be doing just the same.'

'Sam's right. Once you've told her perhaps she might want to ring me and we can talk on the phone first. Whatever she wants. Naturally, I can't wait to see her but it's Christmas Eve tomorrow and you will have plans, so let's see how it goes. How does that sound?' In truth Geordie wanted to get in the car right there and go and see his girl, but common sense held him back.

Leonora placed her hands to her cheeks. 'Oooh, okay then. It will be the longest party in history though, waiting for it to be over so I can tell her. Right, we need to swap phone numbers and then I can send you some photos to your phone straight away. Do you have any of you? Mum only has two, and some of your books so I'm sure she'd love to see some more of you and Sam and your life, so she can fill in the gaps.'

The rush of sheer euphoria on hearing that Carmen had kept his photos and books made his heart so full he could barely speak, abetted by the golf ball of emotion that was lodged in his throat. 'Of course. I have all the photos from our old house, everything your mum left behind, toys and books and her own grandma's dinner service. I couldn't bear to leave them so I brought them here. I'll get everything down from the loft and I also have something I can give her when I see her, to prove I thought about her all the time, especially at Christmas.'

Sam smiled as he spoke. 'Ah, your box of letters. I'm sure she will love them, George.' Looking over to Leonora he explained. 'Every year, since we left London, your granddad wrote your mum a letter and posted it to wherever he lived. He has them all upstairs in a boot box.'

'Oh Granddad, that's lovely... she's going to be so happy. And so are my sisters. I'm going to tell them before Mum, though, because if I don't I will pop with excitement. Wait till they find out we have a granddad at last, no actually, two granddads and one of them looks like Morgan Freeman. I mean, what more could we ask for?'

The laughter in the room broke the ice as Sam thanked Leonora for the best compliment ever and George wiped his eyes.

'Right, let's swap numbers and then I'll ping you over the photos. I'd best get off otherwise she'll be ringing me to find out where I am.' Leonora took out her phone and waited for them to recite their details.

Once they were done George helped her on with her coat and then he and Sam walked her to the door. He didn't want to let her go but knew he had to. 'There's so much I want to ask you, about you and your sisters but we have time for that, I'm sure.'

'We do. And it's going to be so much fun getting to know you both, honestly this is the best Christmas present ever.'

Fearful of becoming a gibbering wreck George chivvied her along. 'It certainly is. Now off you go, pet, and drive carefully. Will you let us know when you've told her? A text will do.'

Leonora gave them both a peck on the cheek before she headed towards her car, waving as she went. 'I will, and I'll see you soon, Granddads.'

They stood side by side as they waved Leonora off, both remaining on the step until she was out of sight. As Geordie closed the door on the cold, December air he followed Sam down the hall.

Sam gave Geordie's arm a squeeze. 'You go and sit awhile, gather your thoughts while I make us some food. My, my, what a day, what a day. And it's going to be a long night, waiting for a call so we need sustenance to see us through.'

Listening to Sam's mutterings, Geordie did as he was told and went into the lounge and stood before the oil painting on the chimney breast, taking a moment to himself. The seascape took him back to his days aboard ship, when the vast expanse of ocean that surrounded him could sometimes seem desolate, mirroring how he felt inside. Other times it would be his only friend, an escape route to far-off lands and respite from living a lie.

He remembered the nights on watch, when he stood alone on deck and wished on every shooting star he saw in the ink-black sky that one day he would see his little girl again. And at last, each wish, each word he'd spoken into the dead of night, all the hopes and dreams that were carried on the wind across the sea, were about to come true.

30

CARMEN

Appleton Farm, Cheshire
Christmas Eve

Carmen didn't know what to do with herself. Her legs kept pacing and even when she sat down and tried to be calm for a second they stood up and were off again. Her hands were twitchy, fiddling with her bracelet or neck of her blouse and she was hot, too, the bloody house was boiling.

Maybe I should turn the heating down, no, stay here, stop fussing, relax.

As if reading her mind Rosina told her exactly the same. 'Mum, for the love of all things holy, please sit down. You're stressing me out now. Pacing won't get them here sooner and you'll be exhausted by the time they are.'

Carmen nodded as Rosina patted the sofa, indicating she should go and sit. 'You're right. I'm just so nervous and excited all at once and I'm already shattered. It took forever to get to sleep but in the end I must have conked out from the sheer shock of it all. Then I woke up at dawn and I swear it was like my earliest memories of Christmas Eve, you know, when you think, *It's here!* and dive out of bed. That was me this morning.'

Carmen sat next to Rosina and twiddled her fingers, giving the pent-up energy a point of release. Rosina glanced out of the lounge window. She was also keeping an eye out for the granddad she was about to meet. 'I have to admit I was the same and I'm so glad we were all here last night to tell you the news. I thought Leo was going to go mad from the exertion of holding it all in.'

Carmen smiled at the memory. Of a Christmas Eve Eve surprise she would never forget.

Carmen had sensed something was up at the party. Every time she looked at her daughters, they were locked in a whispered conversation that abruptly ended when they realised she was watching. At first she'd presumed they were discussing a surprise, maybe presenting her with a bunch of flowers or putting last-minute plans together for her Christmas present so she'd ignored them and concentrated on the magician who was entertaining the guests.

It wasn't until all the presents had been distributed and everyone started heading home with full stomachs and not all of them able to tread a straight line, that she really started to be suspicious. The family had helped with the tidy-up and as she gave orders and made sure the café was left spic and span, kept her eye on her girls. Leonora looked nervous while Violetta seemed to be a bit giddy which resulted in Rosina giving her a stare, not quite a glare, more of a 'calm down' look.

They had all walked back to Appleton, Darcy clinging on to her hand, loving the adventure of being up late and on the private footpath in the dark. Bern and Lou had lit the way with torches while Max and Tilly used theirs to make scary faces that made Ella and Lola scream. Behind her, the three witches of *Macbeth* continued whispering spells and Carmen knew without a doubt that something was up. This perplexed her because after the last few days she'd hoped they'd learned their lesson about keeping secrets so could only hope this one, whatever it was, wasn't a shocker.

Please, Santa, let it be a nice one.

They'd only just taken off their coats and hooked them on the hall stand when she was ushered into the lounge by the witches and the others headed to the kitchen to make hot chocolate. Violetta stoked the fire while Rosina took a seat on an armchair. Leonora took Carmen's hand, her cheeks rosy-red from the cold and the sudden burst of heat as they entered the house.

The pressure was too much for Carmen. 'Okay, what's going on? You three have been acting suspicious all night so come on, out with it. What have you done this time?'

Leonora didn't have to be asked twice. 'Don't worry, Mum... I promise we've been good but, we do have a very, *very* big surprise so you might want to sit down.'

Carmen looked from one to the other and was mildly reassured by the look of sheer excitement on all of their faces that it was something nice but still, she remained cautious. 'No, it's okay, I think I'll stand.'

Rosina sucked in a breath so hard Carmen saw her straighten and Violetta had clasped her hands together and was jiggling on the spot, just like Darcy did when she was giddy. Then when she returned her gaze to Leonora, she saw that her eyes sparkled with tears.

'Mum, I have the best news... it's a bit of a long story but quite by chance, yesterday I found your dad. I met him. I met Geordie, our granddad Geordie.'

It took a moment to process what Leonora had said, and then what it meant and in the seconds before Carmen burst into tears, she managed three words that took her tearful girls and herself by surprise. 'Thank you, Santa.'

Carmen looked at the clock. It was almost ten and they would be here soon and still it didn't seem real and if she'd prayed once that it wasn't a dream and she wouldn't wake up, she'd prayed a hundred times since they told her.

When Violetta came into the room, red hair flowing down the back of a violet, crushed velvet dress, she reminded Carmen of one of the paintings on the art deco biscuit tins down at the gift shop and even that thought made her wonder if she was going mad from nerves.

'Right, the kids are all waiting in the kitchen with strict instructions to stay there until we call them in. Don't want the poor man overwhelmed when he gets there and I swear Darcy has compiled a dossier of questions for him. He doesn't stand a chance.'

Another flurry of anxiety caused Carmen to question her own decisions. 'Do you think I did the right thing though, not talking to him last night? I was too emotional and I'd have only cried through the whole call... but maybe it would've broken the ice because I bet he's as nervous as I am.'

'Mum, stop overthinking it. You were a mess last night and it was late too. Leo said he totally understood and he was very emotional too, when she told him you wanted to see him today. It was a lot for you both to take in. And anyway, it's too late to start worrying now because they're here. I can see a car coming up the drive.'

At that very moment Leonora rushed in. 'They're here, oh my God, I think I'm going to wee. Come on, Mum... are you going to answer the door, or shall I?'

'Flipping heck, Leo. Get hysterical why don't you. We're trying to keep Mum calm here and you're like a bottle of bloody Lucozade.'

Violetta was laughing at her sister as Rosina stood and put a protective arm around her mum and gave her a gentle squeeze. 'So, what d'you want to do?'

Carmen knew exactly what she wanted. The last time she'd seen her dad, fifty-two long years before, was as he walked out the door and closed it behind him. She'd spent so long wishing he would come home, that one day she would open the door and he'd be there on the step. 'I'll go to the door. It's fine, Rosina, I'll be okay.'

The doorbell ringing prompted her legs into action and once again they were on the move, heading into the hall, almost running, on little six-year-old legs, chubby fists reaching for the handle and as she pulled open the door, the years fell away. And there he was.

'Hello Dad.' Carmen took him in. He hadn't changed a bit and his face, the face she'd waited so long to see was smiling just for her.

'Hello pet.'

Stepping forward, just two paces, and she was in his arms, both holding on for dear life and allowing the tears of a lifetime to fall.

To one side, the man she knew to be Sam waited. He was holding a large box. Raising one hand she acknowledged him, letting him know it was okay and he was welcome. He quickly returned the gesture and then wiped away his own tears.

Behind her she felt the hands of her girls resting on her back, and then the sound of footsteps and the voice of an escapee, Darcy, floating along the hall. 'Is he here? Is our great-granddad here?'

Between sobs, Carmen smiled and before all manner of craziness broke loose she managed to speak, her voice cracked and raw with emotion. 'I always knew you'd come back. I really did. I love you, Dad.'

Pulling apart, Geordie Wilson held his daughter at arm's length, taking her in as he replied, 'Ah, pet. And I love you too. I never stopped. And I never will.'

31

VIOLETTA

Appleton Farm, Cheshire
December 28th

Violetta was having a great time with the pricing gun as she labelled the boxes of fairy lights that were going in the New Year sale. Candy totally understood why her part-time partner wanted to call it a day as soon as possible and she herself was eager to embark on her new adventure on the waterways of England. Which was why Violetta was more than happy to get stuck in at the garden centre and help Rosina out while Darcy ran wild up at the house, keeping her new-found doting granddads on their toes.

Smiling as she stuck half-price labels on the next row of unsuspecting baubles, she wondered what the following Christmas at Appleton would be like because the one just gone would be a hard act to follow. Not only did her mum get her Big Christmas Weekend, she also got two extra guests for dinner and a box of letters from her dad. It had been such a magical time and Violetta cringed at herself for even thinking that phrase, but it was true.

They'd all teased their mum on Christmas Eve that she was like an overtired and overemotional child by the time the Two-Granddads (as they were now known) finally escaped her clutches and went home. While the whole family gathered round the kitchen table, Granddad Geordie had shown them black-and-white photos that were a link to their pasts, their heritage and for her mum especially, filled in the gaps. It took a while to explain to Darcy that in the olden days people did wear colourful clothes not just black-and-white ones. She'd wanted to know who had coloured all the 'now days' people in which had made them all laugh.

Her mum had briefly opened the Dr Marten boot box and peeped at the letters but was advised by everyone to leave them until another day because they were running out of kitchen roll and tissues.

Max had secretly touched Violetta's heart when she'd watched him during Christmas Day, quietly taking in his granddad and while everyone chatted, looking through the naval photos again, squinting at the grainy images and shyly asking questions about his life at sea. Perhaps he was relieved to have two more men around the table after being overwhelmed by women all his life – but whatever it was, she could tell he was glad to have Geordie and Sam there and that's all that mattered.

It was only natural that they'd come back the next day for Christmas dinner and after a shuffle round, they stayed the night rather than driving back. All her mother's dreams coming true. And it looked like they'd all be seeing more of the Two-Granddads because they'd been invited for New Year's Eve and would be staying for a few days afterwards so her mum could show them around the whole of Appleton.

Feeling a tap on her shoulder, Violetta stopped labelling and turned to see the woman herself. 'Hello, mother dear, and what can I help you with today? Some candy canes perhaps, seventy per cent off? Bargain or what?'

Laughing, Carmen declined. 'I'll pass, thank you. The last thing any of my grandchildren require is extra sugar, your daughter especially.'

'I can't imagine what you mean but then again, why do you think I'm so eager to drop her off and get down here in the morning?' Violetta gave her mum a wink. 'So, if it's not a box of very nice luxury Crimbo cards, whaddyawant, woman?'

'Chutney, I've run out so I'm going over to the farm shop to get some and I thought I'd say hi. Dad likes it with his stilton and it saves me going to the supermarket.'

'Ah, I see. It still sounds funny you saying that, you know, dad. But I suppose it'd be weird if I had to call someone dad, and Darcy too. Talking of the bossy one, is she being good?'

'Oh yes, she has two willing slaves who are happy to play every single one of the games she got for Christmas. I left them immersed in Operation when I snuck out. That buzzer drives me nuts.' Out of habit Carmen straightened one of the boxes so it fell in line on the shelf then remembered something. 'Oh yes, before I go. I meant to ask your opinion – an idea that I'd like you to think about.'

'Okay, hit me with it. You talk, I'll label.' Violetta carried on with her task as they walked along the row.

'It's about Joel... well, more about the fact he's looking for a job and it got me thinking about the lake.'

'What about the lake?'

'It's the only part of the estate that I haven't bothered with. Bern and I just left it to do its own thing but I think it has potential. I've had a couple of ideas and was wondering about a nature reserve, you know with hides for birdwatchers, or maybe stocking it with fish *and* a really out there one, what about a sustainable salmon farm?' Carmen came up for air and let Violetta speak.

'Ah, I see where you're going with this because what better person to take it on than Joel? Isn't that what he did in Thailand, something to do with water and wildlife, oh and elephants. We should deffo get some elephants, Mum. The kids would flipping love that!'

'Be serious, Violetta. We are never getting elephants although I suspect their poo would be excellent manure for the roses. But give it some thought. The other stuff, not the elephants. I'm going to run it by your sisters when I see them. Right, I'd better get on. It's Ker-Plunk next and Darcy is lethal with those sticks. She stabbed all my tangerines yesterday, the little bugger. I'll see you later.'

Stifling a chuckle at the idea of her daughter jabbing fruit, Violetta waved goodbye and as she was about to start the next row of boxes, saw her mum stop, talking to someone just out of view before pointing in her direction. Suspecting it was a customer in search of ten million cheap fairy lights, she got on with the job and wasn't surprised when she heard a male voice. Looking up, she expected a question. Instead, from the other side of the display she stared wide-eyed and open-mouthed at a face she never thought she would see again.

'Gabe.'

'Hello, Vi. Long time no see. And at least you remembered my name!'

Within seconds she'd taken him in. He looked exactly the same apart from a closely trimmed beard, his blond hair still cropped short. He was even more broad-shouldered underneath his fleece that bore a yellow emblem on the front.

Struck mute, she was still clutching the pricing gun like it was a weapon. His next comment told her he thought the same and as he held his arms up, he tried to lighten the mood. 'I surrender. Please don't shoot, I come in peace.'

Still not over the shock, Violetta was unable to laugh at his joke but did manage to lower her weapon and find her voice. 'What the hell... how did you find me...? And what took you so long?' Her next question was going to be 'What do you want?' but he answered that for her.

Delving into his fleece pocket he passed her an envelope, with *Vi* written in marker pen on the front. 'Here, I wanted to return this. I thought it might be special.'

Her hand shook as she took the sealed envelope and, still bemused, began to tear it open as Gabe spoke, filling in a few gaps.

'I was going to leave it at reception but the lady on there said you were working today so I came to find you.'

Opening the flap Violetta saw it contained a handwritten note and then when she looked closer, the silver bracelet her gran gave her, the one she thought she'd lost on holiday. 'My bracelet. I don't get it. How come you have it? Seriously, my head is so mashed right now.'

Gabe opened his mouth to answer when a couple wandered over to the display and not wanting to be overheard, Violetta made a decision and took a break. 'Come on, let's go to the café and we can talk there, I need a drink but unfortunately they don't sell the hard stuff so I'll get us a coffee or something.'

Moving around the display she was about to lead the way when she was brought to a halt by his sports shorts... and there was something else. 'Oh Gabe. What happened to your leg?'

Looking down at his prosthetic lower leg, Gabe then looked back up at Violetta and answered with a wry smile. 'Well, that's kind of what took me so long.'

Amongst the muddle of thoughts that raced through her head as she bought two mugs of tea and carried them over to the table where Gabe was waiting, top of the list was *What if Mum had brought Darcy with her?*

Trying hard not to think about her daughter, Violetta took him in as she approached. Snippets of their short time together reminded her that he'd been very funny, and relaxed and at ease with himself. He had also loved being in the army with his 'brothers' and she was sure his injury would've put paid to all that.

A rare but crystal-clear flashback to their holiday reminded her that's who he was with, his army mates, a rowdy, fun bunch of blokes. While they'd relaxed by the pool he'd told her more about himself and in between 'his mates versus hers' water polo matches, or beach volleyball she'd been drawn to him and blocked the others out. That's why she'd gone out with him that night. She wanted them to be alone.

Placing the mugs on the table she sat opposite Gabe who didn't look in the least bit nervous which helped her relax. 'So first of all, how did you end up with my bracelet and what happened to you? I mean after you and I, you know, and then you disappeared.'

A cheeky grin spread across Gabe's face. 'I can't believe you don't remember – but then again, you were very drunk that night.'

'And I was so ill for two whole days afterwards. It was the worst hangover I've ever had.'

'To be honest I'm not surprised. Anyway, your bracelet snapped and I picked it up off the pavement. You had that daft, tiny drawstring bag, I took the mick out of it and said it was like the one Scrooge kept his silver coins in. You'd tied a knot in the top but couldn't get it undone, so I said I'd mind your broken bracelet and put it in the zip pocket of my shorts. I've had it mended, by the way. My treat.'

'Ah, I see. And it's a good job you kept it because I lost my bag that night, too, amongst other things. But thank you for having it repaired, that's really kind. So, what happened next?'

Gabe was laughing as he spoke. 'Well, I dared you to climb the flagpole on a dinghy and you went one better and hooked your knickers on the top. Do you remember that?'

Violetta's hands flung to her cheeks, imagining someone finding her undies the next day. 'I didn't... so that's where they went.'

'Yep, that's where they ended up. And you'd insisted on taking a bottle of rakija to the beach so we could drink it under the stars but shall we say, we didn't get that far. We were in the dinghy and I fell asleep but you must have stayed awake and drank the rakija yourself. When I woke up the next morning I panicked when I realised I had to get back to the hotel because me and the lads were flying out later that morning. I did tell you it was my last night.'

Violetta shook her head. 'I swear some of that night is a complete blank but now and then I get a flashback. So go on, what happened next?'

'You were completely out of it and no matter how hard I tried I couldn't wake you, but I had to go. I pulled the tarpaulin over in case you got sunburnt or a seagull pooed on your face – so I did try to take care of you. I didn't have your phone number and your phone was in that daft bag that had gone missing so I couldn't even leave my number. If I'd had a pen, I'd have written it on your forehead, just for a laugh.'

At this, Violetta chuckled and believed he'd have done it, too. 'So you went home and...' She couldn't say what had popped into her mind because he hadn't broken her heart, had he?

'Yep, ended up like this.' Gabe motioned towards his leg. 'I'm glad I wore my training shorts now, so you saw straight away. When I wear jeans it means I have to have the awkward conversation and big reveal later so at least we've got that out of the way.'

'So what happened? How did you get injured?' She had this incredible urge to reach out and touch his arm, knowing before he even began that it wasn't going to be pleasant.

While UK combat troops left Afghanistan in 2014, around 750 remained as part of the NATO mission to train Afghan forces and Gabe was one of them. He went out there two weeks after he left Violetta in a dinghy but he didn't forget her and intended searching for her as soon as he got back from his tour.

He was stationed in Kabul and it was there, in what he described as a random and totally shit piece of luck, he stepped on a landmine and as a consequence lost a limb. He was evacuated and once back in the UK the road to recovery was long, mentally and physically. Being medically discharged from the army was devastating; losing his career and military family another cruel blow. He'd struggled to come to terms with it and suffered terrible bouts of depression.

But out of adversity and after rehabilitation came a new beginning and with the help of military charities he had slowly got back on track and rebuilt his life. His army brothers had stood by him, encouraging him, being there through the really bad times and were there to cheer him on in the good. He'd made new friends when he began cycling for a team of ex-servicemen and had a good job working with a sports education charity, travelling around schools and colleges, inspiring as many young people as he could with his story and achievements.

He'd taken part in the Sydney Invictus Games, winning a silver and then a team gold in the Tokyo Paralympics. His flat was full of mementos, service and sporting medals, photos of him and his military family and in one special box that he looked inside from time to time, was a silver bracelet with a V charm dangling from a hook.

And no matter how much he told himself to forget the bonkers redhead he'd met six years before, he couldn't get her out of his mind, or the strange feeling that somehow, until he found her, his heart would also be dangling on a hook. Not that he told Violetta that part when he got to the end of his story although he was quite pleased to see how moved she seemed by it, reaching out and touching his arm, just for a moment.

Violetta laid her hand on his arm. It was impossible not to. She moved it away though, in case he thought it was too much. 'Oh Gabe. I can't believe you've been through so much.'

And I wish I'd been there for you, but I was probably giving birth to our daughter while you were being flown home from Afghanistan.

'Hey, don't worry. Some had it worse than me and I have a great life now, and, in a way, it brought me here to see you.'

Violetta felt herself blush but didn't care because as much as she tried to be sensible, she was so happy to see him and secretly thrilled he'd sought her out, and dying to find out how he'd managed to track her down. 'I've been meaning to ask that. How did you find me?'

'Well, even though that whole night seems a blur to you, I did remember that over dinner – I did buy you dinner, by the way – you told me that your mum owned a garden centre in Cheshire. I hold my hands up to not remembering the name but I did know it had something to do with apples.

'One of my teammates lives in Manchester and invited me to stay for New Year and before I left, I grabbed the bracelet and decided to stop putting it off and to track you down. It was a long shot but I found this place easily online and then I wondered if Appleton was your surname too. I searched for you on social media but drew a blank so thought sod it and got in the car and took a drive over here. I had intended just to make enquiries and if it was definitely the right place, leave it with someone and hope you'd get in touch.'

Gabe leant across and tapped the envelope and with a grin said, 'All my contact numbers are in there, home address, blood group, national insurance number, just to be sure you could get hold of me.'

If she wasn't sure he felt the way she did, after all this time, after a one-night stand, Violetta was in no doubt about it now. 'Okay, okay, let's swap numbers before you go. In fact, how long are you here for and where do you live? There's so much I want to ask you and there's stuff I need to tell you, too, but now's not the time.'

'What, like you're married with two kids? You're not wearing any rings so please, don't break my heart and tell me you're spoken for.' He was clutching his heart and laughing but there was something in his eyes that was serious, telling her he meant it.

Wording her next sentence very carefully, Violetta put him out of his misery. 'No, you fool. I'm not taken but you still haven't answered my question.'

'Ah, that is good news. Okay, so I live in Oxford and I'm here for two weeks. Me and my mate are going to do some training at the velodrome in Manchester so if you'd like to meet up, you have my numbers, all of them.'

'You really are determined, aren't you, so yes, I would love to meet up and then we can have a proper chat but right now, I'm going to have to get back to work. Even the boss's daughter can get in trouble.'

Gabe looked relieved as he went to pick up the envelope. 'Okay and here, before you go, let me put your bracelet on. Don't want you losing it again.'

Violetta nodded and watched as he slipped it from the envelope and fastened it around her wrist. The feel of his skin against hers made her shiver and their eyes connected for a second once it was done. After shoving his details into her overall pocket she offered to walk with him to the door, ignoring the curious look from Rosina who just happened to be passing by.

Minutes later, after giving him her number and promising to text later, Violetta gave him a hug that lasted longer than expected and waved him off, watching transfixed as his jeep disappeared from view. Once he was gone she smiled as she held her gran's bracelet up to the light and spoke out loud, not caring if anyone heard her.

'Thank you, Gran, for bringing him back to me and Darcy. I don't know how, but I'd bet you a packet of ciggies you had something to do with all this, you crafty old sod.'

Turning, she was almost blown through the doors by a gust of wind that sent leaves rushing across the car park, swirling and skittering in her wake. Violetta knew she was pushing her luck and had work to do, but the days of keeping things to herself were gone so she headed straight towards Rosina's office to tell her the news. And then with the help of Leonora and her mum they could all work out the best way to tell Gabe he had a daughter. And tell Darcy that Santa had been listening when she sat on his knee. Once again, he'd made a little girl's wish come true.

32

CARMEN

Appleton Farm
New Year's Day

'Daddy's little darling, Daddy's little girl. Daddy's little sweetheart, Daddy's little pearl.' Carmen read the words on the back of the blue paper and smiled.

The bedroom was quiet and peaceful, save for the crackle of the fire interspersed by Bern's piglet snores and if she strained her ears, the owl in the tree outside. Carmen was seated in her armchair, warming her feet by the grate, her eyes tired from rereading the letter that she carefully folded and placed back in the tatty box. She didn't want to substitute the battered boot box with a fancy one from the gift shop, preferring to cherish the journey it had made and the markers of history, smiling whenever she saw the pre-decimal price tag.

She was taking her time reading the letters from her dad and with each one, wrote down the answers to his questions and went through them on the phone and filled him in with her life, step by step. She'd reached 1971 where he'd mentioned a place called Walt Disney World in Florida and that one day he'd love to take her there. This had set her mind racing because even though it was too late for him to take her, perhaps they all could go together and make some memories as a family.

It was hard to believe that he was actually there, under her roof just across the landing. Him and Sam in Rosina's old bedroom. It wouldn't have been appropriate for them to stay in her mum's, not unless she wanted to be haunted by the spirit of Saint Sylvia for all eternity.

It had taken some digesting, though, the revelation that her mum had hidden the truth for all those years and in some ways had lived a lie, and in doing so, prevented Carmen from making up her own mind about her dad. Without a doubt she would have forgiven him but she also forgave her mum, too, because decisions like that weren't easy to make or live with. Of that Carmen was certain.

And there was no point in apportioning blame especially when one of the guilty parties wasn't there to speak for herself, then again, there was no need. Carmen and her father were at peace with a past they couldn't alter and had agreed to focus on making the most of the future. Just like Leonora was doing with Joel, Rosina with Lou and all being well and everything crossed, Violetta and Darcy with Gabe.

What a precious moment in their history when the Appleton women had gathered around the table and told the youngest one all about her daddy who had been extremely clever and managed to find them.

Darcy's eyes were like saucers as she drank her milk and dipped her custard cream, listening carefully as her mum explained that he'd been injured in a war and was so brave when he'd been hurt.

'More hurter than when I fell off my bike in the car park?' Darcy had milk running down her chin as she spoke.

Violetta had worded it in a way she'd understand. 'Yes, much, much worse. And do you remember when we watched the Paralympics and some of the people had lost their arms or legs?' Darcy nodded enthusiastically, totally engaged. 'Well, *your* daddy had to have an operation on his leg and now he has a special one, like the people on the telly. And guess what?'

Darcy was completely agog at this point, the drama of it all sucking her in as she listened to her mum. 'He is a super-fast cyclist and won a *gold* medal at the Olympics! How brilliant is that?'

Darcy clapped like crazy and her aunts joined in too. Then she asked a really important question of her own. 'When can I see him? Can he come for tea at Grandma's and she can make pizzas? I bet he likes pizzas, like me.'

Carmen had watched Violetta compose herself before answering. 'Of course he can. He's so excited to meet you. Shall I go and ring him and ask him to come round?'

'Yes, please, and can you tell him to hurry up and bring his medal too.' Darcy wiped her chin with the cuff off her cardigan as Aunty Rosina and Aunty Leonora dabbed at their eyes.

Carmen had been so proud of Violetta, the way she broached it, and Darcy, too, who had then made them all laugh when she lightened the mood with a very wise five-year-old's observation. 'See, Grandma, all the daddies are coming home because it's Christmas. I love Christmas, forever and ever.'

Later that afternoon, when the doorbell rang, Carmen had welcomed in a very nervous-looking young man. Violetta had told him about Darcy when they'd met the following day, after he had blown in with the wind. Leonora and Rosina had advised that she got it over with as soon as she could, no more secrets. Once he'd got over the shock, Gabe couldn't wait to meet his daughter and totally understood the logistics of their situation, saying it was time to move on and make up for lost time. And that's why as soon as she saw him on the step, something had told Carmen that Gabe wouldn't let Violetta or Darcy down.

Darcy was in the kitchen with Violetta, rolling play dough when Carmen and Gabe entered and her eyes were like saucers when she saw him.

'Hey, Darcy. Look who's here.' Carmen kept it light while Violetta focused on her daughter's face.

Darcy stopped mid-roll and pointed. 'Are you my daddy?'

Gabe took a few steps forward, his face beaming and his voice laced with mirth and if you could hear happiness, it was bouncing off the walls. 'Yes I am. And I'm sorry it's taken me so long to get here but I'm really pleased to meet you at last.'

Darcy wiggled down from her chair and made her way over to the six-foot-three man who looked down on his child for the first time. They all waited, holding their breaths. When she held out her hand and took his, her words would go down in family history. 'It's okay. You're a very nice daddy and I knew you'd come and find me one day. Do you know how to play snap?'

Gabe managed to nod and then found himself being pulled towards the table where he took a seat next to Violetta as Darcy climbed onto his knee. Before turning away to fill the kettle, as Carmen watched her daughter hold it together and deal out cards, she was sure of one thing. The three of them were meant to be.

❄

Taking the box of letters over to the wardrobe, Carmen pulled open the door, wincing as it creaked and after placing her treasure inside, nudged it shut. Making sure the guard was over the fire she took off her dressing gown and stealthily climbed into bed next to Bern.

Lying on her back she thought about what Darcy had said, childlike words that over the past few days had haunted her, the ghosts of Christmas past impossible to escape no matter how hard she tried to banish them.

How could it be that even now, when all the fragments of her life and those of her children had come together, all the cracks filled in, that the memory of one man had the ability to smash it all to pieces?

Again, as she lay there in semi-darkness, she posed the question she'd asked many times before. Was it enough? Was it justified, her place on the pedestal? And even now, she could only base her answer on what she saw with her own eyes. The affirmation of her daughters' love for her, the stability she'd given from everything she'd achieved.

Still it rankled. Her dad had come home, so had Darcy's; but Rosina, Violetta and Leonora would never have that option. The grand reunion, or even the hope of that day occurring had been snuffed out on the day he died. No matter how much she'd tried to follow her dad's example of forgiveness and see the wisdom in her mum's last-minute words, *You mustn't worry about anything, what's done is done, do you understand, Carmen?* she couldn't help wonder if things could have been different, if there was an alternative ending to a chapter in Appleton family history.

Turning to face the window, she watched the wisps of clouds float over the new moon and welcomed the droop of her eyelids and the firm voice inside her head that told her to leave things be. Carmen obeyed and closed her eyes and hoped for a dreamless sleep where oblivion would deliver her into the next day.

It was the start of a brand-new year. One that would no doubt bring fresh challenges and adventures for her family and for as long as she could, she'd be there. To guide them, to keep them safe, to put them first and do her best, just like always.

EPILOGUE

Gawsworth
December 1999

I want to wake up, I have to wake up but my eyes are stuck shut by the glue of sleep that holds me down so even if I try to claw my way to consciousness, my leaden limbs refuse to move and I am trapped in the worst of my dreams.

I am being sucked down into a swirling vortex and into the past, a day I try so hard to forget. We are speeding along an icy country road that is slick from a recent downpour and our route is marred by thick fog. It's like driving into the face of death and any second we could smash into a vehicle coming the opposite way. I pray that the quiet country lanes remain so and we are spared, that luck is on my side. My right hand grips the seat, the other is wedged against the dash, bracing myself in case we crash.

It is morning; the clock on the dash says 9.15 and I know that in ten minutes my life will change forever. The ticking starts, loud and clear, counting down. Above us the winter sun has no chance of breaking through the greyness that envelops us and the world that I can glimpse beyond the windscreen looks dismal, it feels dismal, I am dismal.

We are on our way to the doctor's for my antenatal. We are late after dropping the girls at school. Sebastian is driving too fast as always, taking corners that cause the back end to skid and my heart to lurch. I can smell stale alcohol on his breath, the fumes from a whisky binge the night before are making me nauseous and the bruises on my back and arms cause me to wince whenever I am flung against the seat and car door.

I implore him to slow down. 'Sebastian, please, you're going to get us killed.' He ignores me and even pushes on the accelerator, letting me know he is in control.

He is in a foul mood and taking it out on me because as we left I was stupid enough to voice my fears and ask a question that has been burning a hole in my brain. It just came out. I couldn't hold it in anymore. I had to know. The signs of his infidelity have been there for so long but I chose to ignore them until now, after hearing the end of a whispered conversation promising a faceless woman at the end of a phone that he would tell me soon.

I have to know so, despite his anger, I ask again. 'Sebastian, are you leaving us?'

'Leave it, Carmen, I mean it.' A simple question that pushes him almost to the edge, his puce face glistening with sweat and even though I am scared for my life and that of the baby inside me, now I've started, I can't stop.

'Answer me. I know you're having an affair. I heard you just now. I'm not stupid, so tell me the truth. I deserve that at least.'

When the back of his hand hits me square in the face I think he has broken my nose and I cover my eyes, expecting another blow. He rarely stops at one punch so when I feel the car slow I fear the worst as he pulls over to the side of the road. Leaving the engine running he pulls on the handbrake. When nothing happens, no more slaps, I look up and realise we are a few yards away from the level crossing that cuts across the road, a little further down the hill.

It's a favourite place on the route to the village, where the girls love to watch the barriers fall and guess what side the train will appear from. The track runs through the remote countryside and carries freight trains from the city towards Macclesfield and the south, and Sebastian's favourite place, London. Well away from me and the girls and Appleton.

Still stunned from the blow I watch as he fumbles in his pockets and realise he's looking for the indigestion pills that he eats like sweets. Undoing the jar he pops one in his mouth and crunches and while he waits for it to take effect I sob and in the space between, he finally answers.

'I can't do this anymore, Carmen. So yes, I am leaving. I'll go after Christmas. You can tell the girls I've found a job working away. It'll be easier for them to understand.' He speaks so matter-of-factly I realise that he's probably been rehearsing it.

There is no remorse in his voice. In fact, he sounds weary. I am in shock, my lips feel funny and I can't make out if it's because they are bruised or numb yet I make them work. My voice sounds tinny, like it's coming down the line of a transatlantic phone call or from space, not my body.

'Are you going to her? Does she live in London? Is that where you met?'

'Yes.' At last he is honest. I want to ask all about her then change my mind because, whoever she is, we are past the competition stage. She has won already even though I've tried so hard to win him back.

Bizarrely, amidst such utter turmoil my next thought is practical, for my children. 'And when will you see the girls?'

'They can visit or I'll come and see them when I can.'

I almost laugh at this because I know him too well, this constantly absent father who cares more about himself than them. A man who does everything he can to be away from them. I remain silent.

He decides to twist the knife. 'And we will have to sell the house. I'll need the money.'

I reel from his words, my head feels light. 'But it's our home, the girls love it there and what about our baby... you can't walk out now, we can't sell the house, how could you be so cruel?'

His head snaps around and in his eyes I see pure hate. Spittle erupts from his mouth with such vile words they make me wince as does the jab in my chest. 'That's your baby, not mine. I told you I didn't want it from the start when you tried to trap me again. You should have got rid of it like I said. It was bad enough being saddled with the first one and I was resigned to the second but that, in there, is all your fault so you look after it.'

I look to my belly, to where he points and the horror of what my future will soon become hits me full force. I suddenly see what it entails. I have lived it myself and I cannot bear the thought of my girls going through that.

He won't come and see them; they won't go and visit him. Not once he is set up with his new woman. Rosina will be left hating him even more than she does now. Violetta will be left wondering when he will be coming home and my unborn child will be in limbo, caught between two versions of one vile, disgusting man who wanted her dead.

Never have I hated someone as much as I do right now. I cannot bear to look at him and as a huge wave of nausea climbs up my chest I am desperate to get out of the car but my hands are shaking so furiously that I can't find the handle. And then my attention is drawn back to Sebastian when he makes a strange sound and starts to pull at his shirt and tie. I notice that his face has altered, eyes bulging, his mouth wide, gasping for breath and then he creases, clutches his chest before slumping at the wheel, groaning. And then a gurgling, then nothing.

I watch, morbidly fascinated as he slips into unconsciousness. Tentatively, I say his name and touch the side of his cheek below his ear. I feel a faint pulse and I am stunned not that he isn't dead, but by my reaction, a sense of utter disappointment.

What to do, what to do? The answer comes in the form of amber flashing lights on the level crossing and I know that soon they will turn to red and the barriers will slowly come down. The idea invades my head so swiftly I have no time to process the pros and cons. Instead, I do as it tells me.

The road behind and ahead is deserted as I pull off the handbrake and as the car begins to move forward, slowly picking up momentum, with my right hand hidden by Sebastian's chest I easily steer it towards the track. I see the barriers begin to lower and can hear the warning bell as we glide under and once we are on the track, I yank the wheel to the left and the car careers into the post that supports the hinges.

Still Sebastian doesn't wake or flinch so I leap from the car and around to the driver's side and fling open the door. Aware of the cameras that point onto the track, even though the grey mist hangs low, I pull at his slumped body that is impossible for a mere slip of a heavily pregnant woman to move.

Turning, I run to the emergency phone box at the side of the track and pull open the door, lift the receiver and wait. Through the swirl of fog on the track I see the dim glow of the train in the distance hurtling towards us as I give a futile wave with my free hand and grip the phone with the other.

The driver can't possibly see me, not in the fog, and probably spots the car on the track at the same time as another arrives on the opposite side of the barrier. I can only imagine the horror of the man who has leapt from his vehicle but I know exactly what he is about to see.

There is a screech of brakes as the train driver valiantly tries to slow the train, wheels spinning backwards and the noise of steel straining against steel is etched into my brain like nails on a blackboard, a needle scraping a groove across a record.

The freight engine appears from the fog, looming like a growling ogre, swelling with every inch. Yellow startled eyes glow brighter and as it nears I glimpse the shape of the driver trapped behind the dirty glass, waiting for the impact he knows will come.

I cannot look at the car, I dare not, so I turn my back on the breath of diesel fumes and the smell of grinding metal that invades my nose, making it hard to breathe. And then it happens. The voice at the end of the phone line can't hear mine and I can't hear the voice, not over the booming moment of impact and metal hitting metal.

The train carries on, still not at a halt and then it slows gradually and the screeching stops. I can't see on the other side of the train, to the innocent bystander or where Sebastian's car would be, or what's left of it. I hear a voice saying, 'Hello, is anyone there?' And I watch as two men jump from the train cab and stagger onto the tracks, one supporting the other, who I imagine is in shock.

I remain where I am until the train men have reached my side, saying things I can't comprehend as I stare blankly ahead, saying nothing. Instead, I think of my children and amidst a scene of carnage, I know it's going to be all right.

Appleton Farm is safe. No more bruises for me or Rosina. My unborn baby will never know its father's hate. Violetta won't be that little girl who waits and waits, always wondering when her daddy is coming home.

I made the right decision. For all of us. He is gone.

THE END

ACKNOWLEDGEMENTS

Hello. I hope you enjoyed reading Coming Home and meeting the Appleton family because I loved writing their story for you. The idea for this book stemmed from my own fear that Christmas is going to be ruined and after asking friends, I found out that I wasn't alone. We set so much store by one day that we want to be perfect it's like asking for trouble and poor Carmen certainly got her fair share, didn't she.

Also, I'm sure we would all like to forget that the pandemic happened but sadly it is part of our lives and history, so I wanted to include it in the story in a relevant way. The Granny Sylvia scene made me cry because it brought back memories of losing my mum and even though it was pre-Covid, not being there to hold her hand still weighs heavy on my heart. Hopefully, if people read this book in years to come it will all be a distant memory and a blip that we overcame. Fingers crossed.

On to thanking people now. I will begin with the wonderful team at Bloodhound who have worked their magic again and always support me from start to finish.

Tara Lyons, thank you for taking care of my book from the second it gets the thumbs up, and through each stage without getting cross at the stupid questions I ask every single time! And for always making the inside of my books look so beautiful by adding your special flourish to each page. This time, it was snowflakes, they are ace. You are a real gem; a lovely lady and I adore you.

Clare Law, thank you a million times for your support and the fantastic work you do during the edit. I always look forward to the manuscript coming back to me because I know that it will be so much better, and for that I am truly grateful. You are great fun to work with, and I love that you get me, and my words are in such capable and wise hands.

To Abbie Rutherford who is just ace and whose opinion really matters to me, as does her friendship.

Thank you to Ian Skewis for his proofreading skills and eagle-eyed attention to detail.

And to Betsy and Fred who are the best. What else can I say apart from thank you for everything, especially you, Mrs.

Next, to my fabulous loyal team of ARC readers who are so much more than that, you are trusted friends who I count on to give me honest feedback and I don't know what I'd do without you.

To everyone on social media who generously supports and encourages me. I love seeing your names pop up and having a chat and hearing your news so thank you for sharing your time and lives with me.

I must mention my very special amigos Heather Fitt and Nathan Moss. I look forward to our good morning messages and spending the day with you, the laughs, talking mostly rubbish and winding each other up but always being there if we need one another.

And now for another V.I.P, not just in her head but in real life, too. The one and only Keri Beevis - writer extraordinaire, bringer of wisdom, whip cracker, tag-line wizard, banner queen, social media icon, title guru, all round superstar. Once again, she held my hand from the very first chapter of this book and joking aside, I love that she is my writing buddy and most of all the best friend I could wish for. Thanks mate, this book malarkey wouldn't be the same without you by my side.

And finally, to six people who are my world. My precious family. Just like the characters in my book, this Christmas we will all be together and for me, that is the best present of all. Each of you are a gift that I treasure so all of us under one roof, even for a short time will make me happier than I can say. I love you all.

Before I go, I would like to wish you, the reader, a very merry Christmas and all the best for the New Year. Take care, stay safe and be happy.

A NOTE FROM THE PUBLISHER

Thank you for reading this book. If you enjoyed it please do consider leaving a review on Amazon to help others find it too.

We hate typos. All of our books have been rigorously edited and proofread, but sometimes mistakes do slip through. If you have spotted a typo, please do let us know and we can get it amended within hours.

info@bloodhoundbooks.com

Printed in Great Britain
by Amazon

69135022R00190